THE THIEF OF RED MOUNTAIN

Nathalie Andrews

Published by

Girl and Cat Publishing

Cover design and illustration by Alex J Garcia

Copyright © Nathalie Andrews 2013

ISBN 978-0-9927281-1-3

This book is dedicated to Chris Cunliffe, my wonderful friend who will always be a knight in shining armour.

Thank you for all your support.

Further Acknowledgements

Books don't get made in isolation. They are the product of random inspiration, which can come from anywhere and anyone, then the long, hard process of writing and editing for which we all need support. Inevitably, I can't thank everyone who helped me, but a few stand out as having taken an active role in the process…Thus my thanks go out to Asha Chauhan Field, Shannon Urlich, Samantha Bucknell, Zaro Weil and Dave Heaton for the typo-shooting and formatting; Andrew Shore and Ian Crawford for business and tax advice; Steph Sutton for help with a synopsis when I had reached tipping point and finally my mum, Jackie Andrews for supporting it all.

Thanks also to the Facebook writers' communities, Beckenham Book Club and to all the coffee shops that have hosted the creation of this novel, but most especially Starbucks in Hammersmith and Caffe Nero in Beckenham for keeping me caffeinated.

About the author...

"The Thief of Red Mountain" is Nathalie Andrews' first novel and the culmination of many years interest in the culture and conduct of the samurai era in Japan. Nathalie has travelled throughout the world often with little more than a tent, a backpack and a decent knowledge of the local beer. She had always hoped to grow up and be a great adventurer before discovering that adventuring doesn't pay the bills and people don't actually grow up.

Nathalie trained for over ten years in Egyptology and has presented and published academic papers on language and religion in Ancient Egypt. She works as an executive assistant, and is founder of Girl and Cat Publishing. She currently lives in London with her cat, Nefertari and a house full of shiny and colourful things.

Website: http://thethiefofredmountain.blogspot.co.uk/

Twitter: @rukia9chiki   #thethiefofredmountain

Facebook: http://www.facebook.com/thethiefofredmountain

THE THIEF OF RED MOUNTAIN

1. The Red Mountain 10
2. The First Day 29
3. Memories 41
4. The Ways We Lie 61
5. The Sword and the Fox 74
6. To Each a Fate 91
7. The Waterfall 104
8. The Other Side of a Bargain 125
9. The Girl Who Never Was 141
10. The Ghost and her Demon 158
11. Innocence 172
12. Siding with the Wolf 185
13. Snow Princess 194
14. The World we Made 207
15. Two Brothers 218
16. A Silk Peacock in the Rain 232
17. Beneath a Still Blue Sky 249
18. A Teller of Stories 262
19. The Lord of the Mountain 275
20. Demons and a Burning Garden 293
21. Wildflowers 317
22. The Last Dance by Moonlight 340
23. Encounter at Dawn 357
24. Thirty Miles to the West 369

Epilogue 383

THE THIEF OF RED MOUNTAIN

Akayama Province, Japan, 1859...

1. The Red Mountain

Takashi Isamu lay back, lips cool with wine, his mind on fire. Where the screens hung open, he could see the sky, clearer here than it had ever been in the city. Tonight the stars seemed to boil.

An absence of meaning troubled him in the silences between swords clashing. There was no sensuality in his work, no poetry, but tonight he felt as if he might mediate his actions through the woman who now stood watching him from the doorway, or else burn them off in the heat of her body. His own base ego was embroiled in this business, but it was more than that tonight. It was, he thought, probably too much to ask that someone could redeem him.

"Show me," he had told her. She had brought him here to the bedroom in silence. No questions. Just assent. He had asked if she had wine and she'd brought a flask. Then she'd stood there in the doorway, put it to her lips and drunk.

He too had drunk, drunk until his head lolled back and all he could do was watch the stars through the screen and the mesh of leaves and branches outside. The air on the mountains was clean and he liked that.

"Do I scare you?"

She didn't answer.

This morning, his men had rounded up the servants and killed them, to a man, acting on his orders. It was the Head of the Akayama Clan that he had come for, but it went without saying that the servants' lives were forfeit. Those who ran were cowards by his creed. The others had been quiet, and it had been peaceful, their only heralds birdsong and the sound of crickets. He had turned away and gazed out across the valley with its white villages like paper cut-outs. All of Akayama's lands were bathed in this interminable heat. Yet, the sun did not dim over spilt blood; the birds did not stop singing.

This girl had been in the grounds. Some of his men were tired of the heat and of rounding up those who had tried to escape, so Takashi alone had pursued her into a world of white paper walls and delicate murals, pale floors that were soon streaked with the dust from his boots. Her footfalls sounded like those of a fleeing child: soft, quick. Where the corridors opened out onto a broad chamber, the girl fell down onto ornate rugs. Briefly he thought she had collapsed, before it became clear to him that she was shielding something with her body. A pile of rags.

Something was amiss.

There was a body. In the very heart of the manor, covered with sheets and laid out before the fire-pit, there was a body. A dead man with his head split open.

Takashi froze, staring. Here, of all places! Where every line and mural spoke of decadent beauty. How could a man lie dead and yet still be embraced?

His reverie was broken by the arrival of his lieutenant. Inuko did not hesitate as Takashi had. He went straight to the girl and lifted her by her hair, pulling her backwards, even as Takashi stepped forward to study the body. Behind him, her scream was cut short, but he didn't turn to see what Inuko had done, instead lowering the blade of his sword until the tip touched the dead man's chest. A globe of blood appeared. The corpse did not move, so he shifted the blade again until the flat of it was an inch from the mouth. The metal steamed.

With a grunt, Takashi stepped back. Not a corpse at all then, but perhaps not long for this world. "Inuko," he addressed his lieutenant. There was a heavy thump, then the woman's gasping as she fell to the ground, given liberty to breathe again. "Who is he?" Takashi demanded, still without turning round. If this was Akayama, it was a strange end to his day. Time, it appeared, would finish his work for him and his intercedence here was no more than an unnatural interruption of the man's fate.

After a moment, the woman realised he was addressing her and found her voice:

"Akayama Arata."

"Akayama?"

"Captain," Inuko interrupted: "The man we are looking for is Akayama Ryuunaka. He has a younger brother who was married two summers ago."

"What happened here?"

"We called a doctor," she managed. Takashi turned and recognised, in her eyes, the blankness of shock; here but not here.

"Who did this to him?" he asked more softly. "Somebody from this house?"

"No—no."

"An accident…?"

"On the road," she said, her gaze falling back to the injured man, seeking mooring.

"This whole region is under the hand of thugs and bandits. What did your people expect when they turned their back on their own? Loyalty from barbarians?" He turned his away from her, spitting on the dark wood floor as he looked towards the man who was both dead and not dead. "Take her outside, Inuko."

"No, please don't touch him!"

So this was Lord Akayama's brother.

Takashi could see the wounds had been inflicted by a blade; a glancing blow, since anything direct would have finished him, but deep enough, he warranted. The blood was not fresh.

"What are you, his wife or mistress?" Behind him, the sound of the girl struggling with Inuko ceased and Inuko cursed. Takashi turned to see her folded almost double in his arms. There were tooth-marks on the younger man's wrist. "She troubling you, Inuko-kun?" His lieutenant scowled. "You know what I think? That man is already dead." Takashi moved away from the prone figure and took a firm grip on the woman's hair, forcing her to look up: "And his brother's not here. So all I've got is you. Where is he, Girl? Where is the *daimyo* of Akayama?"

"I don't know!"

"Well, think! Stop looking at me like I'm going to kill you and don't you dare speak the first words that come into your head"–he pressed his finger to her lips, leaving them white—"unless you know they'll be of use to me."

Tears sprung up in her eyes. He gave her time. People feared Takashi Isamu because he brought death to walk in their halls and dance at their windows. What they never expected was that, even in its revelry, the tawdriness of life remained unchanged. He needed information, and she would live long enough to give it to him and, in that time, she would come to realise her own life was no great drama, just breath after breath, whether she chose to speak or not. Eventually the knot of muscles in Inuko's forearm would start to dig into her rib-cage. Discomforts did not evaporate in light of catastrophe, and the most remarkable thing about catastrophe was just how unremarkable it became.

"He left for Okiri, two weeks ago today," she said at last.

"He doesn't know his brother's fate?"

"No."

"And when is he due to return?"

"I don't kn–" She caught herself.

Then he was already gone. Takashi turned away.

This was a god-forsaken place. A half day's ride from Okiri. One road. Barely suitable for a good horse. Bandits in the heights. Blistering heat and dry nights. The very edge of civilisation.

More and more these days Takashi's decisions seemed intercut with an absence of certainty. He hesitated. One day perhaps it would overtake him and he would be rendered immobile. And then everything would be swept away, like a canvas washed with salt. Meanwhile, Inuko remained, ever obedient, ever silent.

"What do you want?" the woman whispered, making him realise that he had been silent for an unnatural time. It was not, he realised, a question so much as the beginning of a negotiation, and he glanced back at her appraisingly:

"Oh, you think you can give me something that would compensate me for this day's ride? For a night on this mountain? For the shit and blood on my hands I've had off of your peasants?" he said. "Can you bring me Akayama's head or the duties he owes? Or will you pay me like the shogun?" She moaned softly in Inuko's arms when Takashi pressed a hand to her cheek. "Or do you think you have something else that I want?"

She was pretty. He couldn't deny that. It was hard not to imagine she might be some compensation for the evening. Intriguing pale eyes; they made him hesitate. There again, that uncertainty so alien to him, but this time infused with a thought: "Are you the wife of that man over there with his head cut open?" A small noise of assent was all she gave him as he moved closer. "Then did his brother ever look at you?" She looked up confused. All at once, he lost patience with the idea that she would give it thought. "If you want to live, tell me if his brother ever looked at you!"

His reward was a crimson flush.

He bared a smile at her: "Really? Your own husband's brother? Were you good to him?" He glanced at the injured man who lay by the hearth, oblivious of her body's unspoken confession. "Enough that he would come back for you?"

赤山

"Show me," he had told her.

As the stars turned in slow spirals, he realised he was drunk. Not enough to impede him, but certainly enough to loosen his tongue and lead his thoughts in strange directions.

She had remained on the far side of the room, watching him from the doorway. Calm now; she had been that way for some time and her lingering stare aroused him more than the thought of her touch. It was a long time since he had had a woman look at him that way. Nothing kept her here: no lock, no key, no bars. "Come here."

By nature, she seemed obedient. When she reached him, he heaved himself up, put a hand behind her head and kissed her, and though she stiffened at first, she returned the kiss.

He had paid women often enough to feign their affections. She was not so well-schooled as them. Their first exchange was like a series of challenges. If he kissed her more deeply, she pressed against him, tightening her hold. Her nails dug into his skin. And she was strong.

Stronger than he had imagined, her body firm through the loose robe she wore.

When he pulled back, she left molten kisses across his neck and chest, making him gasp. He had not expected this. Usually women lay there, dead-eyed, else scratched at him. When she reached inside his *hakama* to touch him, he had to fumble with the knots to keep abreast of the clamour of his blood. He knew he desired her, but what strange spell, he wondered, could make her want the same? There were tales of demons in the form of women. This remote estate; the death he'd wrought here; the injured man; it all seemed too strange a series of events for fate to reward.

As she ministered to his shoulder and neck, he reached around her waist and untied the sash that held her kimono closed. It did not fall open at once, but he slid one hand inside. The skin of her belly was soft and flat. He guessed she had never borne a child though she was of an age for it. His palm traced her ribs, up to her breast, lingering there until her nipple hardened beneath the motions of his thumb. The suddenness of her breath against his neck made him shiver.

"Why?" he breathed.

He'd had whores; he'd even had lovers who had not paid such heed to his body. She pressed her hips against his, her own kimono rucked up and heaped against her waist, trailing silk across his skin. And, as if he had always been so blunt and mindless of beauty, he pulled her hard onto him, wanting in that instant to stop her somehow.

She lifted her face. It was beautiful and contorted with an emotion he didn't understand. Her eyes were grey. Until now, he had thought blue. But no, grey.

"What are you?" She didn't answer. His voice was coarse with desire: "What if I take you back with me?"

"You can't."

"Why?" He pulled her down. And now he was moving inside her, she adjusted her breathing to his own:

"I am dishonourable. I could not be seen—at your side." Those words took some of the tension from her body, even as he ran one hand over her hip and thigh, in places finding her skin discoloured with bruises.

"True," he said, letting his fingers rest over them so she knew that he had found them. Her breathing tightened.

In the silence between them then, a deeper absence took root. Even without words though, he could follow the encroachment of his own needs in the rhythm of their breathing. He pulled her tight against him, not wanting to see, in the end, if her affection was real. At the last though, the culmination of his own desire was little more than another hesitation. A spike of pleasure, then all the silences crawling back in.

I am getting old, he thought. Takashi Isamu is too old to slay his own demons, whatever they may be.

She slid off of him and lay at his side, offering him the line of her back, a curve of amber in the firelight. Her hair fanned out across her shoulders, so fine and long that it looked almost like lines of black water following every incline and plane of her figure.

"What will you do?" he asked, his voice sounding brutish in the silence as if, in this scene, he was the one that was out of place. "When your husband is dead, what will you do?"

"I'll bury him."

"And then?" She didn't answer. "What's your name?"

"Akayama Mei."

"I'm Isamu. Captain Takashi Isamu."

"Pleased to meet you," she said. He expected sarcasm, but it was entirely absent. She shifted, curling up a little and he laid one hand on her waist, claiming her. "You're quite the wrong way round, Captain Takashi. You should have asked me for my name first." Her voice was sweeter than he'd expected and he chuckled at the sentiment. She was right though.

"Tell me, Mei, your name before your marriage."

"Chimariko."

"I have not had dealings with your family." He was relieved. It might not do to let her live if she had strong connections beyond these walls. As it was, he might be able to use her, if he so chose.

"Chimariko was the name of my village. Such barbarians live out here as are willing to take their wives from peasant stock," she said suddenly.

"Are you such a one?" He felt her nod. "Yet you speak like a lady."

"Thank you."

They were quiet a moment. The night was heavy and sweet. He thought of what it might mean to live out here, within the bounds that nature asserted: impassable mountains; the depths of the valley. Her world must be a sheltered one.

"I could show you things you've never dreamed of," he said. "The palace of the emperor. The temples in Kamakura, with walls and gateways that reach as far as the ocean."

"Why did you come here?"

He grunted at the question:

"On the orders of my lord, to collect the duties due from the Akayama estate. Word and warning were sent to your *daimyo* weeks ago."

"What was his answer?"

"None came and my own master grew impatient."

"I see."

"You were his lover, weren't you?" he asked. She didn't answer and he wondered if she understood the implications. "He knew we were coming. When he left, he knew the fates of his servants and his men, his family."

"He would not do that. He was an honourable man." It was the first time he had heard something like emotion in her voice and it gave him pause.

"So. Now I see. You love him."

She rolled away from him, sat up and pulled on her *yukata*. "Mei, does he love you?" He paused and watched a blush bloom across her face and chest before she tugged the kimono shut. "Then the bruises are marks that your husband left? It's alright," he said when she didn't respond: "You don't have to answer. I think the story is written there clearly enough."

She glanced up, eyes full of a brilliant anger:

"Or I am an excellent liar, Sir."

"No, I think not. No one lies that well. You love Ryuunaka-*sama*. I'll wager he loves you. Difficult, maybe even dangerous for you to flee with him. He does not know what your husband would do."

"You have a way with stories."

"Is it a story or am I hitting on some facts?"

"Our lives are stories, Sir. Make of mine what you will."

"No, I think not," he scoffed, sitting up and stretching: "A story would have a matter and a purpose. What possible tale would settle around you? Or I?" He met her gaze and realised she was listening, lips parted a little in concentration. "What possible satisfaction could one have of a story that told how a husband beat his wife, then met with a lingering, meaningless death? Does this story please you? To me, it makes no sense. Your audience would tire of it quickly." She took this in and then her cheeks darkened. Sweeter on the eye than her previous blush had been; the colour was of self-awareness. She went back to tying her *obi* and Takashi realised he was speaking too much. It was the wine in his blood that made him believe he was a poet. Still, now the thoughts were there and it had been so long since he had had someone listen the way she did. "I think," he said, "It would be hard to be burdened with meaning, or responsibility for what we become."

"I don't understand you," she said.

"Take Inuko, my lieutenant. It's not his given name. It's one I gave him. *Little puppy*. Always so very obedient. Easy to train, to lead. They want rules. They don't want to choose for themselves. People like walls, you see. The Lady Mei"–she glanced up sharply–"prefers a prison high on the Red Mountain simply because she has learnt to call it by another word: her 'home.'"

He watched her dressing. It had been months, perhaps years since he had opened his heart to someone, and the words surprised him. For all his scars, he was in fine health. He could point at no wound that ailed him, no particular thought or word or deed. Yet he was ill at ease.

The Lady Mei, for so she was in his mind now, seemed too fragile a thing to be a part of this world. Her slender fingers worked the knots of the robes, her lips pursed in concentration like the bud of a flower. "Come back to Okiri with me."

"I wish to remain here, Captain Takashi."

He was quiet while she finished adjusting her kimono.

"You must think me heartless if you believe I'd leave a woman alone out here with only a dying man and rotting corpses for company."

"I doubt they have had time to rot yet. You have only just killed them after all."

He grunted, half-amused at being caught out.

"Well, I could just as easily bind your hands and take you with me."

"You could." She stood up, once more the woman he had first seen flee from him down white corridors. Calm now though. And her hair a little out of place. "I will come back with you to Okiri at the end of summer if you promise me something," she said, and he smiled:

"What?"

"If I can prove to you that Lord Akayama was party to no crime against the emperor, if I can clear his name, then you will let him live."

"How will you do that?" he asked, amused: "He's already far from here."

"You think he will return, don't you? For me."

"And, for you to clear his name, you need to remain here, on the estate?" She nodded. He smiled up at her, more intrigued by this game than he should be. "Love is a dangerous thing, my lady, if it leads you to barter your life on the basis of a hope. I've known men forsake more than their lovers for greed and wealth."

"I have to try." Something in her tone made him sober a little.

He turned away and started to dress, aware that she remained behind him, unmoving.

"You would have to make it worth my while," he said, tugging his sash into an untidy knot: "My lord will pay me only when Akayama's dead."

"If I can find the money, then I will."

He was pleased to hear that the desperation had returned to her voice and hid his smile in the business of tying his *hakama*.

"Four hundred *ryo*," he said.

"Four? I—"

"I'll bring it down to two. The greater part of it can be paid in the manner of tonight. I will have you." He glanced up, watching as realisation touched her features: "Any time I want you."

"No," she said.

"Why?" he asked, collecting his sword from beside the futon. She started at the rattle of steel and wood: "Mei said she was dishonourable. Unfit to stand by my side, she said. So be it, but I find her fit to lie in my bed." He was close enough now that he could lean into her with a whisper: "Or has she found her honour here tonight?"

"No, I...I will come to you. Two payments of a hundred each. I will come to Okiri, but please do not come back to this house."

He touched her cheek. Grey eyes watched him, though she neither flinched nor pulled away.

"Four payments of fifty," he offered.

"Done."

赤山

In the main chamber a number of Takashi's men had gathered, waiting. Inuko was hunched over the injured man beside the hearth. Mei did not follow the commander into the room but leant heavily in the doorway. It was her first concession to the wine, or perhaps simply to fatigue. Heedless, Takashi approached the prone man.

Save for the injury, his skin was unblemished, untouched by the kind of scars that marred Takashi's own. He was not of a heavy build, but he was lean with knots of muscles in his forearms and skin the colour of a labourer's. His hair too had a reddish cast as if the sun had lightened it. No pale, sheltered lordling; he looked like a spirit carved from the very same red rocks as the mountain itself. A perfect stillness rested on his features.

"Mei," he called. She didn't move, but she watched him from the doorway, arms wrapped around her waist. He set his hand on the hilt of his sword.

"Don't," she said.

In front of his men now, Takashi laughed:

"What is he to you?" She didn't answer. He had seen the bruises though, mostly where they wouldn't show. Even so, marriage was sacred amongst the elder clans and there was a strong possibility that, for that reason alone, she would not give him the permission he sought. "I can say he died of his injuries. There will be no mark against your name and no blood on your hands, Mei." Still she gave no answer and Takashi wondered if that was as close to assent as she would come. Before he could act though, she spoke suddenly:

"We called a doctor two days ago when it became impossible to rouse him. A surgeon was amongst those you killed this morning." If she thought she could prick at Takashi's conscience, she was wrong.

"What was his diagnosis?"

"He will die. If not today, then tomorrow or the day after. He cannot eat and I cannot make him drink."

"Then you intend to simply watch him?" As soon as the words were out of his mouth, he realised he didn't want to know the answer. Her decision might be made out of respect; she might care for him then bury him. But he wouldn't rule out revenge as a motivation either; not with her. So far, she had surprised him in all else.

Mei slipped back into the darkness of the corridor and his eyes were drawn to the empty doorway. Inuko interrupted his thoughts:

"Your orders, Captain?"

"Ready the horses. We leave at first light." The younger man started up and Takashi raised his hand. "We'll station six men on the outpost on the way back to Okiri."

"Sir?"

"They are to watch the road. No one is to enter the estate without my knowing."

There were mutters behind him. The outpost was poorly equipped for occupation. Moreover, the stories of roving bands of criminals in this area had not escaped his men. Some of them were doubtless re-evaluating the fate of the wretch who lay before them; he had met his fate on the same road they were now to guard. "The Lord of Akayama will return," Takashi said, "And, when he does, I want him in chains, kneeling before my door in Okiri. If it takes until the end of summer, we will mark this road. No one goes in and no one comes out."

"The girl?"

"She stays."

His men began to file out, going to the horses. Only Inuko remained, standing over Lord Akayama's brother.

"Bait, Sir?"

"Hah, Inuko"–he cuffed the younger man affectionately, messing up an already moppish head of dark hair–"You're the sharpest mind indeed!" His lieutenant ducked away. Just before Takashi followed his men, he turned back to the quiet chamber: "Mei!" No ghostly figure appeared. She had retreated further into the depths of the house and perhaps that was for the best. He was vaguely aware that a part of him wanted to keep on calling. As it was though, she gave him no choice; dawn was coming and, with it, another day on the road. His body ached, but she had at least invested him with the vitality he sorely needed to face the arduous journey back to Okiri. In that respect, he thought, he was still better furnished than his men.

With one last glance at Akayama Arata, he left the way he had come in, through white paper corridors glowing thinly with the first light of dawn.

2. The First Day

A song was caught in her head; something from her childhood.

It was this that Mei hummed as she slipped into the silent house, carrying a pitcher of water. She could remember some of the words, but they and the notes that carried them echoed sadly in the empty hallway.

In the main chamber the fire was unlit, the screens drawn back as they had been the night before. And the man who had lain prone these last four days was hunched beside the hearth, his expression blank.

She dropped the pitcher in her shock.

The water pooled at her feet.

"My lord."

But not her lord. His eyes were empty. Only recently, she had seen the dead, and her whole body went cold with the thought that he was just like them: the same unseeing gaze, lips parted. She could see the breaths moving in him, but never enough to imbue him with life. "My lord..."

She took two steps in haste before she remembered herself, then bent to pick up the tumbler. A little water remained and she crossed to him. His lips were cracked and dry from the long sleep. She had done her best, but had been afraid. Before Takashi's arrival, a surgeon had cared for him and had seen that he did not die for want of water, but she'd not had that skill and her greatest fear had been that he might choke in his death-sleep, that she would cause the fate that, in her heart she had sensed was inevitable.

Yet here was a quiet miracle. "My lord."

He gave no sign of having heard or seen her and so she knelt for a time, feeling the sun that shone down on them both through the open window, simply staring down at the crystal water.

Then boldly, she reached out and took his wrist, his thumb and fingers and pressed them around the handle of the pitcher. "Take this."

He frowned down at his hand as if it were a rare thing. Then she heard his breath catch and, as she looked up, she glimpsed an expression that could be nothing less than the deepest terror. Only glimpsed because he flung the pitcher at her and it struck her shoulder, hard enough that she cried out.

He lurched forward, out of the sheets. Brutish, reaching. She could see nothing that made her believe he lived behind those eyes. This thought, coupled with the residue of slaughter, still so fresh in her mind, made her recoil; the idea that it was still only she who had survived.

With a dry gasp, she fled.

赤山

Akayama, the Red Mountain, rose out of its foothills in the east into rocky spires that vied with the sun. On its western side, the ground dropped away precipitously. A vast cliff of red stone, in shadow for one half of each day, was bathed in radiance for the other. A single road led out of the town of Okiri, cut into the rust-coloured rock for which the mountain bore its name. Where it forked there was an outpost, intermittently manned. And from thence, one way led down to the western valley: an endless plain of scattered farmsteads and human debris at the edge of the world. The other way led further into the mountain and, deepening like a gorge, at last released its captive wanderers into an impossible garden cleaving to the side of the mountain: a sheltered, green woodland of fern, bamboo and ash. And there, two marble terraces connected by the arc of a bridge.

The manor house could have stood proudly in the midst of the capital were it not for the thick orchard of struts and supports that grew out of the cliff itself and kept it rooted, like a strange blossom on the surface of one vast, calcified branch. It was and had always been a fantasy. Nothing of such beauty should exist out here. Yet by chance and the rudiments of nature, the western cliff curled around the manor's delicate frame like a cupped hand and deep wells drew water from the least accessible of the mountain streams.

So had the Akayama estate survived, in written records at least, for the past six centuries.

Mei knew the history. She did not know how dynasties ended; she did not know what came after.

She had been born in a village thirty miles to the west that, on clear days, was still visible as a shadow in a heat haze. It was nestled amongst brown, tepid fields that she recalled, from her childhood, were ever wary of giving up their crops.

Back then Akayama had been the name of the mountain and a name for their rulers, and no one had ever distinguished between the two. Where the mountain's shadow touched the earth, that same earth was ripe for taxation. Between the barrenness of the soil and the meanness of the soldiers who came down from the mountain demanding their bounty, there was a lean existence dictated by the seasons.

It had bred in her, even at so young an age, an affinity for the land. Her hands no longer worked it, but she felt it inside her and always had. The seasons were a long, slow heartbeat. By contrast, her own heart beat faster, but it was tardy compared to that of a mouse or sparrow. And so she concluded everything moved to the same rhythm even if some made greater haste.

She had considered leaving many times over. It was an accident that had brought her to the mountain and an accident that she had stayed. Certainly she had never belonged here, but she had no other home in the world. Over time little roots had grown: the intimate knowledge she had garnered of the house and its grounds; those places that were hers and hers alone. One was here.

On other estates an ornamental bridge might span a gentle brook or pool. Not so here. A narrow path that had once hugged the rock had, in one spot between the main house and the more modest servants' quarters, crumbled away until nothing was left. Long ago in the annuls of the house and its clan, someone had designed this fantastical bridge with serpents that coiled along the balustrade and all manner of beasts and fauna, large and small, carved into its beams. Few stopped to admire them. Fewer still had the time, or perhaps the courage, to glance over the edge and realise there was nothing beneath. All the way down it fell, to the valley floor. And on evenings like this, when the summer mists rolled in from the valley, you could sit above the clouds. Mei's bare feet hung against the yawning dark.

The wind had snatched away a few errant tears and her eyes were dry again. She was trying to catch her courage, which was as fleeting as the last rays of sun.

"Don't," someone commanded her.

She started and gasped, coming as close as she ever had to plunging into the ravine below. He was standing on the threshold, where the path gave way to the bridge, one hand reaching out for her.

She pushed aside the urge to run. He had spoken and that, at least, seemed human. She could see his hand was shaking too.

"I—" she began. He waited.

She swung her legs back over the railings and did not take his hand but joined him on the near side of the bridge. "My lord, I only came here to watch the last of the daylight." It was then that she started to notice the small things that were still out of place. Standing there now, he held his hands at his sides, curled into fists. She could see the way his grip had stained his knuckles white. His feet were bare. His *obi* had been knotted hastily. In these things she recognised little of the man she had known.

He turned away and his footsteps seemed to reach of their own accord back up the path. "My lord, wait!"

She joined him and took his arm. He did not make her take his weight but his very movements seemed heavy. "How long had you been awake when I returned?" she asked.

"I don't remember."

"It doesn't matter. The important thing is that you are here. That you are well." She let her fingers pinch gently at his arm.

"I don't remember."

"It doesn't matter."

"No, I mean I don't—" His breath hitched. In the silence she counted off her heartbeats. "Nothing," he said. "Nothing from before I woke. Nothing." He turned towards her. "Who am I?"

Just the night before she had told Takashi that her life was a story. Not one of words but one of memories. Each caused ripples. And ripples caused waves. They pushed her one way then another. It had never occurred to her that, in a single moment, those tides could be broken, or what it might be to stand outside of them.

"You are Akayama Arata," she said.

"What is this place?"

"Your brother's estate. Your family are named after the mountain, Akayama, see?"

He glanced down at her hand.

"And you?"

"Mei."

"Mei?"

"Your wife."

After a long time he covered her hand with his own.

Yes, she had thought of leaving many times, but little roots grew and wound their way deep.

As they walked, she saw his eyes had strayed to the landscape: the strange spires and crags. Close to the manor, a single tower of rock stood alone against the sky. A fallen boulder had wedged itself between this and the rock-face, forming a natural promontory, and a plateau like an altar. It was on this strange silhouette that his eyes lingered. "What is it you're looking at?" Mei asked at length. He blinked as if she had woken him from a dream:

"This place is beautiful, isn't it?"

"Yes," she said. "It is."

赤山

It was past midnight. He was kneeling on the floor with a mirror, using a knife to shave with swift, efficient strokes.

"We have a morning room should you require use of it," Mei said as she stepped into the chamber. He hesitated, wary.

"I have everything I need."

"I could show you the rest of the house though—"

"No." He went back to shaving.

"I heard one time of a man who was caught in a rock fall, or so they thought," she said, padding across the room. "When they found him, he didn't remember his family or the village where he lived, though he could recall, in extraordinary detail, the place he had called home as a child." He ignored the bowl of food she placed in front of him. "They say that, in the end, all the memories returned." She seated herself across the hearth. He was examining his face in the mirror, frowning at the fresh black scar at his temple. "Your reflection," she said.

"What of it?"

"Is it familiar to you?"

"No, I am"–he widened his eyes and wrinkled his brow, and suddenly bared his teeth, studying the face– "Twenty—"

"Twenty-six, my lord."

He glanced over the rim of the mirror:

"And my wife?"

"She is twenty-four."

She smiled a little as he went back to gazing intently at the glass. He seemed, as yet, oblivious of his strangeness. "They say one of the great vices of the nobility is their vanity."

"Do you know who did this?" he asked, touching the scar and any lightness of mood passed away.

"You had ridden to Okiri. I heard that you were injured, but you'd ridden back without incident, so I thought…But they said you fell to sleeping and nothing they could do would rouse you."

The shock at least had passed from his eyes. In his restless energy she saw the man she remembered. Whether it be virtue or flaw, he was the kind who took what he needed. Perhaps that was why tonight the absence in him was so marked. The will remained but the intention was gone. "Is there anything else you want?" she asked.

"Just give me a little time."

He had no understanding of how apt a request that was.

She sighed and leant over to stoke the fire. She would give him time because she feared his nature. He would act. If there was one thing she had learnt about him it was that he would act. He would not have stood by and watched the household die.

For the first time in two days, she tried, really tried, to line up her thoughts. His brother was gone. The servants were dead. In four weeks time, unbeknownst to him, she would be expected to make the journey to Okiri to spend the night in Takashi's residence.

Ryuu would never have allowed this to happen.

"You must be tired," he said. She looked up and realised he was watching her. "What were you thinking about?"

"When you came down to the bridge and you reached out to help me, your hand was trembling, and the way you stood"–he frowned as she spoke–"You and your brother are both afraid of heights. It seems the most ridiculous thing! Living up here it must be like being afraid of your shadow." She met his eye. "Only, whether or not you think you remember, you were trembling."

Understanding softened his features and he glanced down at his hands.

"It had occurred to me that if I can speak and eat and walk, then something remains. But there is a difference between acting and knowing." She nodded. "Is that all that was bothering you?"

"Yes," she lied, standing up. "And the lateness of the hour." As she stooped to pick up his bowl, his hand closed over her wrist and instinctively she tensed. His thumb slid along the delicate line of the bone.

"Tell me one thing," he said. "Am I good to you?"

"Of course, my lord."

Later, she would make his bed chamber and pausing would check the pale skin inside her wrist. Finding nothing there, she would return to her work.

赤山

She told him, when he asked, that most of the servants had left with his brother. When he had been injured, she had sent others into town to find a doctor, but none had returned and she was afraid they had been killed on the road. There were bandits in the mountains, she'd said

She led him to the bedchamber. His grip was still heavy on her arm. If he doubted her, then he chose not to say, but he did watch her. His gaze was more intense than she recalled, feeding off of his perceptions like a man starved of their succour. His eyes, like hers, were grey. They said it was a trait of the valley people, but here he was and he was just the same as her.

As she finished with the small details of the day, the clothes that the servants should have folded, and the windows that they should have closed, he lay on the futon and watched her. She came and knelt at the foot of the bed.

"Will you stay there all night, Mei?"

"All night, yes," she said, smiling because a thin dawn light was creeping in, between the shutters.

"You are watching over me, I think."

赤山

There were many thieves on the Red Mountain. There were brigands on the road who robbed the unwary. There were those who rode on horseback, wielding blades, who could, in a single afternoon, reap a dozen futures. And there were those who stole hearts, those who snatched words over firelight in the deepest night.

But the greatest thief on the Red Mountain had been born in a village thirty miles to the west. She had often thought of leaving, but in the end, indeed at the very end, she chose to stay.

3. Memories

"Arata...Arata." He tested the name on the tip of his tongue as if searching for familiarity in those syllables. Mei tripped past him, out through the screen door and into the sunlight.

He had spent the morning in the main chamber, searching through documents, fitting them into the spaces between the facts that Mei had given him, gradually building up a picture of his own character. It was an odd way to spend a day, like passing an afternoon tasting new foods, but his discoveries were all short-lived; not one letter or note found its way to a corresponding memory in his head.

"It is a fine name!" she called back over her shoulder.

That girl...She loved the sunlight and she wasn't workshy. She was out there now, barefoot, wringing clothes in a basin, weighing them down with stones to dry on the terrace and humming to herself all the while as if she were born without a care in the world.

"You seem especially happy today, Mei."

"Not really."

"Do you always sing?"

"Oh. Yes." She sounded thoughtful. "I think it's a bit like the birds."

"Marvellous. I married a lark," he said, coming to stand on the threshold between the house and the terrace. "Have I ever told you it's an irritation?"

"No," she said. "You have not."

Still there was something infectious about it, he thought, as he watched her kneading the clothes. Whether she intended it or not, she gave an impression of carelessness, as if all the woes of the world would not reach her. That, in itself, was compelling. Careless but not uncaring. Never uncaring. She was attentive; she was sweet. At some point, those things must have charmed him. Yet with no way to trace his own fascination for her back to anything more intimate than curiosity, he was at a loss. She was quiet now. He waited and, as he knew it must, the silence quickly became as unbearable as nails dragged over glass.

"Mei?"

"Yes?" She regarded him over her shoulder, hair falling across her face. He tried to keep his expression stern.

"You have my leave to sing."

And she did so. Like the birds.

It wasn't just the singing. It was everything about her. She pinned her hair up with jade and gold, wore gowns of silk and embroidery, acted with exquisite etiquette, and yet whenever his attention was on other things, she turned her hand to tasks that should be beneath her and even appeared to take pleasure in them. And she went everywhere barefoot.

That, he thought, would have to stop. They were not children. But still yes, compelling. "Mei, all of this correspondence is in my brother's hand. These are dealings with *hatsumoto,* samurai, traders." He discarded them carelessly on the desk, ignoring the papers that escaped and floated to the floor. "Are there personal letters anywhere?"

"Of what nature?"

"Do we have family beyond the estate?"

"I don't think so."

"Friends?" He looked up and she was leaning in the doorway, her hands tucked beneath her arms.

"You've found nothing of use?"

"Everything is of use and I have a fine impression of my brother's mind now," he said darkly. "Not a coin has passed through his coffers nor a grain of rice through his stores without his having noted it. He must be a fascinating individual!" He turned a ferocious gaze against the stacks of paper. "Perhaps he should have spent more time concerning himself with his neighbours and his family rather than with the running of his estate."

"Is there anything there on duties and trade?"

"I imagine so. Would you care to look? You too can waste half a day."

"Oh, Arata-*sama*," she said, stepping into the room and moving towards him as if she would take his hand. He felt a little of his anger lift. And then, the strangest thing: she stopped. The hand that had reached out closed, dropped away and came to rest at her waist. Her gaze fell away from his.

"Mei?"

"I–I thought suddenly your brother would be hurt if he heard you say such things." She looked up. "But you're right. It is a waste. When the days are as beautiful as this, they should not be spent inside."

"There are more papers. I should keep looking."

"Arata-*sama*," she said sharply and he saw in her eyes a kind of reluctant anger, even as he tried to look away. "What is it about this room?" she said. "What can you possibly find here? It's been three days!"

"I told you that it would take time and you promised that you would give it to me." To his own ears the excuse sounded weak, but she only gazed up at him sadly. "Go outside, Mei, if it's sunshine and birdsong you want."

She opened her mouth as if she would rebuke him, then closed it and turned on her heel. And he watched her go, her feet making no sound on the boards.

The trouble was, she was right. Three days he had spent moving from this room to the bedroom to the bath-house. Three days, and the only time he had left the manor had been on that first day when he'd seen Mei waiting on the bridge, looking for all the world as if she would hurl herself off.

What was wrong with him? It wasn't fear. Not exactly. A sense of dread perhaps. There was too much that he didn't know and out there, instead of answers, were just more questions: on the mountain, in the gardens, on the paths and in the woodland. God help him! Was he going mad? In his mind, they were crowded places; crowded, not with memories, but with ghosts: all the things still invisible to him, so that, were he not mad already, they would probably make him so.

Alone in the chamber now, he allowed his knees to buckle and, free of Mei's quiet gaze, he let his head fall into his hands. It was not over for him. He could see in the way Mei spoke to him that she assumed the worst was past, but he had not told her yet that his head ached sharply sometimes, as if someone had driven a nail straight through to the centre, or that the mildest exertion left patches of shadow swarming across his vision. He was weak and that scared him.

And the world beyond these walls scared him too. And there wasn't a thing in this god-forsaken world that didn't imbue him with some kind of terror. It was no way to live.

He raised his head and looked around. This chamber, furnished with linen curtains, a writing desk and a simple hearth, had become familiar to him. In time, other things would become familiar. The face in the mirror; the woman on the terrace.

Mei. Now there was a problem he had to confront. At a time when he needed allies more than ever, she was lying to him.

Oh, it wasn't just that she was almost too sweet for his current disposition to find her credible, and anyway it was not clear that she was deceiving him in her affections; it was something else. She was cold with him.

It seemed unfair really, to make such a judgement with no point of comparison, but it was there in the way she moved away if he came too close, in the hand that reached out then pulled back. In a marriage, there were no doubt things that went unsaid. And yet her silences were as capable of covering a passing whim as they were a morass of secrets; he had no way yet of telling which. In one thing though he was certain: she had lied about the servants.

She had not sent them away.

It left him to suspect that the two of them had been abandoned here and possibly not just by the servants but by the rest of the household too. Why?

If he had learnt one thing from the papers he had sifted through this morning it was that Akayama Ryuu did not leave things undone. So, if he, Arata, had been charged with remaining on an abandoned estate for a purpose then what, in God's name, was his purpose? And why would she hide it from him? He stood up and began to pace out his frustration on the wooden floor, his feet making a sharp rhythm across the old boards. Perhaps he was being too suspicious; perhaps Mei was not privy to his brother's reasoning. Except no, she had lied, and that meant something was being hidden. And if she could hide something then she could hide anything.

Asking her would be the hardest thing. In doing so he would reveal his suspicions and leave her free to cover her tracks in any way she needed. Better to root out clues from Ryuu's library of paperwork than confront her.

He went back to the desk. Reports, receipts, registers: the depths of Ryuu's honesty were almost as hard to stomach as Mei's attentions. The man must have flaws! He removed the lowest drawer from the writing desk and emptied its contents. His brother struck him as the kind of man who would keep a record of everything, even the less than savoury things, if it meant that he could refer back to them in a moment's need. He was rewarded with the discovery of a small leather-bound book buried beneath all the rest.

Opening it, his mood darkened again as he was confronted with tally after tally of accounts.

"Ryuu-*nii-sama,* I would find your mind an unbearably dull burden."

Only two names in this book though. In one column, 'Ryuu.'

In the other, 'Arata.'

It was one of the few times he had found his name written anywhere in the correspondence. He flicked back to the beginning.

Was he reading this correctly? Did Ryuu pay him a wage? An allowance? It would be humiliating to discover he was on the payroll of the human abacus, but then again no, these were lists of payments being made from Arata to his older brother with, at intervals, large deductions from Ryuu's own totals. These latter were labelled simply 'debt.'

He was borrowing money?

And paying it back. Though irregularly, if the dates were to be believed, and he had no reason to suspect that his brother would have allowed errors to creep in.

A receipt of payment fell from the pages. This time though it was not in his brother's hand. He picked it up.

Two seals closed the missive at the bottom of the page: Akayama Ryuunaka and Kotaro Murasaki.

And a note of guarantee that no more attempts would be made on the life of Akayama Arata following the receipt of three hundred *ryo*. That was all. He turned it over as if there had to be something more. Perhaps if he held it to the light he would see something he had missed.

Nothing. Just those words.

He slipped the receipt back inside the book, closed it and stowed it securely in the front of his kimono before moving swiftly to kneel beside the hearth and pour himself some tea. His hand was shaking. For the first time though it was not from fear.

This was something. Confirmation of his existence. Seeing his name there, over and over. If only he could tell whether those debts were his own or if he was in his brother's employ and, if the latter, what nature of work he had undertaken on behalf of his family. Something sufficiently dangerous to have made himself enemies.

Kotaro Murasaki. It was something.

Now more than ever he felt that Ryuu must have left him here with some purpose in mind and, if it had escaped him, it was known at least to some extent by the figure who now stood in the doorway swaying beneath the weight of a fresh pail of water.

"Did you find something, Arata-*sama?*" she asked, smiling at him, and he shook his head.

"Nothing, Mei."

Because if they were to play a game, and he was certain now that it would be one where the stakes were high, then he had every intention of being the one to make the rules.

赤山

Time passed slowly. Long days gave way to a week.

He watched her.

Mei was happiest alone. For all her sweetness, her presence was a strain on them both, but in the absence of their servants there were plenty of activities to engage her and she was willing to undertake all manner of menial chores without complaint. At one point she explained to him that her lineage was humble and, as a child and young woman, such tedium had been commonplace. This hadn't surprised him. In her bearing and manners she was like one schooled in etiquette. She was graceful with a learned finesse, but when he wasn't watching or when she forgot herself, which was rare, it all fell away like autumn leaves. Beneath, there remained something raw, unworked; exactly what it was he had yet to determine because she would hastily remake herself for him. So no, her heritage was not a surprise, but it did lead to a surprising conclusion: since their marriage could have had no political incentive he must have at one time loved her.

She had not yet shared his bed.

Indeed, since the first day when he had found her on the bridge and she had taken his arm, they had not touched.

At first he thought that such delicate things could be left unexamined until his memories started to return. There were more pressing matters at hand in the form of who and where and how and when. But the more time that passed, the more he began to believe that she was the key, and that the unnatural distance between them was as bound up in her secrets as the fate of their servants and the whereabouts of his brother.

Once he understood her, he might begin to understand himself.

An opportunity presented itself one day. He had begun to divide his time between his living quarters and a library that spanned nearly the length of the house. It was a peculiar accident of design that allowed the walls there to merge at times with the red rock of the cliff so that, walking the length of the windowless room, one had the impression of being in a cavern. The space was lit with standing oil lamps. It appealed to his desire for confinement.

He could while away hours here, lost in books and stories that were, to him, no more or less real than the ones Mei told him of his former life. He had the notion that, seated quietly with his back against the full weight of the mountain, he could be anyone he wished to be, become anything described in these dense words.

"What is it you find there?" Mei asked him one day. She was not at home in a library. Until he saw her there, he had not imagined that anyone could look so out of place amongst books and scrolls. "I thought that you had read all of those and had no time for them anymore."

"Did I say that?" He gave a bitter laugh. If she understood the joke though she didn't find it funny. She stared around at the packed shelves as if she expected them all to tumble down on her within a heartbeat.

He knew that what he was about to do was cruel. "Mei," he said, carefully closing the book. "I remembered Kyoko."

Already pale, her cheeks seemed suddenly porcelain. Her eyes widened. Whatever he had expected, she was giving him more than he could have hoped for. From his place at the base of the bookshelves he watched her, knowing that to miss the slightest nuance of a glance, the hesitations, gestures, doubts, to miss even one was to risk losing the game.

"Everything?" she asked.

"Did you think you could keep it from me for so long?" He rose to his feet. "Did you not think I'd start to ask what this is all about? Why we're like this? Why my own wife can barely bring herself to touch me? Did you think I couldn't see that something was wrong?"

She said nothing but lifted one hand to her chest, her breathing swift.

So he was right? Yes. But how far could he push this?

Kyoko. Not a memory; not at all. She'd been a name in the dedication of a book he'd picked up by chance two days previously; a dedication professing undying love and pressed home with the seal of an Akayama Arata he could not remember. She was another woman then. And he had checked; the book had been a recent addition to the library. According to Mei, they had been married for four years, but the book had been bound last summer.

If this was how it had to be then so it would be. The only way to stop her lying to him was to make her believe she couldn't.

He studied her face. It was so hard to play this right, but she knew the name and, judging by her reaction, she knew of the affair. "I remember when I realised you'd found out," he said carefully. Her eyes dropped away from his face.

She was harder to read if she didn't look at him. He was close though; too close now to lose this opportunity. She took a step backwards and stumbled into the shelf behind, caught in a rain of dust. One of the larger volumes slid forward and he reached for it as it fell, trapping her between himself and the books as he slipped it back between the other tomes.

She seemed to make herself smaller, heartbeats passing.

He was losing her now. No denial; no anger. If she could have, he sensed, she would have faded back into the shadows in which they stood. "She's the reason you can't touch me," he said.

"Forgive me." She stepped forward so suddenly that the impact of her body against his own was jarring. It was an embrace so fierce that, in the face of it, his anger crumbled and he stood for an instant with his hands lifted from the shelves and no means of returning the emotion.

Slowly he let his hands fold over her shoulders. The tension in her made her seem brittle and he was suddenly aware of the difference in their size. He had wanted to scare her; scare her so that she would think twice about lying again, but his mind had been baited by doubts. He had missed the important things: this was his wife and he had loved her.

He might not remember; he might never love her again. But did that mean he should sacrifice his past to defeat her in this? Had it worked, would he ever have been able to forgive himself?

"Mei?"

"Why are you doing this?" she asked him miserably. He could feel her breath fluttering against his chest.

"You've been lying to me."

She didn't deny it, but he felt her sigh and he wished that she would.

"Arata," she said at length, her breathing sounding more even now. "Please let's go outside. It's making things worse if you stay here. You're—you're getting further and further from the truth."

"Mei, you've been lying to me," he said without emotion and she stepped back, her eyes bright.

"There are things I have to show you."

赤山

It was not a paralysing fear. It was not something he could not overcome if he put his mind to it.

Mei was tense, her demeanour changed from any he had seen in the preceding days. She hurried ahead of him. Then, realising that he had no intention of hastening, she hesitated and waited, the urgency an expression of her mood.

It was the first time he'd been out since the day he'd woken and it was cooler today than it had been then. The birds still sung and the crickets still railed in the trees, but today the wind churned in the natural enclave formed by the red cliff and its cathedral of stacks and towers.

"The weather's changing," he said. She watched his face as they walked, side by side now, down from the terraces.

"Not really. The rains have passed, but parts of them linger. We're in the shadow here, but over in the valley they'll have showers and squalls all night." She pointed to a dark horizon where tell-tale verticals of cloud suggested the fields would be wet tonight.

"I thought you said I was afraid of heights."

"You are, my lord, but I don't think the view has ever troubled you. It's more the edges of things," she said thoughtfully and despite himself he smiled at the way she considered that.

He was hesitant on the bridge where he had first seen her. The moisture in the air had left the carvings dark and shining as if the serpents had, whilst he slept, been imbued with life. He was grateful that she neither waited for him nor offered him her hand across the wooden arch. "That was the house for the servants," she said, pointing when he joined her on the other side. It was another building of stilts and struts and overhanging roofs, though in design and structure more modest than the manor house. She led him past it and down a short path that forked, one way leading into woodland, the other to a low building with double doors.

At first he thought it might be a shrine. It was unpretentious though and ivy had grown around the doorway, which no one had bothered to cut back. Belonging more to the mountain than the house, when she opened the latch and pushed the doors wide, all he could see was an empty hall.

As with the library, the red cliff intruded into this room. Though it had two walls made of wood and gesso, the eastern side of the roof was an overhang of red rock. Windows lined the opposite wall but let in only grey light filtered through the trees.

Her bare feet made a soft rhythm on the wooden floor.

He knew this place or at least he knew it to be a *dojo* where men trained in the military arts. As he entered, he paused to take off his sandals and bow to the presiding deity. Mei was already standing in the centre of the room.

"Why here?" he asked.

"Please." She gestured for him to take a seat on the floor, then turned away.

"Mei?"

"Yes?"

He stepped out onto the training floor and suddenly they faced each other across the distance of the hall.

"Do you"–he asked–"I mean–did you–forgive me for Kyoko?" And even from here he could see how she had to think about the question.

"I had the chance to save someone's life once," she said. Her voice was soft but it carried. "I didn't take it and I've regretted it every day since. I do not have to hold you accountable for your mistakes, Arata-*sama*. That is your conscience." He opened his mouth to say he didn't understand, but she had already turned away and he shut it abruptly.

He had lied about remembering Kyoko, but she didn't need to know that yet.

He went to the place she had been standing and knelt. There were memories here. It was worse than standing on the terraces; these felt like watchful eyes. The hall smelt of damp and neglect, but in his mind's eye there were hanging lamps shedding light on the polished floor and the sound of his own footsteps ringing as he moved across the space. Had she known he would remember? Why here?

Mei came back carrying a curved sword in a red sheath in both her hands. Kneeling, she laid it between them, and when he did nothing but stare she sighed and folded her hands on her knees. "I had hoped you would remember. This was yours."

He unsheathed the sword. There was fine workmanship in the tempered metal, from the intricate patterns that wound around the *tsuba* to the blade itself where a design like waves on a storm-swept ocean marked the point from which it had been sharpened to a lethal edge. With it unsheathed to half its length, he hesitated. From that point on the bright metal was stained with blood so dry and dark that it was almost black. "You would never let anyone touch it, not even to clean it, so when you rode back after the attack they just left it. Then, with everything else, they forgot. I think it was a superstition of some kind. Only that wasn't the only sword you returned with. There was another. It belonged to your brother." He looked up. She held his gaze for a moment then dropped forward into a half-obeisance. "Arata, I need you to remember. I don't know why you returned with his sword or even whether that is his blood, but I need you to tell me if he is alive."

He stared.

"Were we at odds?"

"You loved your brother more than life itself, but..."

"But?"

"You had argued that morning. I don't know the details."

Try as he might, he could see no word of a lie in her face. The blood on the blade sickened him.

"Why would I...?"

"I need to know, Arata, if he's going to come back. I need to know if he's going to save us."

A beat passed. He suddenly resheathed the sword and laid it back down, the click and hollow thud making her straighten.

"From what? From thieves? From bandits?"

"Arata, there's no money in the coffers; I've checked. There's no grain in the stores, no rice. We've used the last of the meat, and we have what we can grow when it's in season, but that's all, and there are armed men on the road who mean not to let us through." She looked up. "He left us, Arata, and I don't know why, but you know."

In a sudden motion, he reached for the sword with both hands, but she was quick and her hands covered his own, forcing him to hesitate, bent over the weapon. "You must not use this," she said. "Promise me."

For all that there was pride involved, he understood. She didn't want him running off after a lost cause. And she was right: he was in no state physically or mentally to challenge whoever it was who held them here, if all that she was saying were true. But he had instinctively reached for the sword. And she had instinctively stopped him.

"Mei, why did you show me this?" he asked and, seeing that he had control of himself, she took her hands back and folded them on her knees, a little more hunched now than she had been before.

"I thought that you might remember. They said that you were the best. Your brother never had time for this, but of you they said that you could take on fifteen men and still walk away. And sometimes, when I've seen you angry, I would believe it. You are a different man." She sighed. "You used to spend hours here, practising with this blade. It was your life."

"This—was my life?" She nodded. "My brother had his accounting and I had this."

She had looked away towards the windows and he found himself watching her. She was full of nervous movements. Eyes that followed the branches of trees caught by the wind; fingers that pinched the skin on her wrists gently as if to remind herself she were alive; she chewed her lower lip and seemed to have forgotten him until he reached out and touched her hair. When she wore it down, it was as untamed and unmanageable as she was and it spread across her shoulders like a shawl. Instantly she turned back and brushed his hand away, shock rather than any other emotion registering on her face.

They stared at each other.

She stood up and walked past him. "Mei," he said, "Who were we?"

"You remembered Kyoko. You'll remember the rest," she said from somewhere near the door. He listened to the sound of the latch being lifted and waited until the room was silent again before he took the sword in both hands and rested it on his knees. The weight was familiar.

Perhaps in this he had found something he could trust.

4. The Ways We Lie

Crouching outside the *dojo,* Mei took several deep breaths, waiting for the sense of dizziness to pass. This was ridiculous. Why did she panic every time he tried to touch her? Why was she so desperate for him to remember and yet, at the same time, so frightened. She had taken the fork in the path that led away from the house and into the woodland. Where the trees were thin on the higher slopes, bamboo grew in abundance and she had to be careful, as soon as she was off the path, not to tread on broken canes, each sharp enough to tear through flesh. Once out of sight of the house, she had stopped, her head swimming.

Takashi had said that the house was a prison. She hadn't really understood what that meant until today, and it wasn't because his soldiers were holding her here. It was something deeper than that. A part of her wanted to take one of the horses and ride to Okiri if only to put an end to this. At least it would be over then. She could go to Takashi, tell him everything and ask for mercy. There would be opportunities to escape; there always were.

She swiped one hand across her eyes, half-expecting to find tears, but there were none. The truth was, she wouldn't risk his life. Running to Takashi, however tempting it was, would not clear Ryuu's name. Her only hope was here, in this house, in baiting the brother. Because she was certain that her answers lay with Arata.

The man she had left back at the *dojo* though was much changed.

She had never seen him scared. She had never seen him weak. Always strong, sometimes in the ugliest of ways, but without him, without the person he had been, she felt like a boat torn loose of its mooring. The fullness of that absurdity struck her now. She had stayed for Ryuu, but it was Arata who had loved her and hurt her and bound her up in his life.

"Mei…! Mei!"

She started from where she was standing and gasped as one of the bamboo canes scored a line down her calf. A dark trail of blood appeared. She hesitated, her weight balanced on the other leg as she watched the wound well and start to bleed. "Mei!"

"Here!" she called after just a heartbeat's hesitation. Every sinew in her body told her she should run further, faster, and yet sense suggested she had done a stupid thing by coming out here. If she was ever to cease to be a coward then she would have to face him and the feelings she had for him. With care, she picked her way out of the bamboo grove, now and again stopping to check the scarlet lines that were winding down her leg. By the time she reached the path, it was throbbing and burning by turns. "I'm here, Arata-*sama*."

赤山

"From henceforth, you're to wear sandals when you're outside the house. You're not a child."

She sat on the raised dais where his futon was arranged while he washed her leg. The water was warm. He'd heated it on the hearth and, though she flinched whenever he touched the wound, she never made a sound. She did, after a little time, lean over to see what he was doing and she heard the amusement in his voice as he spoke. "Not very squeamish, are you?"

"I've had worse."

"Really?" he said, starting to wrap linen around the wound. "Then I've not been caring for you very well." She didn't answer.

He wore his hair tied up. He always had. She wondered if it was something he'd remembered or if he hadn't needed to somehow. On a whim she reached out and, mirroring his actions in the *dojo,* touched a stray piece of hair that had fallen across his cheek. His grey eyes met her own.

"You're different," she said.

"How?"

"You're more gentle."

He finished and his hands cupped her foot. His thumb traced a delicate line around her ankle bone, which might have been deliberate though it was hard to tell. "What is it?" she asked after a time, when the touch had become a sliver of sensation in her spine and she had to speak to hide a shiver.

"You asked me if I had killed my brother."

"Yes."

"What kind of man kills his own brother?"

"Ah," she said. This time, when she reached out, she did not stop short of the strand of hair but let her hand rest against his cheek, making him look up at her. "You change when you are angry. Both you and your brother are the same in that way, and you, you have always been so very particular."

"Particular?"

"You must master everything. Everything in its place." As he glanced away she let her fingers slid beneath his chin, keeping him from lowering his head. His pulse was a gentle beat against her fingertips. "It is your right, isn't it, to make everything obey you?"

"Including my brother?"

"I don't know. You left in a rage."

"You said we argued." Her eyes issued a challenge but she didn't look away. She sat back, hands flat on the dais. "No thieves then? No bandits on the road?" he said.

"There are those who are keeping us here now."

"So you say, but I only have your word for it." His hand shifted slowly along the back of her leg to the crease behind her knee. It slid up beneath her thigh. It would be right for her to tug down the kimono she had gathered up to let him reach the wound. Instead, where her hands supported her weight, her fingers curled up against the wooden floor.

"I lied," she said. "I lied because you are—not yet strong."

"To protect me?"

She was ashamed that just the sense of his hand on her leg could still make her breath catch. If she asked him to stop he might, but what possible reason could she give?

"To protect you," she said.

And he leant in so close that their faces were bare inches apart, his eyes studying her own. This time she reached up with both hands, letting the tips of her fingers rest against his cheeks. "Could you see," she asked carefully, "If I were lying now?" On the last word, his lips touched hers.

It was searching, tentative. She found herself leaning away instinctively, only to feel his hands on her shoulders, easing her forward.

Yet the touch was tender; he did not hold her there. And with that realisation came a flood of other sensations. The latent heat in her belly blazed up into her chest. She let him pull her towards him and, from the dais, slid to her knees. All her strength was gone. It was disbelief, more than anything, which paralysed her. Disbelief that he would be kind. Disbelief that he would want her. And delight. And desire. Such fierce desire.

When he pulled back, her eyes were still closed.

"I cannot tell," he said, and she heard him shift and stand before she opened her eyes. It took her a moment to comprehend what he was saying. "You can lie quite well with words, I think. But in some things you cannot." He straightened his *haori* and she watched him brush it down as if wiping dust from the cloth. "I am flattered," he said as he turned away.

赤山

Perhaps, she thought, it was because, having been born up here, up above everyone else, and having looked down on the valley for so long and seen how small the rest of the world was, he had thought it would be easy to control it.

She watched him in the days that followed their encounter. There was a change in him. The energy she remembered from before spilled over now into something more than nervous searching. He seemed to have regained a purpose.

He spent a night and a day cleaning the sword she had shown him in the *dojo* until no trace of blood was visible on the blade. Then he spent each afternoon practising in the sunlight before the great vista of the western plain. And she watched him. Because words between them were no longer easy.

It was two weeks since Takashi's men had come; another two before she would have to leave for Okiri. She was not as afraid as she knew she should be, but she was concerned for their more basic needs. Before the summer was out they would run short of their meagre foodstuffs, and she had no way to pay Takashi yet with anything but herself.

And that was why the spectre of a rider dismounting in the grounds one morning came as both a warning and a relief.

She stood stock still on the terrace. It was barely dawn and the light was still pale, having not yet climbed over the jagged rims of Akayama's peaks. She wore just a simple *yukata,* her hair loose from slumber, her feet bare again since she saw no virtue in following instructions when their enforcer was absent.

At first she could only think that it was a dream, but as the rider heaved bags from the horse's back and turned towards the house she came to life again. This was one of Takashi's men. She didn't know what he would do if he found Arata, but she wasn't about to test him. She jogged down from the terrace and headed him off on the near side of the bridge, recalling, as she did, that this youngster was Takashi's second, the one who had gone by the name of Inuko.

He blinked at her attire.

"Akayama-*sama,*" he addressed her.

"Inuko-*san.*"

He smiled at her use of the nickname. He was young. Had he really been so young before? Those were the same broad hands that had lifted her and nearly choked the life from her body, and which now offered her a drawstring sack. He tugged it open and let her peer inside.

"Rice," he said. "You have no reason to come to Okiri now until such time as the captain requires payment."

It had never crossed her mind to ride to Okiri for food. She had nothing to pay with after all. And now it seemed there was no need. From afar Takashi was mocking her with her own salvation. She drew the sack closed and bowed her head, a willing prisoner. "His instructions were," Inuko said, "To check that the princess was still in her castle. And to ask as to whether her prince had awakened."

She looked up. Dark, lively eyes met her own. He had a mischief about him which, in such a line of work, bordered on pleasure in another's woes. For all that he was young and handsome, she trusted he could hurt her without a thought: an intelligent mind rankled by boredom and forged by a blunted conscience. She would not test him, but she would make him leave.

"He died within two days of your coming."

"So you would say."

"You may look around if you wish," she said, stepping aside from the path. "Inuko-*san* will find the house empty. I buried him with my own hands. The solitude up here is suited to mourning."

"I have no intention of looking for things I won't find. You can show me the grave-site and that will suffice."

She hesitated barely a moment, knowing that he would be waiting for her to slip. A nod and she turned away. He fell into step a little behind her, heaving the bag of rice over one shoulder and following her across the lower terrace and into the copse.

"Take care since the path isn't even," she said.

Indeed at dawn it was wet with dew and springy underfoot, as if they walked across a blanket of moss. Water vapour hung in the air. She turned right at the well, heading deeper into the undergrowth.

"You buried him all the way out here?" Inuko asked, out of breath under the weight of the rice bags. She let him pass her.

"I still have to sleep in the house you know."

It was a grave and not deep. A single stave of wood stood upright at the head, bearing no name and no symbol. A mound of disturbed earth. Mosses and grasses and little striplings had started to grow over it and Mei, who knew when and how and in which season each one grew, wondered if the man beside her could tell how long ago the soil here had been turned.

"Do you wish to exhume the body? It has only been two weeks. It would be...recognisable."

The scowl he threw at her was answer enough.

"You are cold. I don't know what Captain Takashi sees in you, but you are cold." Relief struck her like a wave as she followed him back towards the house, the moisture in the air leaving enough dew on her skin to hide the sweat that had broken out, and by the time the terraces and struts of the manor came back into view the relief felt like a sickness. He heaved the rice sacks from his shoulders and Mei watched him, feeling the sun creeping across the tips of the awning like a meter counting out her heartbeats.

The dead man whose grave they had just visited would soon come down from the house to the *dojo*. He'd done so every morning now for nearly a week. "Where do you want these?" Inuko asked.

"That's fine."

"You have a storehouse, don't you?"

"Yes, but I'll need some for the kitchen and I can soak it here before I store the rest. Really, it's fine." Too much. He hesitated, looking hard at her, and she was aware her fingers were curled into the silk of her gown.

"You're easy to spook. Do you plan to stay here?"

She said nothing. Sunlight, like embers brightening the limits of the higher crags, reached towards them with the advent of morning. "Takashi has set guards on the gates of Okiri and if your lord passes the outpost my men will arrest him. In all likelihood, he'll have been captured and executed before you've had word. All you've done is delay your fate with solitude."

"You don't know him. He's found me before," she said. "He'll find me again."

"Is he worth such faith?"

"It is not faith." She glanced up, letting him at last see a hint of the desperation she was feeling, if only to let him know that he had crossed a line. "It is many things, Inuko-*san,* but it is not faith."

"Hm." But something in her vehemence stopped him and he scratched his temple, glancing at the house in a way that made Mei fix her eyes straight ahead in silent prayer. "Your decision," he said and, with that, he turned away.

She waited, counting his footfalls to the bridge. The hollow ring of his boots on the wood. The horse standing by. He mounted and glanced once more towards her. Her, and not the house. Then he dug his heels into the beast's flanks and set it to a canter. The rhythm of its hooves took longer to die away inside her head.

"Arata-*sama*." And, as if the name had some power of its own to release her, she turned and ran back towards the house, lifting her skirts so that the dust kicked up over her bare legs. "Arata-*sama!*"

He was not in his chamber, nor the main room. She jogged out to the bath-house. She could not hear water, but she checked each room anyway, apologising outside the first two, then letting her manners slip as she felt a spike of fear lodge in her belly. The *dojo* was empty. She tried the library. She lit the lamps so that she wouldn't miss him in the shadows. His brother's quarters. The servants'. Room after room until the snick and shuffle of the doors as they slid back became a counterpoint to her bare feet across the floors. Room after room, down to the cellars and the storehouse and, at last, the stables.

Where one stall stood empty, she swayed and dropped to her knees.

She had never been under the illusion she could control him. He was like a force of nature when he moved, like the wind that had come roaring down from the crags that morning, chasing the sunlight with a coarser passage. Her mind returned to Takashi's words: people made their own prisons.

There was so little to hold on to in this world. It was easier to find the things that would hold on to you. The heartbeats that held everything steady.

The trouble was that some were not willing to relinquish their grip. They were perfectly willing to change the night to day, or die trying. He was one such as this.

She clenched her hand into a fist. It wasn't fair! She had seen things she shouldn't have seen and had lived through times that should have changed her, but she had survived because she had learned to subdue in herself the impulse to change the world from what it was. She had no desire to foster that in him, but she had thought, no she had hoped that, given all he had lost in this fight, it might have humbled him enough to give him pause, to make him think that perhaps, just for once, he couldn't win; that there was a virtue, not in resignation, but in pressing forward with what remained. If he was as willing as he seemed to be to dash himself to pieces against a tide they didn't even yet understand, then she was powerless to stop him.

But something in her found that sentiment hard to swallow and it took her a moment to realise that the feeling, like a weight in her chest, was actually hope. He had mocked her with tenderness; he had lied to cover his own weaknesses, and he had been cold with her this past week, but some part of her believed he was far from helpless. If anyone could change night to day, she thought, it would probably be him.

5. The Sword and the Fox

He had been watching from the doorway.

He could see Mei on the terrace, speaking with a straggle-haired, rattish-looking young man who wore a sword on his hip and, despite his stature, carried a large and obviously heavy sack with ease. The stranger's acknowledgement of Mei, with little more than a nod and a gaze that roved uncomfortably across her slight figure, told him all he needed to know about who held the power. She was scared. And it wasn't that she showed it, but he could tell. Perhaps he had become more accustomed to her than he liked to think because he could read her body language like an open book now and she was stiff and humble in the stranger's presence.

He did not yet know enough of the situation to act. Nothing in her demeanour suggested she was trying to escape. Indeed he watched as she led the man away towards the bath-house and the well, and his blood thickened with an emotion he was at pains to place. If the soldier touched her, if he hurt her; well, it mattered little that his own affection for Mei was little more than a distant acceptance of his dependence on her; there were other things at stake, like respect, and honour.

He hadn't moved. His knuckles were white from holding the doorframe, his body damp with a cold sweat he hadn't noticed until now. Why had he frozen?

This was fear, binding and all-consuming. The soldier could have cut Mei down and here he would still be, watching in passive bewilderment. He cursed, turned back into the room, and took up his sword, sliding it into his belt before heading for the door. And stopping.

He couldn't.

It wasn't fear of the stranger; it was the sense he now had of seeing two things at once. Overwhelming. There in the small details of his life; it cleft his world to its core. When it came to something as big as this, he was rendered helpless.

Because he knew things he couldn't possibly know. Because thoughts blazed up into his head that weren't his own.

Taking up the sword had been one way to contain the sense that his own mind was splitting. Its routines were simple and forced him to experience firsthand how it felt to know something, know it so well that his muscles responded instinctively and his focus was always two steps ahead, while in actuality he knew nothing at all. Not consciously at least. On the one hand, he experienced the sensation as contradiction; on the other, he recognised two people acting as one: the man he had been before his injury and the man he was now. In the simple meditations of the sword form these two people seemed to coordinate and he could believe that there was a calm beneath the turbulence he encountered in every other action. But when it came to other things, and exploring the grounds had been one of these, witnessing the arrival of the soldier another, it was as if both body and mind froze up under a deluge of impassable contradictions.

He knew that the stranger was a swordsman, probably a *ronin* turned mercenary, or even a samurai, though a poor one if so. He knew these things, but he had no way of knowing how he knew, whether the man was familiar to him or if he had read something of a warrior's poise in his movements. Either way, the thought trampled on his more delicate insights like a wanton child. Knowledge, when he was in this condition, was a bully, allowing him no room for doubt and no room for sentiment. His head hurt.

He wasn't sure when he decided to follow the stranger, but he must have chosen it nonetheless because he found himself in the stables, tacking up one of the horses. It was a bay. He didn't know why he chose it or why he threw a blanket across its back instead of a saddle, or how he mounted and rode out when at last he saw Mei return to the house. It was, he realised, far simpler to act without thought. Thought was as dangerous to him now as vision to a man blind from birth.

He didn't ride fast. There was little need. Mei had told him there was only one road and anyway it was as familiar to him as the rest of this landscape of double layers and ghosts, of memories present yet absent. Only one thing stood out as distinct in this world, he realised, and it was the first time he had given it any real thought.

Mei.

His present self dared not trust her, though, for the sake of his past, he dared not lose her. He must once have loved her, yet that was gone and with it any sense that he had once known her. What he had discovered of her so far was down to observation, not instinct. With Mei there was no sense of overlap, no past superimposed on the present. She trailed no ghosts into his chambers; no echoes lingered in her eyes. She was simple, infuriating and perfectly and wholly a part of this new world. It was a train of thought he might have followed had he not at that time emerged from the narrowest part of the gorge, squinting in the bright sunlight that seemed all the more rich in cast for the russet hues in the rocks all around. He was face to face with two riders. The first was the young man who had come to the house; the second was of considerably larger build, with a brutish look about him, though the sword on his hip suggested that he, like the first, was probably of samurai blood. Nevertheless the first expression that registered on both their faces was shock.

The younger put his head on one side. Though he was a scruffy even dirty waif of a man, if a man he was and not a boy, still he had, on second glance, fine features and delicate brows: a brightness in his eyes that suggested he was not yet so jaded as to have renounced all pleasures.

"Unexpected," the youngster said.

Mei had been right. Until now, her husband had acted solely on instinct. Well, perhaps not instinct exactly, but at the command of a shadowy self who still existed, though smothered, gagged and bound, and who controlled all the thoughts and decisions that boiled unbidden into his consciousness. Yet like a turncoat at the last this shade melted away the moment he was confronted with two sets of curious, even hostile, eyes. It was the younger who spoke. "Akayama Arata, I was under orders to kill you, a fate that, up until just a moment ago, you had escaped by already being dead. Why dig your way out of the ground to follow me here?"

"Dead?"

The young man snorted and glanced at his partner then back at their pursuant.

"Did you intend to challenge me, Akayama?"

"Who are you?"

The youth rewarded him with a small smile, a sign he took as evidence that it was not a question to which he was already meant to have an answer.

"Keisuke Ibuko, Lieutenant serving under Captain Takashi Isamu in Okiri."

"Soldiers?"

"Soldiers," Inuko confirmed, frowning and lightly touching the hilt of his sword as if it should have been obvious. In the silence they weighed each other up and his hand fell away from his weapon. "You seem confused," he said.

"What business brought you to my estate?"

Ibuko smiled like a blade.

"They did a good job with you, whoever it was gave you that scar. You look like a man who's lost. I'd guess they took more from you than you're willing to let on, but at least you're not dribbling, spitting up your own food and railing like a tortured beast, like some I've seen. I doubt she'd have put up with you for long if you'd woken like that. What is it though? Can't think straight, Akayama?"

The youth's words crept in on his mind, which had been trawling through a mire of what-ifs and supposed-tos, desperately aligning Mei's words with this new information. It had not occurred to him that he might have let that blankness show on his face. It had not occurred to him that he might be outmatched the moment they saw it.

"Who ordered me dead?"

"Captain Takashi," drawled Ibuko.

"For what crime?"

"You're in the way." Without fuss Ibuko drew his sword. "It's very simple and, if I'm honest, I think Takashi's already got a soft spot for the girl."

"The…? Mei?"

"Takashi had the notion she wouldn't hide anything from him. He's quite the romantic when you cut through the layers of shit. Though we all have those, right? Still I figure this violates whatever arrangement they came to. After all, she did tell me you were dead, Akayama."

"What arrangement?"

"The kind where everyone gets what they want." Ibuko grinned and for the first time the other man felt his anger rise up and become something unmanageable. Distantly, he heard Ibuko address his comrade. "Homura, fetch the girl. She can join us in Okiri. We don't have to spend another night on this godforsaken mountain—"

And, with that, the once-dead man cut him down.

The motion was so fast that awareness seemed to lag. There was the larger man riding towards the gorge, half-turning back at the sudden clash of swords; Ibuko's blade lifted to the vertical in a parry a second too late; his opponent's blade sinking into his arm, enough that it wouldn't come loose without more than a little force, and then the sound and swell of blood, eclipsed a moment later by Ibuko's guttural scream.

It wasn't the kind of thing to leave unfinished. The sword hung brightly in the air, slick with blood and bits of muscle. But the victor had frozen, intent suddenly upon the sounds and colours, the confusion as to who had acted when he had made no conscious choice . Just beyond his focus, Ibuko slid sideways from his mount, his body falling in the dust. Save for his blood, which was forced out in steady gushes, he was still, though he continued to choke on his own screams, the most appalling of sounds.

The other soldier rode back, hollering, his sword raised. Empty-eyed, their enemy slid gracefully from his own mount's back, barely aware as Homura's sword whistled through the air where he had been sitting. As the soldier passed, he swept his sword in a semi-circle, letting his weapon collide with the horse's back legs. It let out a shrill scream and buckled, dumping Homura in the dust.

Once on their feet, they faced each other, the soldier and the nobleman. The latter was aware of his own breathing, coarse and fast, as if he had already overexerted himself. Homura looked like a madman. Inuko just kept howling and twitching in a growing pool of his own blood. And, all these things registered as disparate parts of a dream.

Homura flew at him, sword brandished above his head as if the soldier could cut through the very fabric of the bright morning. And, an instant later, their blades met. The impact woke him from the last remnants of his slumber. Homura was stronger than him. But it was worse than that. With a growing sense of sobriety, he found himself trying to anticipate his opponent's motions. The instant he set his mind to it, the sword became a clumsy appendage; the rhythm of his parries became erratic. Homura's blade slid down his own and sparked against the guard, forcing him backwards. With the next blow, he defended his face by a hair's breadth. At the next, Homura bared his teeth, hardly letting the swords touch before side-stepping and swiping his opponent's leg.

The pain came a moment later.

He hadn't realised, until he stumbled, that the soldier's blade had done anything more than rent the fabric of his *hakama*. The pain was a shock coming, as it did, from the length of his calf. In that moment, to fall was certain death. He gritted his teeth, his breaths hissing, refusing to give ground. His clothes were dark. If there was blood, he couldn't see it and that meant Homura couldn't either. Standing in the shadow of the gorge now, he had nowhere else to go, but he took his stance, trying not to wince as he put weight on a foot he now felt as nothing but forks of pain snarling up towards his thigh.

"Homura!"

Ibuko's cry registered as a flicker in the larger man's face. Homura almost ignored it in favour of finishing their enemy, but none could be in any doubt as to the effort it took the lieutenant to form those syllables. "Homura! Help – me!"

The nobleman licked lips that were suddenly as dry as the red rock of the gorge. Homura hesitated for only a moment before starting to creep back to the prone bundle of rags and blood that had once been his commanding officer, not daring to turn his back on his opponent who, for his own part, kept his weapon drawn as he limped to where his mount now stood in the shadow of the rock wall, its ears flicking at flies, its face turned away from the storm of swordplay in a picture of bland indifference.

"I'll be coming back for you, Akayama!" Homura shouted at the man who now sheathed his sword, mounted and urged the beast into a trot, glancing back over his shoulder several times before his sightline to the two samurai was lost in the folds of the gorge.

Satisfied though that Homura, if he really intended to save his lieutenant, would make for Okiri, he let the beast slow to a walk.

He didn't know if the young man would survive. He was certain his sword had gone through bone and blood...A wave of dizziness made him rein in. He pressed the back of his arm to his mouth and retched. The smell of sweat and gore was strong.

He had done that. Not him though, no. His shadow self; a self that now leered out of his past and laughed at his delicacy. Who was he, he wondered. Capable of fratricide. Capable of killing strangers who were barely more than boys. His own wife distrusted him; his brother shielded him from those who wanted him dead. Had they been justified? What had he done? What had he done that had made his brother abandon him here?

By the time he reached the edge of the estate he was shaking. He untacked the horse.

He no longer felt the pain in his leg though he walked with a pronounced limp as he returned the animal to its stall. It wasn't that the pain was gone. It was his mind; it was breaking loose, fracturing and leaking into the abyss that was the valley, now filled with summer mists. He started to cross the bridge, feeling light-headed, and came to a halt staring at the terraces.

A fox sat on the uppermost, watching him with jade eyes. Man and animal stared. In its mouth, it carried a single piece of carrion, and it gazed down as if daring the human to take it. Yet this treasure it so guarded was a human hand, with skin the colour of porcelain and five perfectly manicured fingers. Its teeth had sunk into the fleshy portion beneath the thumb and, so burdened, it stood up, shook its russet coat and trotted unhurriedly down onto the lower terrace.

Forgetting himself, he started forward and almost fell as his leg buckled. The fox took its opportunity to pass him on the bridge, only breaking into a run on the far side as he staggered to his feet and gave chase.

By the time he lost sight of it, he was all but lost himself, deep in the forest that clung to the side of the mountain. He had followed it down through grass and shrubs, through the trees where they grew in thick clumps and through thinner patches of silver pines. So when at last he burst from the undergrowth into the open air, he thought it would be to a sense of relief. The blue sky formed a dome above. The ground fell away.

Two more paces and he would have plunged over a cliff-edge limned with red scree. He heard himself cry out. There was a sickening loss of balance. He landed on his back on blankets of grass and moss with flies and iridescent beetles that flew up in a storm from where he lay. The blue dome still hung above. The day was bright.

He scrambled backwards, unwilling to sit up until he was certain he was far enough from the edge so as not to see the drop. Yet even from the safety of the first trees, his heart still thundered in his chest when he raised his head to see how close he had come.

The fox, with its grizzly prize, had vanished.

There was no way down from this mountain. There was one road and it led to Okiri, and there were soldiers on the road, and there were secrets in the mountain.

赤山

Had it been Mei? The slender forearm and the fine fingers. How though? How, in leaving her had he sealed her fate?

He could take no pride in the breed of horror that racked him in the discovery that he was alone. She who had been guardian to his past, who had held him in place and moored him here when all else had fallen away; she who had told him that this was his home, was gone.

Long after he should have given up he continued to go from room to room, calling her until his throat was hoarse and her name a stranger on his lips.

Eventually he collapsed by the hearth, head down, hands in his lap. She chose that moment to walk in.

She was dressed in a lavender kimono, hair tied in a yellow ribbon. In her hands she carried herbs and grasses and a garland of red flowers. She was clean and hale with no mark on her, and a flush had bloomed on her cheeks as if she had been climbing.

He rose to his feet and embraced her. Though she stiffened, his force made her body mould to his. She cried out once at first, then fell silent, her breathing fast and taut against him. He could feel her heart beating in her chest like a bird fluttering against the bars of a cage.

"Arata, you're hurting me."

He loosened his grip and staggered like a drunkard. She would have reached out for him, but she saw blood spattered across his wrist and pulled back. The anguish in her voice was like a knife. "What did you do? Is this your blood?"

"No, no." he touched her cheek, leaving a smudge at which she understandably balked, but when he looked again her eyes were full of tears. He embraced her more carefully this time and she stood obediently, arms full of crushed flowers.

At length, when his breathing was steady again and he found her presence credible, he asked where she had been. "I thought they had found you," he said.

"Who? Inuko?" He didn't answer. "I went walking."

"Walking?"

"To find berries and wild mushrooms."

"What–what are you?" Wide, pale eyes gazed up at him and he thought of wraiths and creatures from stories that lived only in the fine spray of waterfalls and collected berries in the sunlight. "What are you?"

"We have to eat," she said. He slumped down on a low bench by the door, his head resting in his hands. It was almost dark outside. He'd spent all day chasing stories, finding beginnings and no endings. His head ached. He'd not eaten or drunk and, as to his leg, the blood had dried, sticking his *hakama* to his skin so that, every time he moved, the surface of the scab broke a little and the pain beneath blossomed afresh. All in all, when he reached for her hands his own were shaking, and that was all she really needed to know.

"Mei, I need you," he admitted, "But I need you to be just a little more—ordinary."

"I can do that."

"Mei, why do you…?" He hesitated, realising that the question would be clumsy but knowing that it needed an answer nonetheless. So when she sat down beside him and their eyes were level, he felt less ashamed to ask, "Why do you love me? Mei, don't look away!"

"I don't know," she said quietly.

"Am I wrong though?"

"No, but I ask myself the same. Every day."

He let go of her hands as she shrugged and dropped her gaze.

"I think I killed Ibuko."

She stiffened. He had a feverish light in his eyes. "You were right about the people on the road who will kill us sooner than let us leave, but you didn't tell me why. They're soldiers, Mei. *Bakufu* soldiers."

"I knew you would go after them the moment you saw them! You were always like that!" she scolded him.

"Why are they here?"

"They came for Ryuu."

He frowned.

"My brother? Why?"

"They say he didn't pay the duties. We didn't, I mean. Except he is our lord, so it falls to him. They will not return to Edo while he lives."

"That's impossible." He rose to his feet, glancing around the room at the cabinets of papers and accounts. "My brother..." He hesitated, an image in his mind of two columns of arithmetic, Arata and Ryuu; of large sums of money paid to Arata and only irregularly paid back. "Mei, I need you to tell me honestly, was I ever in my brother's pay?" She looked confused. "Did he ever employ me? It doesn't matter how sordid the job. Did I do the work he didn't want to dirty his hands with?"

"I don't know what you're asking. Why would you need money?"

"Why would I need...?" He trailed off. The answer to that was a hair's breadth away and yet he felt like he was back in the forest, standing on the edge of that cliff.

"Arata-*sama*—"

He raised his hand for quiet. He was standing in the middle of the room now, in the heart of this house. This empty house. One road leading over the mountain. Just one. And only the two of them on this estate.

Yet he had followed the fox down to the cliff-edge.

"Is there a graveyard close to this house?"

A little of the colour drained from her face.

"There's a grave—"

"No, not a grave; it wouldn't be a grave," he said, turning to her with a vivid light in his eyes as something fell into place. "Fresh bodies!" He clicked a finger at her as if it were a question she could answer, then without warning he turned and hauled her to her feet. "Mei," he said, holding her there by her shoulders and forcing lightness into his tone, "Where are the servants?"

"I told you they left with Ryuu! All but the ones who attended us and they—"

He smacked her across the face.

In the silence that followed, she straightened with one hand on her cheek.

Her eyes were bright. And at last she answered quietly, "They're at the base of the cliff."

He swallowed and swayed on the spot.

It wasn't even the information; it was the unblinking gaze with which it was delivered. If he had never found her frightening before, he did now.

"Oh, Mei…"

"I had to do something!" she said wildly. "He'd slit their throats and I couldn't even lift them. It was all I could do to take them that far. But I couldn't leave them!"

"They were people you knew! You—you were singing aloud the next day as you washed my clothes! What's wrong with you?"

"I don't know!"

"You are cold."

"People say that, but"–she pursed her lips–"But people die. If you knew how many people died in one day, how could you mourn them? One or two perhaps, but if it's a household or a village or a town?"

"You mourn them because you have feelings!"

"I have feelings!" she snarled. She watched him cross to the screen door, standing there as the blue dusk deepened into night. "You know, most days I feel like I'm going to burst right open. Why do you think I don't?"

"Because I couldn't do what you did. I'd be sick to the stomach. You're not what you appear." He glanced at her appraisingly. "What does Takashi want with you?"

"I agreed to pay him if he let me live."

"I see. So I'm a loose end."

"I told them you were already dead."

"Somehow I think they know I am not." She turned away and collected up her pile of herbs and fruits and flowers, then came to stand beside him in the doorway. "Would you mourn me if I died, Mei?"

"Your leg is bleeding, Arata-*sama*," she said without emotion. "You smell like horse and some other vile thing I can't place."

He chuckled as she stepped past him out into the night.

She was something, he thought; he just wasn't sure quite what.

6. To Each a Fate

It had been the strangest of days.

Mei sunk down in the tub, her body concealed by the black and white reflections of candlelight on the surface of the water. The thick smell of steam and the delicious warmth loosened her muscles and washed away the dust from the hills.

Something had changed tonight. She saw in him more and more of the man he had been and yet, for the first time, she found herself thinking that something might be permanently lost. This was not Arata; this was a man who called himself Arata because she had given him a name; a man who was only just beginning to recognise himself and, even then, it seemed to be a self he found unfamiliar.

It occurred to her that there were some things she yearned to forget, things that dictated her actions in any given moment because her decisions were harnessed by emotions that ran deep, like precious ore through the veins of her memory. To be free of them, she thought, might be liberating. Liberating and frightening. Like the sun forgetting to shine in the morning. Or the winter forgetting to follow the fall.

Takashi had said that no-one was free to write the story of their own life; given freedom, they sought imprisonment; given the lead, they would choose instead to follow. But would a man willing to chase possibilities he did not yet understand, willing to draw a sword and fight for things he had barely glimpsed, would he be satisfied to follow? No, over the years, she had watched him grow, becoming more headstrong, more sure of himself, more stubborn. She might almost believe that he could stop the earth in its course and order the sun not to rise tomorrow and both would obey, as would all things in nature.

But if he proved Takashi right? Torn loose of his past, given that rarest of freedoms born of loss, he had come as close to breaking today as she had ever seen him. He had told her that he needed her. And with that she had discovered the full weight of her responsibility. When all else was gone and she could not promise its certain return, she at least could remain.

She liked bathing on summer evenings when the air was cool enough to make her skin prickle with life, but not so cool as to sting, and her only light was a single melted candle in an alcove by the tub.

She sat up and leaned over to where a mirror rested beside it. Her face in the glass was marred by a smear of blood. He had left it when he embraced her. She washed it off. Whether it had been his or Inuko's she didn't know, but now that it was gone she checked her cheek for bruises. He had not hit her hard, but her skin was pale and bruised easily. He had done worse in anger, though not to her. Tonight, there was no mark.

She washed her body, then climbed out of the tub and dried her hair, letting the water on her skin trick her into thinking it was cold. Then she put on her nightclothes and her sandals, and headed back to the house.

She was fairly certain they would be safe tonight. They had talked over dinner. It had been a simple exchange, but she had wrung from him the details of the event. If Inuko were dead or dying the chances were that Homura would have returned with him to Okiri. It would be a night and, if they were lucky, another day before Takashi could attack, assuming that he was with his lieutenant and would need a little time to organise his men. He would come though; she was sure of that. But she was not yet certain enough of what Inuko had meant to him to predict how he would react.

"Arata," she called as she entered the house, not yet willing to come upon him unannounced. He had been too wild tonight, too lost. She sensed he needed respite, but how to give it she did not know, when their fates hung as heavy as the summer mists.

The injury to his leg, which she had suspected but only seen when he had returned from the bath-house, had looked far worse than it was. Homura's sword had shrived off a layer of skin from his calf, which left a bloody mess, but it had not incapacitated him. If anything, he had seemed unaware of it, and that was perhaps worse; something of the day had rubbed off on him; it had shaken him to his core, which in turn left her with her sense of certainty torn asunder. If Akayama was her prison then he was its walls and to see them torn down affected her deeply.

She stopped by his chamber. He was kneeling on the pallet, his back to the door and, when she slid the screen aside, he quickly closed the book he had been reading. So quickly indeed she might have questioned him were she not tired. She bowed.

"Stay tonight," he said without looking up.

She glanced at him quickly to see if she had understood. It struck her that it had not sounded like a request. "You used to sleep in my room," he added.

"I never slept," she admitted, recognising that by 'used to' he referred to but a week hence. Beyond that, she suspected, he still could not recall. "I just stayed in case you needed me."

"Do so then," he said shortly.

Obedient, she crossed to the window sill where she had sat each night for the first week since his waking. He ignored her and set the book down on the dresser, then crossed to the futon and snuffed the candle. In the silence that followed, she felt him watching her.

There was enough light from the moon that she could see when he pulled aside the sheets leaving space on the futon beside him. She slipped down from her place in the window and knelt beside the bed. Unthinking and, under cover of darkness which, after all, forgave all things, she began to untie the sash of her robe.

His hand touched hers. She couldn't see his face. "I didn't ask for that." His voice was cold and she hesitated, taken aback before she realised that what she had taken as anger on his part was something closer to shame. She flushed. It was too dark for him to see, but even if he had she suspected he would not understand how he affected her. For a long time she didn't move. When next he spoke, it was with raw confession. "You are a stranger to me."

"Is this alright?" she asked, shifting to lie beside him. Her body felt clumsy as she settled, but his hand slid over her side and round her belly.

"Perfect."

They lay that way for a time and, though she barely dared breathe, she was aware of the exquisite play of moon-beams in columns of dust and the way shadows picked out imperfections on the wooden floor. His breath against the back of her neck made every hair on her body stand on end.

"Arata-*sama* is most tolerant of strangers," she whispered at length and she felt the change in his breathing that told her he had smiled. His fingers pressed against her stomach.

"You are warm."

"So are all things that live."

"You are here."

赤山

In Okiri, it was raining.

Takashi paused briefly in the gateway. The monastery was modest, appearing to be little more than a town-house from the outside. Hidden behind thickets of trees and ornamental shrubs, it was a low-slung, sprawling building that served the town in a myriad of ways. The shogunate supported an educated clergy, so it from amongst the monks and novices that small towns like Okiri procured surgeons and healers.

Shaking the worst of the squall from his hair, Takashi crossed a fragrant garden and was at once assailed by the perfume of incense, burnt in liberal quantities to disguise the butchers' smell of the hospital wing.

He looked out of place here: muddy, wet, dressed for riding rather than a social visit, cutting an imposing figure as his boots made hollow thunder on the decking. One of the monks came rushing out to meet him, holding his robes in his hands to keep them from the rain as a woman might clasp her gown in modesty. He bowed deeply and apologised before Takashi could speak.

"Please, please." The man gestured towards the house.

"Ibuko Keisuke is a soldier of mine. He was brought here with a man named Homura."

"This way. We have been expecting you, Captain."

Takashi hated doctors. It was the smell. The stench of blood on the battlefield could make your senses sharp as knives, but in a place like this, where it lingered and made the air rich and rank, it only made him sick to his stomach. His father had died in a place like this, so long ago that he could not remember where it had been or indeed whom he had left with thereafter. But he could still remember the smell.

It was a small room, panelled in dark cherry wood and choked with incense. Homura was standing inside the door; Inuko seemed to be sleeping. His commander kept his voice low and level as he slid the door shut against the encroaching rain and faced his subordinate. "What happened?"

"He followed us from the house. We were talking. He attacked out of the blue."

As Homura spoke, Takashi glanced at the figure on the futon. Anger curled in his belly, its long fingers tightening on his gut. He was not sentimental about his men, or so he had told himself, but Inuko was an exception. He was the only one he had ever taken as his second; fierce yet obedient, he was the kind of soldier Takashi might have liked to be if only the profession had held satisfaction for him. It didn't, but he had at least taken some pride in training the young man up.

"Have the monks said anything?"

"They might try surgery."

"Bastard." Takashi turned away from his subordinate, clenching his jaw until it ached thinly. The bandage on Inuko's arm was more scarlet than white now; his skin was ghostly pale. If he survived, he would never wield a sword again and that would be if they let him keep the arm. "Akayama should have finished it."

"He hesitated," said Homura.

"Hesitated?"

"He seemed not to be himself. It's hard to describe. I think that was part of the trouble." He licked his lips as if ashamed of the admission he was about to make. "Inuko was joking with him, seeing how far he could push him. Seemed like he wasn't there exactly. He just sat and took it. Looked lost, I thought."

"He–was." There was a rustle of movement from the pallet. Inuko had turned towards them with a gaze like glass. It was with difficulty that he formed his words. "He was empty. I looked at his eyes. There was nothing in his eyes." Takashi crouched down to better hear him. "You told me that…Always look at the eyes."

"…You'll see the moment they make the decision."

"He never did." A feverish light touched the young man's features as he reached for his mentor. "I swear, Isamu, his eyes were empty."

"If he carries anything like the reputation of his brother, we were probably out-matched from the start. There's no shame in it, Inuko. No shame."

As if satisfied, the boy's eyes fell shut and his breathing evened out. Takashi sighed. He was young and strong and stubborn. He wasn't sure what kind of life would lie ahead for him, but still he wanted him to live. It seemed that even he could be sentimental at times. "I'll stay, Homura. Well done in bringing him back."

The large man bowed and, sensing the words as a request for privacy, left the room. Takashi sat with his back to his lieutenant, resting his chin in his hands.

Two weeks had passed since their arrival. Okiri had plenty of distractions. As he had suspected, corruption was rife and, with few men to keep the peace, it was enforced by ruling factions whose only real concern was to keep themselves in coin. They had been hostile and suspicious at first. Still, Takashi had proved that he could drink and gamble with the best of them. The ones who held authority gave themselves away these days by their knowing smiles as he passed them in the street: you're one of us, they said, and he had no mind to correct them. He had gambled. Within the first week he had doubled the payment he'd taken to come here. He'd been losing thereafter but no mind; at the time, he had taken it as a good omen.

Mei too had been a gamble. One option had always been to kill Arata and return to Edo. Any way you looked at it his job was already complete: the Akayama line would end here. In keeping Mei though, he was playing for higher stakes. If she kept her word and paid him, he would rake in nearly as much as he would have on completing his mission. If, in addition, he succeeded in luring Ryuunaka back to Okiri, he would have double.

He had once despised men who worked for pay, believing they lacked dignity. Then he'd spent a winter starving, sleeping in doorways or stables or by the roadside, and he'd come to understand exactly what dignity was. Since then he'd taken the bones the nobility threw, earned himself a name and a reputation. Better to be a lapdog to the shogun than a cur to a peasant.

"Inuko?" he said at length. "Are you awake?" His lieutenant grunted a response. "You saw the girl, didn't you? Is she there of her own volition?"

"She protected him," he said without opening his eyes. Takashi frowned.

"I had wondered…She asked me not to kill him. She has feelings for him then. And there I had thought she might have guts enough for revenge, that she might finish him while we were away." He was disappointed.

"The captain," Inuko said softly, his lips curling into something like a smile, "Prefers a girl who'd kill him in his sleep…"

"Have to find ways to keep things interesting. Better than dying of apathy."

"I'll bear it in mind."

Takashi glanced over. Inuko's eyes were still closed; his lips pale but drawn into a smile that seemed genuinely oblivious of his pain.

"Pull through this one and I'll forgive you for being a cocky bastard," Takashi said. The words registered as a flicker on the younger man's face.

"One thing, Captain," he managed after a moment. "If you do go after him, be careful."

"I always am."

"No, it's more than that…I don't think either of them is what they seem."

赤山

"Arata-*sama*," Mei had asked suddenly one morning. "Now that you know the servants are dead, what are you going to do?"

"Do? What do you mean?"

When the soldiers had not come to the house the first day, or the second or the third, he had begun to get restless. He dallied with the thought of riding down to the outpost. Better surely than to wait for death to come knocking. Then again, at least by staying at the house, they could be under no illusion as to where the threat would come from. Every day, he trained within sight of the road through the gorge.

Mei, for her own part, seemed largely unaware of the straits they were in. Perhaps she had had more time to accept the fact that they were little more than hostages in their own home. Then again, with Mei, who genuinely seemed to exist in a world of her own at times, it was hard to tell if her lack of concern was ignorance or a strange breed of indifference.

She had changed though. No, they had both changed. An alliance had been forged between them and, though he spent a large part of each day training and she was away for hours at a time foraging for food that would make their rations more palatable, once night fell, by an unspoken contract, they were rarely if ever out of one another's sight. In the days following his confrontation, she had watched him with a concern bordering on genuine anxiety, so much so that he had eventually asked her what was wrong, and it was this that had elicited her question about the servants. "What did you think I would do?" he asked.

"If it's all gone: the household, the money, the clan?" She pursed her lips, cheeks pale, searching for something in his face.

"I'd rather be alive, wouldn't you? And anyway, all of that was – is – Ryuu's concern, not mine. You don't need two of us to bear that responsibility."

She seemed to cheer up a little after their conversation. She went back to singing as she walked through the house.

He couldn't decide if she was naïve or brazen. A part of him wanted to shake her and force her to understand that their lives were at stake. Yet he also knew that if she stopped singing or laughing in delight at the most trivial of things, he might have stolen something beautiful from the world. Since he had no right to do that, he let her continue, now and again chiding her if she forgot the words.

Time was stretching on though. Soon only a week remained before she was due to leave for Okiri. Out of respect, he had not asked for the details of her arrangement. If parts of the contract were to shame her, it would do him no good at all to make her put them into words. Now that it was close though, it was a shadow over everything he did. He had been convinced Takashi would make his move before she was ever required to fulfil her part of the bargain. Now it looked as if he would hold off and that was somehow worse. Takashi was laughing at him. It was sufficient punishment. He'd imagined soldiers on horseback pouring out of the gorge and setting the house ablaze as they slept, but in the end this was far more effective. And Takashi hadn't even needed to draw a blade.

You took my man. I will have your wife.

And worse still, she would go willingly.

It had crossed his mind that there might be some way to stop her leaving. He could physically prevent her, but even then he could not imagine a method that might not put her life at risk if Takashi came looking for her.

So he lay awake most nights with her curled up beside him, his own body cold with dread and hers burning with the heat of the summer's day, and he thought to himself that there was one small mercy in all of this: he still could not recall ever having fallen in love with her.

It would be, he convinced himself, far worse if he had.

7. The Waterfall

Mei joined him as he trained on the terraces. He wiped the sweat out of his eyes and glanced over to where she sat. The day had dawned bright and warm and still. Peaceful, he had thought, like a painting that would soon be torn in two. The terrible truth lurking behind was that, tomorrow, Mei would leave for Okiri, and he had found no way yet to stop her.

She sat cross-legged on the terrace above this one and smiled when he lowered the sword and looked up at her. "What are you doing?" he called. "Come down here!"

"You come up! I've brought water." The pail was on a rope over her shoulder. It spilt clear water onto the stone as she rose to her feet. Instead of going to the stairs though he merely sheathed the sword on his hip and crossed to where she stood. Reaching up, he took hold of her bare ankle. "Got you." He leant his chin on the terrace, watching her playfully. His body ached. The constant training took its toll, but he could think of no better way to spend his time. "Where are Mei's sandals?" he asked, keeping a firm hold of her foot. She hopped a little and, perhaps intentionally, let some of the water spill in his direction.

"A ghost came in the night – a terrible, moaning thing – and it took them away and said I could never have them back."

"What did a ghost want with your sandals? It couldn't wear them."

"Precisely. That's why I felt such pity for it."

He sighed, let her go and reached for the water, which she duly let him have, slipping down on her knees.

"Mei has such a soft heart," he said and she smiled as she watched him.

"Have you remembered anything yet?" His eyes darkened, but she pressed on. "Only I had hoped, seeing how well you practise with the sword, that if you could remember that—"

"It's different," he said.

He didn't want to disappoint her. He was well aware that exhuming some memory of Ryuu might prove useful currency in Okiri. He had considered making something up, but his knowledge of the world beyond this estate and of his brother was so slight as to make him useless on that count. He had already decided that, if he lived through the next few days, it would be under a veil of self-loathing. A better man would have found a way to stop her.

"Your body remembers," she said.

"I know."

"It's alright. You don't have to be ashamed."

"I'm not ashamed for myself," he said and left it at that. He had no inclination to insult her.

He stood for a time, leaning back against the terrace, his eyes on the blue sky: high cirrus clouds like horses' tails; flies that whirred past them, living for a day and dying at dusk. At least they had no time to learn to dread.

He was hot. He was miserable. He might have to concede that, with all the training in the world, he was not going to walk into the midst of twenty or thirty men and defend her honour with any hope of success. Even if he died trying, it would likely be for nothing. The bargain would still be played out. "I'm tired, Mei. Trying to remember anything at all feels like digging into a hole where the loose soil keeps falling in. I'll never reach it."

He felt her hand on his shoulder and turned to look, only to see that she was staring out across the valley.

"I was born out there. I don't remember, but it's still a part of who I am." The wind snatched her hair back from her face. In this light her eyes were the colour of storm-clouds and the idea that she was beautiful sprang into his head unbidden. "What I'm saying is, even if you don't ever remember, I don't think it has to change who you are, who you were." She looked at him.

It was something he needed to consider, but it was horrifying to hear it put into words: the sheer enormity of what he had lost.

"I've been careful, when we've talked about the past, to ask for names and dates and places," he said. "I was afraid, if I asked after my character or passions, I would find out too much or perhaps be steered wrongly. Now I think I have to."

"It's—it's a lot to put on one person."

"If you took it lightly, I wouldn't trust your replies."

They were silent for a time. He could feel her hand resting on his shoulder, her thumb making delicate circular motions of which he suspected she was unaware. Yet the aches in his body seemed to recede a little. "Let's begin with us," he said.

赤山

A short time later Mei, having retrieved her sandals from the wandering spirit who, it seemed, no longer had need of them, was leading him down through the forest. She treated the paths as subtle conveniences, following them at times but giving them little heed. By the time she turned away from the valley and started leading him up a gentle incline, he was thoroughly lost.

"We need to climb from here," she said. She had no compunction about digging her hands into the mossy weeds to aid her balance when she needed it.

"Are you really a noblewoman?" he called after her. "You move like a snow monkey!"

"Come, come, come." She helped him over the last rise. Here the ground flattened out. Covered by a blanket of rust-coloured leaves that seemed to have lain undisturbed since autumn, the clearing was devoid of any paths or traces of human influence. In its centre was the source of a noise that had been lapping at the periphery of his senses: a waterfall pouring down between pillows of moss and red rock into a dark and deceptively still pool. A shimmering mist formed half-seen rainbows where white water struck black. He stared and walked past Mei to the very edge of the pool. "Up above the falls is a meadow where we used to go; a field, filled with wildflowers," she was saying. "Come on, I'll show you."

"Wait a moment. Something…" That sense of overlapping worlds. For once though, Mei seemed a little impatient. She came padding back through the leaves, barefoot, her sandals in one hand.

"You have to climb the rocks themselves. The mud's too slippery."

"I said wait."

He frowned, eyes on the falling water. It was something about the sound and the rhythm and the smell. "Why did you say we used to come here?"

"Privacy sometimes." He glanced at her. Her cheeks were flushed, possibly from exertion. "And somewhere you could be free to talk."

"Why here though?"

She shrugged.

"You were always so busy. Always busy. I told you once that you had to stop. It's like you wanted to keep a hold of so many things, but eventually they were going to bury you. And that's why we came. Just to get away."

"Funny. I had pictured myself as a good-for-nothing. While my brother ran the household, I trained all day." She was standing beside him now, watching the bright spray. A quick glance in his direction.

"Maybe it would have been better that way."

"You think I worked too hard?"

"I don't know," she said. "I think you look younger now than you did then. There are fewer lines on your face."

"But Ryuu must have done the lion's share of the work."

"Yes, of course." She dipped her toes into the water and he watched as she bunched up her gown and tucked it into her *obi*, modesty briefly forgotten as she stepped into the water up to her knees.

He tried to find within himself the ghost of a man who might have found peace in the rush of falling water, but try as he might he could not sense that delicate aesthetic within him. He could understand getting lost in work, in exertion; he had enjoyed their ramble to this place, but was disappointed to discover the lack of a more noble mind that might find poetry in the landscape. The sense of familiarity was receding.

Mei was speaking animatedly of a time they'd come here, to the field of wildflowers at dusk, and there had been fireflies, which had seemed to her like stars waltzing between the trees. In their vanity, they had tried to chase them, she said.

He watched her in the water. It was licking at her thighs now as she stood gazing at the top of the falls where lines of sunlight blossomed from a shred of sky. She was unaware that the back of her gown, where she had knotted it into the sash, trailed in the water. Her pale legs disappeared into the pool, but at the backs of her knees the skin was near-translucent and he could see the dark veins. And her fingers, trailing the surface of the pool, catching ripples of sunlight.

He closed his eyes and the world shuddered as if caught in the percussion of a drumbeat. It hadn't been here. There had been no trees, nothing to shut out the bright blue of the sky. Another place then. Another time.

"There was a waterfall," he said. She turned back to him, eyes widening as he spoke. "It wasn't here. There were men…boys. That girl! That poor girl!" He sat down heavily and put a hand to his head, not because it hurt or even because he could be sure it was where the thoughts originated, but because he needed to steady himself within the moment. The touch of his fingers against his temple was wholesome and immediate. "Some boys killed a girl. She could have been no more than a child. They were barely children themselves, I think but, fancying themselves thieves, they must have set upon her." He heard rather than saw Mei wading back to the shore. "I came too late, but there was another girl. She had hidden herself beneath the waterfall…Looked half-drowned when I found her." He looked up. "Was it you?"

She didn't answer. She had turned away from him, her shoulders hunched in a manner quite unlike her. Her breathing was strange and jagged, but it wasn't until he approached and, kneeling down, tried to touch her, that he realised she was crying liberally. Blinking so that she could see through the tears, she jerked her arm away from him. "Mei?"

Did she know it had been nearly a week since she'd pulled back from him?

He knew. He had taken note the first time he had touched her and hadn't felt her stiffen.

The memories he had made in these last few weeks he coveted. He told himself it was because they were so few compared to what he had lost, and there was nothing wrong in the attention he paid to a woman who was, after all, his wife. Yet he wondered sometimes if the feelings he had for her were indeed a residue of his past, those of a husband to a wife. He was jealous, but in itself that bore little mystery; it could be the possessiveness of a husband or simply that of a man who knew he was being made a fool of. He had, perhaps idealistically, believed that with time and the gradual return of his memories, he might have rediscovered something of a routine with her, a settling into one another, of becoming each other's habit. Instead she continued to surprise him every day and no gesture, no turn of phrase or tilt of her head, stirred any memory within him. He kept forgetting that he had lost everything and instead found himself more and more curious about this woman who had bound herself to him. Even today, he wondered if his motivation had been, as he had claimed, to recall his own past or if, with the events of tomorrow wearing heavily on his mind, he was not trying to find out as much as he could about the one thing he would be forced to relinquish. It grated that, while all the rest of his world shimmered with ghosts of familiarity, she was more ephemeral. Even now he could not understand her or why her words smacked of reprimand:

"You remember that? In all things, you remember that?" And she covered her mouth with the back of her hand as if she could hold back the emotion. She turned away from him.

"Are you angry? Just tell me if it's true and not some phantasm I've dreamed up now." He sounded impatient. He already knew; it had been her. But now he wanted why and when; the part before; the piece after; memories that were, by rights, his. As usual though he lacked the finesse to ask without the words sounding somehow brutal. "Why are you crying, Mei?"

"I'd not thought you would remember. We were children."

"Then is it true?"

"Her name was Yumi. She kept on calling me. I thought if only she would stay quiet they wouldn't hurt me. I didn't see when they killed her, but after – when you came – I wondered if I could have saved her." Mei was still for a moment, save for her shoulders which rose and fell with each breath. One finger remained pressed to her lips. "Arata-*sama*, I might have saved her. That's why I had to do everything I could to keep you safe after the servants were gone. If it were only me, I could have fled; Takashi would have let me live. But the moment I'd left, if I had left, I would have become that girl again. The one who hid."

"Tell me this is not why—tomorrow…" He trailed off, realising the half-spoken question required no answer. "Don't go," he said quietly. Her eyes flicked towards him.

"Takashi will send men to kill you tomorrow," she said simply. He didn't respond. He had already guessed at such. "You know the path we took today?" she said. "Down past the bamboo forest? If you follow that to the end, there's a point where it once wound round the side of the cliff. It crumbled long ago, but I found some good, strong saplings. A few lashed together will take your weight. If you lay them across the distance and cross over, you'll be able to haul them with you to the other side; then there's just enough of the path left; you'll be able to hide on the far side of the rock face. I left everything you would need in a hollow tree to the side of the path." She waited, eyes on the water.

"No." That didn't even seem to register though; it was as if she had not heard. "I said, no."

"Then I won't go. I'll stay with you. They can kill us both."

"No!" All at once he took hold of her and shook her.

It was more savage than he intended, but her body was limp until, a moment later when she wrapped both arms around the back of his neck and held on with her face pressed into his throat. He let go of her shoulders, defeated entirely. It was not even her touch; more immediate was the whisper of her breath along his collarbone. The sense that he was meant to protect her, that he was going to go mad if he let her out of his sight, crashed in on him, and he dared not return the embrace in case, in his desire to keep her, he crushed her entirely.

"Promise me," she said. "If you promise me, then I can go."

He pressed his lips into her hair. She smelt a little like the waterfall and of fresh rain, two analogies that seemed too fanciful to have come from his own mind. At last he wrapped his arms around her.

"Do you know what you're asking of me?"

"It was the first time we met, the day Yumi died. You wondered if it was a dream? It was years before I came to the estate and there have been times I thought it was a dream."

"Did I love you all those years?" he asked and he felt her sigh.

"I knew—the moment I saw you."

They remained that way. He realised that her breathing had slowed. Her embrace becoming heavy as she relaxed.

He had then the most ridiculous notion that he was lucky. Ridiculous because of what would come to pass tomorrow; ridiculous because he had lost the full extent of his past and was a most unfortunate, rootless creature. And yet lucky. The sun was shining and she loved him. Briefly these two factors converged in the most extraordinary of coincidences. Here he was, alive and empty, and it took only this miracle to fill him with the sense that past and present alike watched him here.

He leant down and kissed her.

赤山

If it were possible to fall in love with the same person twice then no doubt everybody would choose it, over and over.

It had been spring. He had been riding when he'd come across the youths: famers' sons perhaps. Discontents. It was not unusual in these parts. This, he had been taught, was the challenge he would have to undertake. Akayama's lands were known for their lawlessness, known for being too far from the capital for the iron hand of the government to cast its shadow over these people's lives. But this was his land. Every rock, every tree, every village, every turned patch of soil, and every river snaking between road and hill, belonged to the House on the Mountain.

The youths had killed a girl. They put up a fight at first. He took down one without ever drawing his blade and the others fled like feral dogs.

The girl was a few years older than him. It seemed they had tussled over the bags she had carried. They probably had not foreseen her death. They'd simply done what they had done. She was the victim of an indifference he could barely comprehend and he stood for a long time beside the pool where she must have come to swim, thinking that he had never before seen a corpse. There was nothing terrible or sickening about it. She had been discarded; that was all. And abandoned, had fallen asleep in the mosses and weeds at the base of a shallow waterfall. The grass was dark and her skin was pale and her fingers still clutched the drawstrings of the bag she had sacrificed herself to protect.

He leant over, retrieved it and, sitting at her side, emptied out a handful of coins, some bread and a folded blanket.

Disappointed, he set them down on his other side.

Then realising that she would never reach across him to fetch them back he returned them to the bag and the bag to her outstretched hand. He got to his feet.

Perhaps there was a slight change in the rhythm of the falling water; perhaps a movement. He tensed and turned towards the falls, searching for motion, and was rewarded a moment later with a violent coughing from behind the white curtain. A few steps took him over the shining rocks to where the water had, over the centuries, hollowed out a cavern behind the falls.

If you could fall in love…

赤山

A curving rock face formed a bower behind the veil of white water.

"Listen," Mei said, "It sounds different from this side, doesn't it?" It did. It sounded hollow and it seemed that the water sang with a single long, low note beneath the barrage of white sound. And, if you started to focus on that, then even the empty noise began to divide into rhythms and cymbals and drumbeats. "Do you hear it?"

He nodded, eyes on her and her alone. "It's like everything," she was saying. "You can't escape it. The whole world has a pulse."

"Mei…"

At the sound of her name, she rocked forward and put her arms around him, forcing him to duck beneath the falls, so close to the sheaf of cold water that he expected to feel its lash across his shoulders. Instead she pulled him into a kiss. She was delightfully bold, brilliantly clumsy in the narrow space; all knees and hips and it seemed to him he had not only to navigate the rocks but also the obstacle of her body to reach her mouth. It was too soon to think he was at liberty to touch her. Just her lips then. And she must have felt the same uncertainty because he felt her hands on his cheeks and neck, but when she touched his chest where his *kosode* hung open, she withdrew her hand. He pulled back and saw that her eyes were dark and unfocused. "We're married?"

She sighed. He sunk down, half-expecting her to push away, but she gave him liberty to rest against her chest. Her fingers combed through his hair. This was like the nights they had spent together. It was easier. "I know you want me to remember," he said.

"Hush. I said listen. You never did listen."

He did. To the sound of the falls. And to the soft drip-drip of water trapped amongst the leaves and rocks.

"I think you can hear things I can't hear," he admitted. "I think Mei is in her own world." She chuckled, a soft sound that joined her heartbeat briefly.

"That's the trouble, Arata-*sama*. When you're born to work the land you hear them instinctively. You and I were born into a pattern that will go on long after we are gone. Like a dance or a heartbeat." He shifted a little against her as she went on. "We can't change it."

"Do you really believe that?"

"I know it. I...I've seen some things that don't make sense if you try to imagine the world is good or bad. Once you realise that it's neither – it's just dancing – well, everything else falls into place." Smiling indulgently, he closed his eyes and she asked him, "Why? What do you believe?"

"Well," he said softly, "I honestly can't remember."

She laughed, her fingers sliding down his cheek to his neck. He couldn't decide if it was harder to kiss her or to lie here burning to death so very slowly beneath her touches. "I think people can change," he said.

A man whose wife flinched every time he reached for her. Whom she derided for his temper, for the hand he'd raised against her. "I hope people can change."

Her fingers stopped drifting over his skin.

"I wonder if you could make me believe that, Arata-*sama*."

There was a sudden depth of emotion in her voice that he hadn't heard before.

He sat up. She shifted to lean back against the rock face, her eyes on him and the playfulness gone from her gaze. When he reached for her again, simply to brush the hair away from her neck, which was a ghost pale curve, she dropped her eyes. She was a cut-out; a painting. He traced the line of her neck to her shoulder and wondered what strange enchantment she possessed to remain so perfectly still.

"Make you believe it?"

"You can't. I already know how this will end."

His fingers stopped beneath her chin, tilting her head up, and there was an apology on her lips when he kissed her.

She did not respond as she had done before, with any kind of fire. He pulled back, a question in his eyes: was it tomorrow that troubled her? He wanted to tell her no, that is was only now that mattered; it mattered more than anything because, unless she understood that, Takashi had already won. He kissed her neck, lifting her body this time, and she placed both hands against his chest, initially as if she would hold him back. Yet as he drew on the delicate skin at her throat, he felt her fingers sink in, hard points against his skin. Her body felt heavier than before.

She tasted sweeter than he had imagined, of salt and sweat and the residue of tears. With their previous lightness abandoned, he knotted a hand into her hair and drew her head back, letting his lips and teeth mark the paper-fine skin beneath her chin.

They would see. Let them see.

Then he kissed her full on the lips and felt a tremor run through her, an all but involuntary motion that pressed her hips to his.

When he pulled back, her eyes were closed, her breathing fast. Behind him the water sang louder than ever.

He leant down and ran one finger along the edge of her kimono. She didn't move. That intangible stillness, and yet he recognised her sense of him in her breaths; they grew more ragged with each motion. The gown slid back from her shoulder.

As he kissed her again, he slid his hand inside her robe, beneath her breast, and trapped the nipple between finger and thumb. She shifted beneath him, curling into the touch. She was not resisting, but it seemed to him that she was overpowered. She kept moving as he followed the line of her neck with his lips, lingering on the collarbone, then descending to the tip of her breast; it was hard now beneath his tongue. Her back arched and she put one arm around his head, holding him there.

Her heartbeat. It took him a moment to distinguish it from his own and then he realised how furiously it hammered against her chest. Without much grace, for he feared he had little left to give, he tugged the kimono back from her other side and kissed the point above her heart.

"There," he said.

To his surprise, he found that he was smiling and her incomprehension at this was delicious. He took one of her hands and laid it flat against her chest, leaning enough weight on her that she could not easily escape. "You listen," he said.

She caught her breath, her face animated again.

"To what?"

"Your heartbeat – your pulse – the one thing you can't change – the one thing you can't escape."

She laughed suddenly at his sincerity.

"What?"

"It's faster now," he said.

"I know."

"You said we couldn't change it."

She blinked at him, then laughed again, tipping her head back as the sound burst out. He wrapped his arms around her, buoyed up by her strangeness.

"Oh, Arata-*sama*….."

"I told you people can change. People change people." He kissed her shoulders again, distracted from their conversation. He liked the way she shivered when she laughed. She had released her arms from the long sleeves of the kimono and boldly now she began to untie the sash of his *hakama*. It occurred to him that he had been too intent upon her body; such that his own was almost overcome with desire for her now.

She lay back against the stone, her kimono becoming a patchwork of patterns and colours against which the pallor of her skin offered smooth contrast.

He touched his lips to her belly and he moved up an invisible centreline, until he was above her and, where their hips met, a motion on her part pushed him inside of her.

His body responded violently. Stripped of his control, a kind of convulsion passed through him.

He felt her nails digging into the back of his neck and he slid one hand into the small of her back. The change elicited a sound from her. She stifled it against his lips and, this time, smothered by the rhythm of their bodies and the heartbeat in his head, their kiss was clumsy. He could no longer tell where his breath stopped and hers began.

They found their way through each other.

It was the cold stone beneath her kimono, the tightness of the space, the tentativeness of her touches, that made things real for him. Kisses that missed and found his nose and chin. Nails that dug too deeply and his breath against her neck. These were the things he could commit to memory. These were the things that would last.

He saw her caught in the instant of her desire.

His own came like a wave then. Her body responded with a series of after-tremors.

And then he was lying on the silk of her kimono.

For the first time, she seemed unaware of him. Her head was tilted away. Coils of her hair, dark with sweat and spray, made spiral patterns across her shoulders down to her breasts, as if her upper body were painted with black henna. He tried to memorise the details: the finger she lifted and ran along her collarbone as if she too was mapping his touches; the moment when she turned towards him and he became aware of every curve of her body against the white falls behind; how brazen the gaze in those grey eyes.

He expected her to speak, but at the end she kissed him slowly.

Desire abandoned, in this last, he sensed an emotion deeper than lust. He had thought that, in the roughness of his affections, he had marked her for Takashi to see. But in her last kiss, deliberate and unrestrained, she claimed him.

She buried her face against his chest then and all the dark enchantment fell away, leaving her body, delicate and pale as it had always been. When he held her it was as if he could break her, and he closed his eyes and listened to her breathing.

How long they stayed that way he didn't know. It was perhaps the cast of the afternoon sun that made him realise the day was stretching on. Unfair that their time together had been so brief.

He didn't know much about the man he had been or even about the boy who had saved a girl who had fallen in love. But he did know that, at some point in his absent past, he had made a good choice. And given the chance to make it again, hold her again, save her again, he realised, he would choose it, over and over. Until whatever rhythm her world danced to faded and fell into silence.

8. The Other Side of a Bargain

Mei waited while the men looked through her belongings, sifting through one bag after another and, with dour expressions, noting the contents. They had thought she would bring money and had not been prepared for this, but after a short discussion her offering was deemed acceptable.

"I have thirty *ryo,* Arata," she had told him that morning. "That's from emptying the coffers and going through the servants' quarters and your brother's. I need fifty." She'd been lying with her back against his chest and shoulder, his arm wrapped around her belly. Since their afternoon spent by the waterfall, it seemed to her he had been unable to let go, both figuratively and literally.

"Payment?" he asked.

"Yes, he has asked for our payments of fifty *ryo* each in compensation since he should otherwise have been paid for his bounty. We're paying for Ryuu's life."

"Is that all he has required of you? Money?"

She didn't answer but lay there a moment before removing his arm from where it lay across her body. She stood up and crossed to where she had laid out her clothes for the morning. "Twenty more," he said, and she was glad that he was not going to ask any more questions. "It should be simple to furnish you with goods worth that much."

And that was what he had done. Mainly dresses and gowns since silk was still expensive; knives from the *dojo,* and one of the horses from the stables. It was, she thought as she had left him that morning to ride alone through the gorge, a most generous dowry.

He had asked to come at least as far as the outpost, but she did not trust Takashi's men. And even if he had returned to the house unseen, the journey would have wasted valuable time.

"Prepare yourself," she said. She had kissed him on the side of the mouth.

She could see by his eyes that he was angry. She was glad. She wouldn't say farewell; she couldn't risk drawing out that fury into a more tangible emotion. Whilst he remained so, with it coiled inside him, he was strong.

Without another word, she mounted and started towards the gorge only to have him intercept her a moment later; it was not what she expected.

"I don't know if he will give you any freedom in Okiri, but I think this is important." And he had pressed a folded piece of paper into her hand. She opened it. A name. "We need to find Ryuu," he said, keeping pace as her mount moved forward like a tide. "That's the most important thing. If we find him, this is all over, one way or another. I wouldn't ask you to do this. I could be putting you in danger, but I've considered this from every side and this may be the only opportunity we have."

"Kotaro Murasaki," she read.

"You don't know him?"

"No."

"Find out who he is," he said, stepping back to let her go. His reluctance was tangible. "He did business with both my brother and I."

"If I can," she said, careful not to let any emotion show on her face. A hand raised in farewell was her last acknowledgement. Then she kept her eyes straight ahead.

Be angry, she thought. Stay angry, stay strong and stay fierce.

Takashi's men took their time going through the silks and fabrics as if she would try to cheat them in this. She saw the money, the coinage at least, disappear into a coffer in a corner of the room. "Will the captain not ask for this money once I reach Okiri?"

"I think she's saying we're thieves," said one of them. Someone cuffed the back of her head and laughed when she nearly fell. It had not been hard; just unexpected.

She had grown soft, she thought. These last few weeks, she'd let down her guards. But here, now, she would need to remember that nothing was sacred. Funny. She hadn't expected to long for Takashi's company, but compared to these men, he was at least a known quantity.

"Our salary," said another, looking with interest at an inlaid bowl amongst her goods. "Hardly fitting for him to ride all the way out here with our wage. When we're relieved of duty, we take our share back to Okiri."

"Why not send your wage with your replacement?"

"The captain wouldn't trust any one of us not to steal the others'!"

They laughed amongst themselves.

There were thieves in the mountains. So she had been taught as a child. She had stumbled upon them sometimes: thugs who could take a life without a thought; there were those too who dressed as warriors and rode in the name of the shogunate.

She watched as one of the men, the leader it seemed, looked up from his task and gave a nod to the company. Half a dozen rose and, without another word, filed out. They carried swords to a man, and one had a flintlock, a pistol, in his belt.

"You won't find him," she said when, in the wake of their departure, no others in the room acknowledged their leave-taking.

"He has nowhere to run," someone said.

"Akayama Arata died four weeks ago."

"That's not what I heard."

"I showed your lieutenant his grave. Did you think it was a man who attacked him? It was no man. No, nor any living thing."

"Are we meant to believe it was a ghost?"

She was quiet.

"I heard," said someone on the far side of the room, "That Homura cut him in the leg and he limped well enough to be a man."

"Ghosts have no feet to limp," said the first.

"No, this one had feet for sure."

"He comes in any form he chooses," Mei said, lowering herself onto a seat by the door. From here she could see the gorge and the way the swordsmen had taken back to the estate. She kept her eyes on the passage through the rocks as she spoke. "Sometimes he's the wind; sometimes a wild dog hunting for scraps that passes through your town; sometimes he's a rock fall that catches you unawares; sometimes he's the heat in the heart of a storm. Sometimes though he comes as a warrior. You would know only if you fought him. The devil himself is in his blade."

By their silence, she knew they listened, but she dared not turn to meet their eyes.

"I'm not afraid of the devil," someone said suddenly, "But I'd not choose to die like Inuko." There was a general murmur of assent and Mei realised that the young lieutenant's death was still fresh in all their minds. The wound had been to his upper arm. Either infection or blood loss then. She hadn't heard the details.

"I am marked," she said.

It was a long time before anyone spoke. There was the soft scritch-scritch of one of the soldier's cleaning his sword.

"What does that mean then?"

"It means," she said, turning to the room at large, "That he protects me. No matter where I go. And it doesn't matter how far you run. He will find you."

"I'm not scared of fairy stories, Woman." The man closest dragged her to her feet: tall, lanky, with a mane of dark hair to his waist. Without any ado, he cupped her breast in one hand, firmly enough that she was pushed back against the wall, and squeezed hard. The laughter from the others was a soft ripple of sound. Yet all she could hear was her own breathing, deep and steady.

"He'll know," she said. "You'll die by his hand."

"A dead man's hand?" He squeezed harder still, pressing one knee between her legs so that bile rose up in her throat. "I'd sooner be afraid of what the captain would do to me if I ruined his prize." The others jeered and he let her go, jerking his head back as if he expected their adulation.

"Inuko raised his hand to me," she said, trying to resist the urge to fold her arms across her chest and hold herself. "He is dead. Arata will not rest until he is certain I am free of you. All of you."

"If Inuko is dead, then why is Takashi alive and well? I heard he did more than touch you."

"We made a bargain," she said and flinched as something soft struck her on the shoulder.

"Change out of your riding clothes, Little Devil." A pale pink gown lay folded against her ankles. She took it and turned away from them and they mocked the modesty she tried to retain, facing into the corner as she shed the *kosode* and *hakama* she had worn for the journey. No-one else touched her though.

Soft, she thought. Grown too soft.

They could do far worse, but she suspected it was Takashi's influence from afar that protected her and, all through the miserable ride down to Okiri, she found her mind wandering between two images: the half dozen men who had ridden away towards the estate and her memory, now somewhat faded, of Takashi Isamu, who had stormed into her world and torn it apart. And it was with a bitter taste that she acknowledged her gratitude to him for, whatever orders he had given to his men, they were neither rough nor, for the most part, cruel with her, save in the cheapest of ways. A touch, a grope, the brush of a hand; these things, she told herself, she could endure. And it sickened her how swiftly gratitude came to mimic a need for him. She thought of the man she had left back on the estate and of how he had but yesterday delighted in her, and she wished that she could recall in perfect detail those touches, those kisses, the way his eyes had found and committed to memory every detail and every flaw of her person and yet, as the road descended into a bank of cloud and warm summer rain, she realised that the distance between Akayama and Okiri had become like a pane of glass to her and her memory hammered impotently against it. No time has passed between the afternoon when Takashi had descended on the household and now.

And that was better. Her time on the estate was a dream. She could please Takashi. She could lose all the rest because it had never existed.

And somewhere her spirit dashed itself against the glass and split into glittering pieces.

赤山

"You must be hungry. Please take a seat. You'll forgive me that we are not so well furnished here as you are in Akayama."

It was a small room, very meagre, very plain. The futon was in a recess on the far side of the chamber. Three walls were white-washed stone; to Mei's left, the fourth was made of shelves and cubbyholes and nooks. Takashi noticed the way she stared. "An ammunition store. Maybe Okiri was wealthy once. Now they'll sooner employ vagabonds like me than fill the space with expensive foreign arms. Does it surprise you that I didn't object to staying here? My tastes should be more refined perhaps, but this is what I am now: a weapon of the government, Lady Mei." He handed her a half an orange, freshly cut. "Fruit costs, does it not?"

She didn't answer but ate it nevertheless and he could likely guess, from the way she sucked it dry, that she was starved of such extravagances. She turned away. "Inuko died," he said.

"I heard."

"He was the only one I gave a damn about."

As they ate in silence, she found that she was able to take in details she hadn't seen before. Takashi had perhaps a decade on her, but time it seemed had only served to add layers of muscle to an already thick-set body. There was nothing elegant or graceful in him, save for his eyes, which seemed to show too much: emotions too refined for such an exterior.

Yet it had not been simple, she recalled, even during their last encounter. She had expected a barbarian, and he had acted like one in front of his men, but alone with her she had sensed a desperation in him. He had talked. Her experience was not broad, but she suspected men who sought only conquest were not so eloquent. And, for all that he had forced her, he had been gentle. "Why didn't you let me kill him?" he asked, offering her tea. She drank and set the cup down. She could think of nothing to say. "You told me to let him live."

"He is my husband."

"I thought he struck you."

"He is different now."

He got to his feet. He moved, she realised, like Arata and Ryuu. Years of training, worn like a cloak; he was leagues apart from the rest of his men, yet he hid it well. Crossing to a shelf, he poured himself a cup of wine and stood drinking, with his eyes unfocused as if solving a difficult problem. "Who are you really?" she asked suddenly. "You're not like the others."

"What makes you say that?"

"I can see it in your eyes. The others look straight ahead at each moment when it arises. You look through things."

"Through?"

"Through me."

He frowned as he crossed back to her and took a seat then glanced up. His eyes were sad, she thought, but it was nothing so easy to explain as that. She had sensed it the first time they were together: the idea that he was not fully present; as if his mind were always elsewhere, searching. And his actions, for all that they were brutal, could never be anything more than half-hearted.

As he drank, she reached over and touched his cheek with the backs of her fingers. He froze. Then his other hand reached up and covered hers and he held it against his face, eyes closed.

"I wondered why, after I left Akayama, I wanted to return," he said. "Why, despite everything, I became convinced that you did not hate me. I thought about you many times, Mei. Mostly I found that I was curious that one could live who is so forgiving." He opened his eyes. "I know what I am after all."

"It is why you are that puzzles me."

A ghost of a smile appeared on his lips.

"I puzzle Mei?"

"You lack conviction," she said, trying to put into words the strange hesitation she had sensed in him. She had come to recognise the signs of someone having lost themselves. That same emptiness resided in Takashi's eyes; the same loss, though brindled with a depth of pain she didn't understand. "You yearn for an end to all this."

"An end to what?"

"You seem tired of bloodshed."

He bridled:

"Is that what you think? That I have become sentimental in my dotage?"

"Or simply that you see now there is no glory. You've followed the road, haven't you, to its very end, and the thing you were looking for? It isn't there. Arata and Ryuunaka are warriors, but they never sought honour through violence." She could see from his expression that some of her words sank in. And in that moment he seemed young again, perhaps angry, perhaps insulted, but vibrant in a way he had not been before.

"You cannot understand what honour is," he said.

"You cannot steal it."

"I never have!"

"Do you think if you ride in his name that the shogun will someday recognise you? Do you think if you take another man's wife, she will one day love you? We are nothing but the trappings of something you lost long ago—"

He raised his hand to strike her and stopped. She neither moved nor flinched, but his voice was like steel.

"The truth is not always yours to state so liberally, Mei."

And he rose to fetch more wine.

Already on her knees, Mei bowed forward and put her head on the ground.

"Please let Akayama Arata go if he lives through this night."

"Begging doesn't suit you."

"You want to end this, don't you?" she asked, more desperate now.

"I want my money."

"Do you hear yourself when you speak that way?"

The next thing she felt was his hand in her hair, dragging her out of the bow.

"Starve!" he said and his face twisted with anger. "Starve with me one wintertime and lie in the ditches and pig-sties, and fight the dogs for their scraps! Starve and then tell me if you prefer your honour to my coin!"

"I would!" she hissed, reaching behind her head to keep his hands from pulling in her hair. "I would if it would save his life."

"That's very virtuous! But I would not be lectured by a woman who is sleeping with her husband's brother!" He shoved her backwards. Then, almost delicately, he lifted his foot and planted the toes against her sternum, gently pressing her down until she lay flat. She turned her head to one side. She knew the faraway look had gone from his eyes and that scared her. "Let's be who we are tonight," he said, stepping over her and loosening his belt. "Not who we wanted to be."

She lay there, not wanting to look at him, though she was aware it was growing darker outside and, when he lit a candle, the scent of the smoke licked across her heightened senses. She kept her eyes on the door, her hands across her chest, though he moved them to strip her. And when she was lying against cold stone, still she kept her head turned away.

When she felt his hand between her legs, then his body bearing down on hers, she closed her eyes and braced herself against the wall behind. Funny, how cold her shoulders were and how warm his body.

He pushed inside her and she screwed her eyes shut and clamped her mouth shut, not willing to give of herself a single breath, a single sound. It made his own panting, rutting noises all the more ridiculous for that he was so alone and, if she let herself step sideways out of the picture, there was still a place of silence in her mind where beams of light dissected themselves into rainbows beneath a waterfall and he had no hold on her.

In the end he lifted her and held his face against her throat, in his last stirrings of passion clamping her hips against his and bruising her. She reached out and held him, digging her nails into the muscles in his back as she stifled a cry against his shoulder. The pain was brief but intense.

He pushed back from her and she slumped against the wall.

It had not taken long. She curled up around the burning, aching sensation: a scarlet line through her body; pieces of him taking root inside her. She pressed her hands to her stomach. "You had no intention of coming here for me," Takashi said. "Only to beg for his life."

"I would have," she whispered. "And I would have given it freely; you had no right to take it. No right."

He stared at her as if considering the truth in those words. She thought that she might cry, but the only sound she made was a low moan as she picked up the kimono that lay tangled about her knees and covered her body with it. She turned her face towards the wall. It smelt of the damp, stale air of Okiri.

"I think it would be better if you hated me," said Takashi as he lowered himself to the floor before her, "Since I am going to take away everything that you love."

"Why?" And this time the word was a dry sob.

"It's not your fault." He ran a finger along her jaw and sighed. "When I was twenty I found a child living on the streets, a wretched little thing; he'd come and beg for bones and bread off me. And I gave them. He amused me. I saw in him who I had been, and one day I found out that he and I were not so different; both good families; both fallen on the worst of times; parents killed; our holdings seized. Figured I'd teach him what I knew of the sword, then see if we couldn't get hired by people better than drunken merchants and wealthy gamblers. We did. We did well. Like I said, he was the only one I ever gave a damn about."

He straightened, took some wine from a nearby shelf and pressed it into her hands. She was too numb to really feel it. "You ask me why I am what I am. I am the sum of every opportunity and injustice done to my family. And that, Lady Mei, is exactly what you are too. It's just, on this occasion, you picked the wrong family."

She looked away as he stood up again, and unstoppered the bottle with trembling fingers, surprising herself with the first swig because it was plum wine and strong enough to make her eyes water. Holding her breath she took down as much as she could, eyes closed; draft upon draft until the next swallow stuck in her throat and she gagged.

The bottle rolled out of her hands.

Sometime later he walked past her and picked it up. Her body was too heavy to move.

Time dilated.

She had been sitting against the wall forever when Takashi was suddenly there beside her again, dressed in a dark robe, his hair loose now. Her eyes roved towards him. Lifting her head right now would be too much, but he held a small piece of paper in front of her eyes. "Explain."

"Something," she murmured, "To do with Ryuu."

"Kotaro Murasaki?" He sounded surprised, but she was too tired to think of why. It was important though, wasn't it? Something nagged at her about the name.

"Who is he?" she managed. Takashi laughed.

"Kotaro runs a money lending firm if you ask for him openly. Ask for him in private and most will know he runs the whore house and the gambling ring." He folded up the paper and slipped it into the sleeve of her kimono. "I like your family, Mei. I like that they make things simple for me."

With that, he lifted her up. Her head nodded backwards over his arm; her world was spinning, turning to a slow beat, and she shuddered suddenly, thinking there was something she should remember.

Six horsemen.
She dreamed.

9. The Girl Who Never Was

A light shone brightly in the residence, a fire that had been glowing since dusk had sapped the colour from the landscape. From his place above the gorge, the last and only soul left alive on the mountain could see both his house and the one road that led away from it to the east. He shifted a little to relieve the cramps in both his legs.

He had been here since noon and had deserted his post only once, to light the lamps before nightfall. To his right, a bow lay flat on the path. It was not that he felt Mei's plan had been flawed, but he had found the bow and arrows nearly a week ago, had practised and judged himself proficient. It wasn't enough for him to hide, not when his mind crawled all over the thought of another man with his wife. On one hand he told himself that she could handle herself. She was fierce; not in her demeanour, but there was an iron strength beneath her convictions. On the other hand though, there lay all his darkest imaginings. She saw this as her side of a bargain. He recognised it as a convenient revenge and the thought that she might have gone, blinkered to her fate, terrified him. If Takashi wanted her, she would likely live, but if Takashi wanted him above all else then he could use her in all manner of ways to reach him.

No. She had believed Takashi would let her return. She would not have believed so without good reason. She had not left as a martyr or a sacrifice. He had seen in her eyes the intention to return to him and it was that, above all, that would keep him strong tonight.

He caught the sound of distant hoof beats deep within the gorge. He let his lips curl into an ugly smile.

Let them come. There would be nothing finer than making somebody pay for the way he felt tonight.

They were more cautious than he had imagined, choosing to leave the horses in the gorge rather than ride to the house itself and, as they approached, they kept their eyes on the rocks all around. It was of course a perfect fortress in many ways and perhaps defence had been on the mind of the architect when he created a house accessible only by narrow passages and wooden bridges.

Two men. Four. Five. Then six.

As he had practised so many times that afternoon, he raised the bow in perfect silence, took aim, and fired. He was nocking a second arrow as the shaft of the first passed through the leading man's chest. The only sound was his body slumping to the ground. The second shaft stuck in the neck of the next man. He was noisier, falling to his knees, bubbling.

Despite the elegance of the weapon, with his whereabouts revealed, it became useless. He leant down to discard the bow and take up the sword that lay behind him.

And something lashed across his cheek.

It felt like a feather, stung like venom. A sound exploded in his head and then on the rocks behind, and instinctively he dropped to his belly, hands over his head as dust fell around him like rain. There was blood on his cheek. A wound no deeper than a scratch, though now perhaps he better understood Mei's fears.

He had neither heard nor seen gunfire before, but he knew a little about the weapons. Like so much of the knowledge stored in his mind, it had no source but hung suspended. Guns were less accurate than the arrows of a skilled archer, but more destructive. Clean. And fast.

He scraped forward across the rock face. The sword clattered as his fingers closed over the *saya* and then he was up and running. Staying low, he descended at a sprint.

At the base of the track, he was barely metres from the four remaining men when he took up the end of a rope he'd laid down earlier and heaved the full weight of his body against the slack. All through the thick grass on the edge of the woodland, it dragged up a series of metal trays. In daylight, they would have stood briefly on their edges before falling back again. In the darkness, the effect was far better than he imagined. Not only was the sudden flurry of movement enough to draw his pursuers' attention, but it was brilliantly reminiscent of footfalls through the long grass. An invisible fugitive appeared to flee from the scene and run towards the house. It had been Mei's idea and he had been quick to dismiss it, but, like the woman herself, over time, it had grown more compelling.

As the swordsmen gave chase he stepped into the moonlight.

Four of them remained. It might be possible with four. The energy running inside him was cool and clear and, this time, his desire to kill was unfettered by doubt.

Yes, it might well be possible, but then the truth was she would never forgive him. Hers hadn't been a simple appeal to him to live. It had been a promise. Do this for me and I will come back to you.

With a hiss of frustration at the departing figures of his enemies, he slid the sword into his *obi* and ran towards the woods.

赤山

She had polished off the wine and fallen into a death-like sleep.

Takashi sat in a shaft of moonlight slung in through the high window, his skin and the girl's the same milky cast, softened by shadows. She had been right about him in every single way and, in turn, he had thought he understood her.

Let us be, he had said, who we are, and not who we wanted to be.

Words spoken in the knowledge that she must have strayed far and long ago from the path she might have chosen; spoken in the knowledge that she had come here to please him as payment for the life of a man who had already rent apart her own marriage; spoken in the knowledge that she was, by her own admission, dishonourable. He believed all those things.

Let us be who we are.

Then why did he feel guilt? Why, when he had taken women as plunder before, when he had looked into the eyes of boys barely out of childhood as he'd cut their throats? Why would this, of all things, leave him with a sense of loss? And angry, as if it were he and not she who were humiliated.

And why was it so important that he prove to her there was no good in this world? Why not let her go on believing until the rest of the world betrayed her and she was forced to open her eyes?

Because.

Because so long as she continued to believe she could never look with anything but contempt upon him.

She should not have refused him tonight. She had come from nothing; she had a place in this world because she had once caught the eye of nobility. What dignity she had was borrowed, so upon what grounds did she assume she was too good for him?

Yet in his mind's eye he recalled a woman who had breathed life into him, with whom he had spoken freely. He had not lied when he had said he'd thought of her often. He had imagined her alone and untouched in that exquisite house clinging to the side of the Red Mountain. Never once had he imagined Arata had woken, until

Inuko's fateful encounter had changed everything, and then he had considered returning for the girl. His revenge on Arata though, he had decided, would be twofold and sweeter for it. Not only would he let the man see that his wife would leave him for another, but let him see too that she would come willingly. That, Takashi had thought, would be the true prize. And up until the last, he had believed she might be willing.

What had changed? In the space of four weeks, what was so different?

With a grunt he stood up and crossed to the shelves, eyeing the dark shapes of wine bottles and flasks of sake standing in rows. She had drunk enough for them both though and he didn't feel like getting drunk. As much as it pained him, he felt as if he might be seeing things clearly for the first time in a long time. He stepped back and stretched broadly in the trail of moonlight.

Tomorrow a decision would have to be made. Of one thing he was sure, he did not want to keep her here against her will. Fool, he thought; sentimental old fool, to think that it was anything but too little and too late. And yet, if at the end of all this she turned to him with softer eyes, then it was worth a little whimsy. He understood now that she would need her spirit broken if she was ever to accept him and who he was, but tonight had taught him one thing: he did not want to be the one to break it.

Let her go back to the mountain then, he thought. She had been alive there. Afraid, desperate, manipulative but alive. He wanted to see her alive again.

At least one good thing would come of this night, he consoled himself: her husband would be dead.

赤山

The very same man who occupied Takashi's thoughts was partway through the woodland when he realised he was no longer alone. There was no cover thick enough and no shadow long enough to hide in tonight. He found himself running from shaft to shaft of light while, over to his left something or someone was keeping pace.

It was a trick of the night that all things, once bathed in moonlight, whether stone or tree or deer or man, lost elements of their form. It could have been a beast or a spirit. If it were a man, and he suspected that were the case, then he wished that the moon, in her mercy, might show him the eyes or the face. It was hard to judge a challenger with no expression. Harder still to know when to stop, turn and fight. Soon, soon. And then there would be others.

So he had been less discreet than he'd intended, or perhaps he had simply underestimated them. At this rate, they would catch him before he reached the collapsed road and long before he could find the tools Mei had left for him.

There was a shout from his right. A second shadow. The chances were high that all four had realised their mistake and followed him. And why not? He had already shown that he was a worthy match for two of Takashi's men. Why take unnecessary chances?

The path dipped down into a stream-bed. Lightning flashes of water marked the periphery of his vision as he crested a small slope and turned. He drew his sword.

There was no-one there.

He was not delirious enough to have imagined them. He was not afraid either. If anything, his blood was singing for this confrontation. But perhaps they knew that because how better to play this game than go to ground when he challenged them? If they thought he had a chance then stabbing him in the back was a far better tactic than facing him.

He thought he understood now why a hunted beast sometimes froze, eyes wide and seeing nothing. He did not trust this moonlight.

And when he started to try and listen for them it seemed that the forest could have hidden an army because every leaf conspired against him by shifting in a sudden breeze. The sound was like the whisper of fabrics. They would use that to their advantage, he realised. They would be closer now than a moment ago. His mouth was dry.

To his right. Yes.

He kept his eyes ahead, both hands on the sword, allowing his glance to brush across the featureless shadows as if he was still searching, while every inch of his being instead focused on the shape to his right, ascertaining its height, the slight tilt of the head, the undrawn weapon, because a blade would catch the licking moonlight too soon. If he took a step back, then this shadow assailant could pivot onto the path and execute a swift cut or a single stab. The latter would be most effective, particularly if he lowered his sword. Then one of the others would finish him from behind.

He watched the scene in his mind's eye, mapping the locations of the other swordsmen onto an imagined landscape. He dare not let himself wonder how he knew these things or if they were right; the scene would start to collapse around him if he did; the shadows would close in. And he was reminded suddenly of the way Mei sang, often without realising she did. Like the birds, she had said. As unintended as a heartbeat.

It was like that. There must be a pattern, and some part of him understood how the notes must fall and the cadences rise. He needed only to set it in motion.

If he lowered his sword, a thrust to his belly or chest would be the most efficient end.

He sighed aloud, slumped his shoulders and switched the blade back across his left arm to resheath it, turning to continue on.

And as a man pivoted onto the path behind him, instead of sheathing his weapon, he stabbed beneath his arm, parallel to the *saya* on his hip. He caught someone or something, the same spirit that had tracked him, still faceless but grunting and choking now, cut out of the dance. Engaged in a simple play of motion and rhythm he tore the blade out and swung it in a half-moon, creating a crescent of reflected light before it slumped into the belly of the next man. The soldier folded, gagged and started to scream.

He stepped over the bleeding heap, hearing only the staccato steps of a third attacker. There was only so much of the melody he could prepare for. The third man's doubt and the step he took backwards were not a part of the score. And the fourth should have shown himself by now.

He could hear his own breathing; it was deep and almost calm, and he wondered at that; it was another clue to who and what he was.

And to think that he had once had the audacity to call Mei cold.

赤山

It was too late, or perhaps even too early for the knocking at Takashi's door to be anything mundane. It did at least make him realise that he had been kneeling at the foot of the futon for hours now and, within that time, his thoughts had meandered, but ultimately wormed themselves into circles. He was tired, she had said. That much was true. He had known there was something wrong with him, inside him. Like a cancer but growing so slowly that it had taken this long for the seeds to form shoots and the shoots to bloom into something ugly.

More knocking. A muffled shout. He got to his feet, disorientated. It was too soon for news of his soldiers to reach him from Akayama. He had the sudden absurd notion that Arata might have come down from the estate like a whirlwind to wreak revenge. Right now Takashi wouldn't have had the stomach to stand up to him.

He tore open the door and tried to set his face. Shuru, one of his men, was standing in the courtyard, still dressed in his day clothes and pale with excitement. He bowed, one hand still on his sword: a slight that Takashi noticed but didn't comment upon; he was too curious as to the young man's distraction. "You have a good reason for disturbing me?"

"Yes, Captain, we do." Shuru smiled like a wolf. "We have Akayama Ryuunaka in custody."

Takashi stared. The words shook away a little of the indecision that had been paralysing him tonight. This was good news. He had rather forgotten what it felt like to achieve something. "Wait there." He closed the door in Shuru's face and turned back into the room to dress, keeping half an eye on the woman who was hidden, still all but unconscious, in the folds of his bed-clothes. She didn't move, but her breathing was deep and strong and regular. He had been concerned at first by how much wine she had consumed, but it seemed that she would be alright and, guessing at how she would feel tomorrow, she was unlikely to do anything rash. Fixing his sword into his *obi* he stepped out into the courtyard and locked the door behind him. "Set a guard here," he told the younger man. "Don't tell her she's a prisoner, but let whoever stands here know that if she is ill they should fetch her medicines."

"Yes, Captain."

"Why isn't Akayama Ryuu dead yet? We could leave this godforsaken place tomorrow." And how neat that would be. Arata dead; Mei already in his bed, and their lord's head severed and ready to be brought before the court as proof of his success.

"It was the opinion of the men that brought him in that he should be sober when they killed him."

"I really have no interest in giving him an honourable death. He's caused me enough trouble from afar."

"They lashed him to make him speak, but even after that, he is still denying everything. Homura's of the notion we'll not have the full story until he's spent a night in chains."

They were descending the stairs to the prisoners' cells now, cut into the black stone beneath Okiri. The stench of damp was enough to mask the more nauseating odours left by the few denizens who had stayed down here in recent months. The irony was that the greatest criminals roamed the streets above and left the lesser here to rot.

"Do we really need a story from a man who's done no more than fail to pay his duties?" asked Takashi, stifling a yawn. Out of the corner of his eye, he saw Shuru's lips quirk into a small smile.

"Oh, I think you'll like this one. In fact, I'm inclined to think if there's one thing this man is good at, it's stories." Takashi glanced up.

"Oh?"

"Indeed."

Shuru stepped back to let them both into the guards' room. Homura was standing over a table, his hands resting on crumpled papers and notes of promise. He straightened to attention as his commanding officer entered.

A suspicion bloomed in Takashi as he glanced between the two men: Homura's stoicism; Shuru's knowing smirk.

"What then?" he asked. "Has he mentioned the girl?"

"There is no girl," Homura said.

There was a silence that stretched thin in the stuffy room and Takashi recalled suddenly that it was still several hours before dawn and he had not yet slept tonight. He lowered himself into a seat and frowned. "There is no girl," Homura continued, "Because Arata's wife died in spring."

"She's dead?"

"The exact manner of her death isn't clear, but I checked and the death itself is verified in Akayama's records. Her family were Shirakawa." He pushed a note towards Takashi. "A noble lineage. Her name was originally Shirakawa Kyoko, but, for two years now, Akayama Kyoko."

"Two years...She said they were married for four."

"It's a fiction," said Shuru, the smile falling from his lips for the first time. "She's taken us for a ride. The noble lines, even Akayama, wouldn't stoop to marry village girls. Doesn't it sound more like a storybook to you? She made it up."

"There's more," said Homura. Takashi looked up. "It's probably better you hear it from him though."

"He's inebriated. Wine and something else I think," said Shuru, joining the other two at the table. "What I want to know is, who is she?"

"We could probably get a name out of him," Homura said.

"It's alright," said Takashi. "She told me that first night. She's Mei. Chimariko Mei."

赤山

The danger was in thinking.

The third swordsman stepped back again. Outlined in moonlight, blade raised; his face gave little away and it was for this reason that his opponent was hesitant, feet sliding through the grit as he advanced. The nobleman still let his instincts guide him, his focus cast outwards like a net into the surrounding shadows, dark pools between patches of silver grass and glass-like leaves. The fourth man was out there. He inched closer to the third swordsman on the path. They were still more than a blade's length apart when the latter panicked and lunged. He sidestepped. And something changed. Perhaps it was desperation, perhaps a hardening of resolve, but as he twisted into a cut that should have rent the other's shoulder, the swordsman was gone. Steel flashed to his left; he changed his cut to a parry and grunted as the blades clashed and their edges squealed.

The young soldier bared his teeth and sprung into a series of ferocious cuts that pushed the him backwards towards the trees. Every time he thought he might lunge or cut, the soldier was gone. Every time he tried to gain ground, a blade stopped him. Desperation flared even as both men engaged in a frenzied clash of swords between shafts of moonlight. The next strike brought the soldier's skull-like, terse-grinning face close to the noble's above a cross made by their two blades. It was close, too close for comfort. His breathing was faster now, as he tried to let his body dictate the motions, to know and not to guess. A second later, his opponent twisted and rammed the pommel of the katana into his chest.

A sudden dark. He choked and his next breath was a wheeze filled with all sound, colour and sensation. He was falling backwards, the soldier standing over him; the descent of the youth's blade, a single line across the canopy above.

He lurched to one side. On hands and knees now and his heartbeat trying to burst out of his temples. The soldier raised his weapon above his head and ran at him, screaming like a banshee. His own sword was missing. He crashed into the undergrowth at the side of the path, consumed now by both the need to escape and to find something to protect himself. Too many thoughts. His hands closed over a thick branch. He turned just as the soldier's blade howled again, passing through the wood, sending splinters boiling into the air. He screwed his eyes shut against the shrapnel, heard the steel whine again, a breeze across his cheek, and his momentum carried him backwards into the leaf mould. He kicked hard.

His feet collided with the soldier's belly and hip, making the next strike fall wide. A heartbeat later, he was up and running again.

His katana was a shadow on the path. He fell on it. In his mind there was only this, the ink dark blade, and the soldier who pursued was just another patch of dark against the feast of moonlight. The youth was flying at him, unaware that he was armed again.

He had lost the steps of the dance a long time ago. It was luck and not skill or fate tonight. He turned at the last moment and slashed the young soldier across the chest. As he fell, the youth's lips parted in a blossom of blood and surprise.

Victorious, the nobleman stood over the body, his own weapon remaining at the final point of the cut. The tip shivered, the tremors in his body magnified along the length of his blade.

As he began to breathe more normally, something hard and cold was pressed firmly to the back of his head.

In the same way that one might note the time of day or a change in the weather, he recalled suddenly that there had been a fourth soldier, the one who had carried a gun.

His shoulders shook with soft laughter as the last of Takashi's men cocked the weapon and pulled the trigger.

10. The Ghost and her Demon

Mei turned onto her back and tried to open eyes that were thick with sleep. There was a pain in the base of her skull, just as if someone had driven a nail straight through, and it dug further in as she realised where she was. She sat up. Several glances around the room convinced her that she was now alone. That at least was a relief. Beneath the covers she was still naked and she curled up a little as she recalled what he had done. She had misjudged him. She had thought he could be reasoned with, but even now she could feel his touch all over her. Not as it had been before, when they had lain together in Akayama. This was different. His intention had been revenge and her body ached as if he had impressed his cause upon her person.

If she had misjudged him in this then there was a chance she had misjudged him in other ways. He had kept his word so far, but there was no way she could be sure he would now. Standing, she dressed and crossed to the door. It was locked.

It was clear then. He didn't intend to let her return.

She felt as if someone had reached inside her and tugged a single cord beneath her heart. She tried the lock several more times. On a distant, sunlit terrace, one man awaited her return, but she would never meet him, while in this world Takashi would come for her night after night after god-forsaken night.

No. This was the wine and the pain in her head filling her mind with ill thoughts. She was not given to despair; there was more inside her than that. With a snarl she threw her weight against the door.

"Hey, hey, are you alright? Don't break it down!" She jumped back. The latch was pulled and a young guard stared in at her. His face was soft. He didn't look immediately hostile. "Are you sick?"

"No."

"Then just be good and wait for the captain." The door closed in her face.

So, she thought, the world would continue; hers might crumble but it was perfectly possible that no-one here would even notice.

She glanced around the room. It was not a prison cell, but it was secure. There was no other way out that she could see.

"I need to relieve myself, if you'd be so kind," she told the locked door. "Unless you would have me use some corner of his quarters." After a moment's hesitation, the door opened again. The young man stared at her suspiciously. "Well?" she said.

"Fine."

"I could freshen up for him," she suggested, stepping out into the bright sunlight, trying to think wildly of way to prolong her liberty.

"I'll bring water to the room later." They crossed an empty courtyard and he gestured to an outhouse.

"There you are, my Lady. It might not be to your more noble tastes…Not quite what you're used to."

It was actually far, far better than she had hoped for.

The facilities, being of the crudest nature, were fed by a stream that entered at one end of the building, itself in a state of some dilapidation, and went out at the other. Closing the door behind her, Mei went hastily to the far side of the room and crouched down beside the point at which clear water flowed in. Already there was a gap nearly large enough for her to wriggle through on her belly. It looked clean, as if the water had come down from the mountains rather than passing between the buildings. Even if it had, she didn't think she'd have minded or noticed. Her mind was already far from this place. She didn't think it was possible to long for a person more than she did right now. It was as if a hundred thousand threads connected her body to the Red Mountain and pulled her home.

Standing, she kicked hard at the wall, then crouched and pulled away a couple of the loose bricks. Enough. She went down on her front and slithered out into the stream.

No-one looked too hard at her in the street. The kimono may once have been fine, but it was dirty now and, by crossing her arms, she hid some of the ornamentation. Her hair was unbrushed, her face likely wearing the blush of last night's wine. Head down, she started towards the city gate.

赤山

It was evening.

The walk from the city to the outpost covered nearly fifteen miles. Mei had started out with her mind working fast on the question of what to do when she arrived. It would not be left unmanned. She had hidden too when two horsemen came racing up the road from Okiri, perhaps searching for her. They knew, as she did, that there was just one road to Akayama. The outpost was close enough to the gorge that the rock walls served to secure the way naturally. Only a ghost could pass unseen.

Fifteen miles on and she was no longer entirely sure she wasn't a ghost, having shed her skin and left her body collapsed on the road some half a dozen miles behind. She was faint with the heat. Her mind had slowed down to the most fundamental of thoughts: she needed water and shade, and if she needed to beg them from her enemy then so she must.

Hooves thundered in the rocky gully ahead. This time there was nowhere to hide. She flattened herself against the rocks and waited for them to find her.

Two riderless horses, reins flowing, swept past at a gallop, sides salty and mouths frothing.

She stared.

They were gone, the sound echoing like a long note off of the stone walls.

A few more paces brought her within sight of the outpost. Her mind told her to stop, but her legs kept moving in a rolling gait for several heartbeats more before understanding struck her: Takashi's men were dead.

Not just the two who had come after her on horseback, but the others too, the ones who had stayed behind at the outpost. Their bodies lay like meat in a butcher's shop. Sand soaked up the blood. There was a neatness in the scene that made it unnatural, that made her look twice and still not see it for what it was, and yet, amidst all of this, there was movement. He was a whirlwind of dark cloth and bright steel.

She watched, blinking. The figure clad in black was driven back by a soldier. Their fight was desperate and yet, at this distance, it felt unreal. A back and forth of crossed blades. The man who had done all this, the man she barely recognised, but whom she had been trying so hard to protect, was driven backwards again. This time stumbling. Of a sudden, she started forward.

He must have seen her but he gave no sign. The soldier's back was to her and she stooped, picking up a long, flat stone from the road. With a cry, she threw it at Takashi's man. It struck his arm. A small thing. But as he started in her direction, the other man's sword passed through the crown of his head down as far as his jaw.

Mei stifled a scream with both hands.

In the sudden silence there was only the sound of her heart beating. A slump as the body fell.

For a long time, nothing moved. When she did, she stumbled and her legs gave way. There was a snick as the only survivor sheathed his sword. He said nothing but hastened forward to catch her and, lifting her, carried her away from the bodies and into the shadow of the gorge.

赤山

Night fell early. Offering only the narrowest ribbon of dusky sky. The shadows in the canyon were soon long, its colours rinsed by the encroaching dusk. When everything had become grey and outlines began to bleed together and even the air had grown cool, Mei at last began to look around. The man she had never thought to see again now walked beside her in silence, one hand on the reins of the horse she rode.

His presence was both a shadow and a force. The emptiness she had seen in the days after he first woke had returned to his face. His body was a testament to what he had done. Where his clothes were not stained with others' blood, they were soaked with his own, wounds that she judged were, for the most part, shallow: grazes, scratches, bruises. He did not limp or wince, but nor did he show any sign that there were thoughts behind his eyes.

"Arata, you're hurt," she said at last, and quietly, as if she daren't disturb the fading afternoon.

"My mistakes."

"I told you not to confront them."

They walked on in silence, the air between them as heavy as a wall: everything she didn't want to tell him but could hear behind the barbs in his voice.

"I was inconsistent," he said. She felt the effort it took him not to ask her questions. It was easier to talk of other things. "Each time I could have as easily lost as won. Each cut, and from one moment to the next, I was calm, then afraid. Inconsistent. I loathe that uncertainty."

She reached forward and put one hand on his shoulder.

"You sound—you sound like you," she said.

"What do you mean?"

"That you hate uncertainty. I don't think you've spoken that way since you woke. As if—as if you know something about yourself."

"What does it matter?" he asked and she found herself unable to explain, unable to put into words how her heart had leapt at sensing his surety, and contracted just as quickly as she realised what it would mean.

Yet, if he ever asked and no matter what he came to think of her hereafter, her first emotion had been joy.

"It matters," she murmured. He stopped and turned suddenly and he pressed his face against her leg. "Arata—"

"It was luck. Only luck."

"It was never only luck," she said, resting one hand in his hair. "Do you know what I think? That our souls are bound up in that house, these mountains. No matter what comes for us, so long as we're here, we're safe."

He shifted a little so that now his cheek rested against her calf and his eyes gazed back the way they'd come.

"No one guards the road to Okiri now."

"I told them you would come, like a wind down from the mountains, I said. And I warned them you would kill every one of them."

"We could leave. We could reach the town at very least. Once out of the mountains we could take to the fields. They needn't find us."

He sounded like a man describing dreams. In the silence that followed, perhaps they both felt the weight of the canyon around them and the night that now flowed fast into the fissures and cracks. The thin train of sky above was weighty with stars. Very quietly she said:

"I don't want to go back to Okiri."

And when he looked up he saw something in her eyes that made him turn back again to the road ahead.

"It's not far," he said. "I left the lamps burning."

"He wasn't going to let me come back," she said.

"I know."

And that was all there was to say. It was not, she thought afterwards, a choice. When she had said their souls were bound up with the house, she might have added that they were woven into it, irredeemably tangled. She might have said too that it would make no difference if they fled to Okiri. She had sensed the change in Takashi too late. Now things were slipping, sliding off of a level plane, and their whole world was tilting. Okiri would not change things. Nor would flight. What remained now was the time they had borrowed.

赤山

It was a difficult night.

Mei had thought at first that she wouldn't want him to touch her, but the contrary was true. When they were at last alone in the darkness of the old room that still smelt of summer flowers, she was glad of the arms that enveloped her and the soft rhythm of his breathing.

She hadn't known what to do at first. It was as if her mind had drawn a blank. And it wasn't just the events in Okiri; it was the changes she saw in him. He was filled with a dark energy. He had collected the swords and a gun from the men he had killed and the weapons were laid out on the terrace like trophies.

She wanted them away from the house. The spirits of the dead hung on them. But she did take up the gun and, never having seen one before, looked it over. It seemed such a blunt, empty thing to cause harm. "It doesn't work," he told her. "See, you raise this and set it so, then press your finger here. He held it to the back of my head, but – well, try and you'll see – it just makes a click." She aimed it away at the valley and did so. The weapon in her hands exploded with such force that the sound seemed to rend a hole in the night.

She cried out, dropped it and all but fell over the threshold and into the house.

"Not very reliable," he said, following her in. She found herself wishing that his responses seemed more human.

"Take it away! All of it! Anything they touched. Take it far away from the house."

While she sat at the hearth with her back to the door, he did so. Even when he returned though, it seemed to her that death still lingered about his person; his eyes were vacant as he stoked the fire.

"There was honour in the world once. At least with a sword you are close to your enemy when they die. Those modern weapons can take a man down from a hundred paces. Wielding one means you never have to look at what you've done."

"Times change. The codes men follow change."

"In the past, we followed ideals."

"The same ideals that would have a man take his own life if he were shamed?" He continued to stoke the fire. "The ideals that say a woman should slit her own throat sooner than let a man force himself upon her?" He stood up and turned away from her.

She bit her tongue. It was impossible to explain that she wanted him to scream at her, that it had been easier when his brother had struck her because at least then she could feel that things weren't fine. She wanted to tell him his eyes were empty and that she had grown used to seeing them full.

He was already gone, out into the night.

She stood up and went to the bath-house. There, while she bathed, she heard him vent his anger, as if it had not been enough, a feat near impossible, to kill twenty or thirty men as he must have done today. Even so, it was not enough for him. She left the bath to see what he was doing. He was slamming one of the swords again and again into the stone terrace and, when it broke, he took up another and kept up the rhythm without ceasing. It was mindless and so full of poison she had to turn away.

So she had thought perhaps it would be hard to have him touch her tonight. But as soon as he had, she'd felt nothing but gratitude. He had started to talk to her, as if telling a story to a child.

"I had meant to wait for you here in the house, as we had agreed, but when it came to past noon and there was no sign of your returning to the residence, I had to go at least as far as the outpost; it seemed to me they might be holding you there while they waited for the others to come back from the estate. And I feared perhaps I had paid for killing them with your life. It seemed to me then that, if we had to die, I would not let them live."

"I understand."

"I remembered things. I remembered training. Sometimes I remembered faces. Everything jumbled together. Who I was." She tensed a little and his body seemed to follow hers: his hold on her tightened. "I trained hard, didn't I? To be nothing more than a murderer."

"That is not who you are or who you were."

"Then what? Who was Kotaro Murasaki? Did he hire blades like mine?"

"He runs a brothel and a gambling ring."

He shifted away from her and she lay for a time on her belly, just drinking in the smell of him from the sheets; trying not to think about what he was saying.

"Gambling. Of course. Of course." He laughed drily. "Ryuu leant me money. I was never in his pay. He leant me money to cover my own debts." He stood up.

"Don't. Come back to bed. It doesn't matter now."

"Do you understand, Mei? It was me! I'm the one who has done this!" She didn't have to turn to know that his gesture took in everything: themselves, the house, the soldiers and the servants. Ghosts that would haunt the mountainside long after they were gone. "You were right! The answers were with me! How can you stomach listening to me talk about honour? Save Ryuu. He was no part of this. He was right in what he did." She turned to see him gesture at the scar on his head.

"Save Ryuu, save Ryuu," she chimed and buried her face in the pillow.

"Don't you understand, Mei?"

"Even if we told Takashi it was Arata and not Ryuu, it would not matter now."

"I thought you wanted the truth," he said and, despite herself, she laughed softly and turned so that her back was to him. "I was a gambler," he said, "An adulterer, a man who turned against his own brother. All I am good for is killing."

"You are not those things."

"But I was." She felt him kneel down on the bed beside her.

"Arata, what if I told you I had done things far worse than you have ever done, that I am a most accomplished thief?"

"A thief?" He lay down and slipped an arm around her belly. When he pressed his face against her shoulder, she was surprised to feel the dampness of tears against her skin. She pushed back her own emotions. There was so much she wanted to say, but it was already too late, she knew. "Did you take something from Takashi?" he asked softly.

"You could say that, but I was thinking more about us." She turned over and kissed his brow, then pressed his face against her neck. "I suppose we should have died today, but we've stolen a little time. Whatever comes of it, I won't regret." His lips touched her collarbone, his breath warm and, for a time, she lay very still counting the rhythm of his heartbeats and the soft rise and fall of his chest.

Sleep crept up on them, a bounty granted by the day's exertions. She waited until she was certain, then pushed back from him a little to see his face. Even in slumber it was, tonight, marked by lines of concern. A thin graze across his cheek marred the symmetry. The dark knot of scar tissue near his temple. And, still bright, the remnants of a tear on his cheek. "When you wonder, and I hope you have a chance to wonder," she said softly, "I hope you'll realise what I stole and why, Ryuu."

11. Innocence

As a child Mei's life had been centred around the toil of the land: the sunrise, the sunset, spring and summer and the quiet red and gold descent of the landscape into winter. Her parents were old and it had been a disappointment, to her father in particular, that the only child they had brought into the world was a girl, so from a young age she had set about the task of making herself as useful to him as a son would have been. Years of labour had made her strong, though she never grew tall or large or stout. She had a practical, curious nature. Her father had once said she asked too many questions: why did the crops grow only if the sun shone? Why did the birds sing most at dawn and then again at dusk? He told her there was no why. The birds and the seasons needed a purpose no more than music needed a reason for its melody. She took his answer to heart and didn't ask anymore, and the years rolled round and round.

When, in her twentieth year, bandits came and burned the farm to the ground, murdered her parents and left her for dead, it was, she understood, her youth and a strong body that saved her, and a man from the residence of Akayama.

Akayama Arata, the real Akayama Arata, had a kind of wildness about him, but one that drew people to him. His eyes danced; he laughed often; he wore his dark hair long and loose. Unlike his brother, he cared little for manners, or for leading men, but when he put his mind to it, he was capable and fierce: a fine soldier who had led soldiers down from the residence to exact justice on the lawless of the valley.

Seventeen sick and injured travelled back from Mei's ruined village: those not yet strong enough to rebuild. Medicines were brought from Okiri. They were tended to and gradually, gradually couples and families left and returned to their lives.

Mei did not return. She had nothing to return for. Here in Akayama she had all the food she could eat and the attentions of a young nobleman who instructed the household to dress her in fine clothes and keep her well. It was everything a young woman could wish for. And though he never courted her, he praised her or teased her liberally whenever they passed in the mansion's grounds.

This went on for two years. Emerging from the events that had stolen her parents and her past was like swimming for the surface of a dark river, but when she did emerge it was into a world inhabited by dreams. Arata, always peripheral, was nevertheless their focus and, though she kept them to herself and never dared to hope for more than a kind glance, she did give free rein to her daydreams, imagining worlds in which he would look at her with bright, kind eyes.

She never gave much thought to Ryuu, the head of the clan. In many ways, he was overshadowed by his younger brother's charms. He was sullen and always busy and it wasn't until her second year that chance would have it they passed one another on the wooden bridge. She noted that Ryuu paused the way Arata did, both brothers uncomfortable with heights. It was the first time she had looked properly at his face. His features were not dissimilar to his brother's. If anything, they were a little softer. His hair was dark, but in places it had been licked by the sun so that, in the light, it was the same rusty brown as the mountain and the terraces. It seemed to her then that she knew him from somewhere, and not just from the half year she had spent at the residence. From somewhere, from before.

So serious. And somehow tired.

She passed him with her eyes down and yet thereafter he played upon her mind in a way that Arata never had. And so, though she continued to wish for and dream about a charming, rapacious man who had rescued her from the farmsteads, there was now another, forever present, whose eyes did not dance but ran deep like a channel beneath more frivolous dreams.

赤山

In the evenings, she dined with the servants. Usually she would eat and then Harumi, a round-faced woman, second only to the head of the household, would comb her hair and tie it up before she went to bed. She had her own room here, which was more than she'd ever had before. While the other families from her village had moved on, no-one had ever asked her to go with them. She was content here. It was pleasant to be treated as a woman and not a child.

Tonight though there was a strange atmosphere.

The kitchens were stifling. The staff either knelt or sat slumped against the wall as Harumi moved from one person to the next, serving each with a bowlful of soup and one of rice.

"Have you heard Lord Arata is getting married?" Kimiyuki, the youngest of the household, chirped. For his efforts, Harumi cuffed him across the back of the head.

"Shut up and get," she said.

Mei sipped at her soup. Gradually though she became aware of the servants' eyes on her and of the whispers rippling between them. Harumi lowered herself to the floor with a grunt and dug into her own bowl of rice.

"Don't be too disheartened," she said. "I'm sure there will still be a place for you here."

Mei stared hard at her soup as her cheeks grew hot. "There's no need to be modest," Harumi continued. "Why do you think I've treated you like my own daughter all these months, and dressed you every morning? Did you think that was just a courtesy we extended to our guests?"

"I don't know."

"Then in all this time he has never—?"

"No, he has never!" she cried. All this time, she realised, they had been watching the passing of her most intimate dreams. She had been living in a fantasy, but she had never imagined that it was one the others participated in. Did Arata know then? Did he realise?

In the corner, Yuri, the swordmaster, had been motionless throughout the conversation. Now he lifted his head:

"However you look at it," he said slowly, "He's nobility."

"He's the second son," said Harumi. "And, like all of his ilk, he's afforded greater freedom than his brother. He told me himself to take care of this one, to see she wants for nothing—"

"Let it be, Harumi-*san*. It's lost on her. Leave innocence for the innocent. A man like him would spoil her."

"Yuri-*san!*" Harumi looked scandalised. "You shouldn't speak that way of our master."

"I serve the lord Akayama Ryuunaka. Not his brother."

Of them all, only Yuri ever spoke out of line in the household.

Mei continued to eat in a silent blush, no longer particularly concerned with the taste of the food. She excused herself as soon as she could, staring out at the fragile and even gaudy shell her life had become. It was unfair, she thought, as the cool evening air licked her face; she had liked those dreams. She could have gone on dreaming them a little longer.

She went to sit on the bridge with its ornamental dragons and serpents.

"Mei-*san?*" When she turned, Yuri was standing behind her. "You're not afraid of falling, are you?" he asked, smiling a little. She shook her head. "Do you have somewhere to go? I mean apart from Akayama?"

She considered him, heels swinging over the drop.

"People have been kind to me."

"Yes, but you are not a servant. Nor are you anybody's wife. It would be wise to consider who you are before others make those decisions for you." He bowed. "I'm sorry if you don't like my words, but that is my advice to you. Good night, Chimariko Mei."

"Yuri-*sama*?"

"Yes?"

"I was curious about Ryuu-*sama*." He turned towards her. "I overheard old Koban say one time that he was a demon, but he doesn't seem that way to me."

To her surprise, the swordmaster grinned.

"Ryuu-*sama* could be if he so desired."

"Is he happy?"

Something in Yuri's expression changed.

"Why do you ask that?"

"It must be hard to be a demon if you do not choose to be."

"Is that what's troubling you?"

"It must be hard to be all that he is if he did not choose to be."

"A *daimyo*? A man who demands the world and has it handed to him? You think that would be hard?"

"Yes," she said and, after a moment, Yuri's smile returned.

"You are sharper than you pretend to be, Mei-*san*. Be careful it doesn't get you into trouble."

赤山

Akayama Ryuu was not a dream. He was a thought that crept into her head and wouldn't leave. He was there when she turned her mind to important questions like where she should go if she could not stay on the estate. She did not think of him as she had about Arata, not as part of a story in which she was the heroine and he the hero. He was simply there whenever she tried to pull herself away from his world.

Arata was married in the springtime. Kyoko was gentle and polite. Beautiful too, and they suited one another: her quietness in the face of his ebullience. She was all that a woman was meant to be and, warrior, lover, husband and protector, he was all that a man should be. For all that Ryuu was *daimyo,* he lived in their shadow.

It was *uzuki,* the month of flowers. The orchard was a feast of blossom and Mei had cloistered herself between the roots of one of the oldest trees, with a twisted trunk and constant fall of petals. She had fallen asleep sometime after lunch and she woke in the full glaze of the afternoon sun, the earth around her and her own arms and legs littered with blossom. Somewhere people were talking.

"Your parents write to me often and ask how you are. I tell them you are well and that you have brought great joy to this family. It has been so long since we have had a woman's touch in this house, since my own mother died—"

"It is my honour."

Mei recognised Ryuu's and then Kyoko's voices. If it struck her as strange that the two of them were alone, it was stranger still to hear Ryuu speak so frankly. "That is one of the reasons why I brought you here, my lord," Kyoko was saying. "I would like to visit my parents."

"Of course. We should all go."

"No."

Mei realised that they were approaching her. She should stand up, make herself known and yet it seemed to her already that the conversation was private. She had trespassed too far. And it was Kyoko's next words that convinced her: "I wish to go alone."

"As you will."

"It would be for some months."

Mei heard Ryuu's footsteps stop and, shortly after, Kyoko's too.

"Then tell me," he said, "Have we wronged you?"

"Only grant me this one request."

"A month is too long, Kyoko-*san*. The servants will talk."

"Does it really matter what servants say?"

"When they talk in Okiri, yes." He closed the distance between them. "Kyoko, is something wrong?"

She was silent for a long time. The wind came fretting in from the valley and Mei stayed perfectly still as another down of blossoms gathered against her fingers; the soft illusion of snow. Very close to her now, she heard Kyoko gather her skirts and seat herself on the ground.

"My lord, I am not happy here."

He did not answer at once. Mei imagined he did not even move.

"Kyoko-*san,* in married life" –

"Do not lecture me on married life!"

"Do not raise your voice to me."

The new silence curled around the three of them like smoke.

"My lord, there will be no dishonour on your family," Kyoko said softly.

"What are you suggesting?"

"We would still be married. I would merely live at my parents' residence—"

"No."

"My lord, this place is a prison! We are half a day from anywhere!"

"And what does a woman want in Okiri?" Ryuu demanded and at once Kyoko threw the words back at him:

"Ask rather what my husband wants in Okiri! Ask that!" Ryuu fell silent. "I know why he goes there," she said more quietly, though it was clear from the clutter in her voice that she was tearful. "He drinks and he gambles, my lord."

"Who have you told?"

Kyoko's breath hitched in her throat and, to Mei, it seemed she took a moment to steady herself. When she spoke though, it was with a masterful lack of emotion:

"I see. His habits are of little interest to you then."

"I am aware of his indulgences. They should impinge on your marriage no more than they impinge on our life here. He can do as he pleases so long as our name is not marred by it."

"That is your advice? And is that your counsel when I find the marks of other women's fingernails on his skin?"

There was silence again, broken only by a series of muffled sobs.

"Kyoko-*san.*" Ryuu's voice was softer. "There were sacrifices I could not foresee when I undertook the affairs of this family, but we live with them because there are things of greater value than you and I in this world." He must have crouched down to speak to her because he was so close now. Just the trunk of the tree and a few low-lying bushes between the two of them and Mei's hiding place beneath her camouflage of blossoms. Kyoko must have shifted because there was a sound like fabric being pulled across the ground, and then a most unlikely request:

"Kiss me," she said. The hope in her voice, and it's frailty. "I did not know anyone could feel so lonely as I do."

"This is my family," Ryuu responded with a slur of emotion.

"But you are lonely too."

Mei held her breath, uncertain of what she was hearing. Then Ryuu spoke thickly:

"In the end, our sacrifices define us."

"Name your price," Kyoko's voice broke with despair. "What is too high to protect this family?"

"A bloodline unbroken for a thousand generations. I find no cost too high." Mei heard him shift, a tentative stepping back. Kyoko, still seated on the ground barely yards from Mei, began to cry, forcing anger in between her sobs:

"One day–one day you will find something more precious to you than all this."

"Until then, I protect what is mine," he said, "And I expect no less from you."

She heard Kyoko rise and hasten away, her skirts catching in the grass and foliage. Silently Mei leant forward, peering around the side of the tree. What she saw would stay with her for a long time after.

He was standing where Kyoko had left him, his figure rimed by the evening sunlight, his shoulders hunched and the wind catching at his hair. As she watched, he turned towards the valley, towards the vast cliff that marked the edge of the gardens, and he walked towards it, each step as slow as a drumbeat. He reached the edge and, for an instant, she thought he wouldn't stop. She was up on her feet. He gave no sign of having heard her. He swayed a little; she could see now that his eyes were shut.

It was a moment only and then he stepped back.

His whole body heaved with a breath and then it was as if he remembered himself because his eyes widened and he staggered backwards, all at once returning to the present. He turned away gasping.

There was a terrible vulnerability in what she was seeing. She didn't fully understand it, but she did see something, something that, in all the time that she had been here, she had missed: she knew him. Not as Akayama Ryuunaka, lord of the estate; she knew him before.

He was the boy who had saved her life on the day when Yumi was killed. He was the same boy who had pulled her, choking and half-drowned from the water. He was much changed. Not just in years, but in the weariness in his eyes. But he was that boy.

He didn't see her that day. He didn't know what she had witnessed and she never told a soul.

By the time Takashi arrived in their world with his men and his bloodshed, everything had already descended into chaos. Kyoko was dead; Arata and Ryuu had turned one against the other.

All she had needed to do to save his life was ensure that 'Ryuu' was gone. Long gone. Disappearing off the page and into another story.

So she told them that Arata remained. The younger brother.

Arata was not Takashi's target.

Comfort, then companionship, then something more.

At that point, it was already too late to confess. It was not the need to protect him now. Nor even the need to protect herself. It was because, as Arata, he was alive in ways he had never been alive before. He was young in a way that he had never been young.

As somebody else, he was everything that he had never dared to be.

Her conscience. His past. These, she realised, were the sacrifices that would define them.

12. Siding with the Wolf

Once in his childhood, Takashi had, while hunting, stumbled upon an injured wolf. The animal, he had been taught, had a kind of majesty and whenever he had seen the packs before, always at a distance, he had admired them. They were strong, unyielding, and yet like ghosts in their comings and goings. The injured beast, lying across a huntsman's trail, had seemed to him a travesty, with its bloodshot eyes and its elegance drained, leaving only muscle, sinew and heaving flanks. Yet his father warned him not to approach. The wilderness, he said, never left anything that was born of it and, in death, it would sooner take him than in life.

It was this memory, one of very few he had of a time before his parents' deaths, that surfaced as he approached the man they held in custody. Akayama was kneeling on the floor, his hands bound behind him. They had stripped him to the waist to deliver the lashes that Shuru had claimed had been necessary to control him. He did not seem to be putting up a fight now, but perhaps that was why Takashi thought of the wolf. Dangerous when cornered; dangerous when quiet. Or perhaps he was just being more wary today, since he had been plagued with ill fortune since the morning.

The girl was gone. He had sent two men after her. Assuming she had taken the road to the residence, their task should not have been a difficult one, but neither had returned. Nor had the party he had sent ahead to kill Akayama. Gradually word began to spread that there was silence from the mountain. Those who left for the checkpoint or the estate did not return. Shuru had asked to go. His brother had been stationed there. He was the first and only one to return, having ridden his horse so hard that it was ruined. Shock was plain on his face. At that point, Takashi knew, he should have stopped him reporting back to the others, but it was done now. And so it had spread, from one to the next, between those that remained: they were all dead, to a man. With that news, a strange fear seemed to take hold. Someone said that the girl had told stories, had claimed that Akayama of the Mountain was a ghost, a spirit bent on vengeance. In the light of day, they might have dismissed it as a fairy tale, but faced with their comrades' deaths and a long, dark night, their tales took form, grew powerful, wormed their way in amongst their truths until the world rewrote itself. No longer hostages, the last wretched vestiges of a clan put to death, the man and woman on the mountain were now a demon and a spirit.

 Takashi had no time for their stories. A part of him was dislocate, aware that in the space of a day his force had been halved. That was the equation on paper. In truth though these were men he had worked with for years. Suddenly gone. It wasn't something he could swallow all at once. If he tried to consider it, there was a void and all he knew was that the one person he could blame, who was still within reach and was neither witch nor demon, but could still bleed and could still bruise, was this man.

"Ryuunaka," he said. His prisoner ignored him. "You prefer 'Arata?'" Bloodshot eyes flickered towards him. There was a tremor in the man's body, which Takashi suspected was a mark of heavy drinking.

"The council confirmed her death for you," the prisoner said. To his credit, it was not a question.

"Akayama Kyoko? Yes."

"Since I have told you the truth in all other things, why don't you believe me in this?"

"Because it would be to your advantage if I believed you were Arata and not Ryuu."

"And it was to his advantage, wasn't it?"

"That's fair. It seems like everybody wants to be Arata," said Takashi, moving fluidly into a crouch. He hadn't meant to make the motion threatening, but his prisoner tensed.

"What do you intend?" Akayama asked.

"I intend to kill the man who resides on your estate. His name means nothing to me now, and then I shall deal with you."

There was a silence in which Takashi realised he had already said too much. Akayama studied him, weighing him up. There was a dark intelligence in the prisoner's eyes.

"You need me to kill him for you?"

Takashi frowned, sensing danger.

"Are you offering?"

"How many are there on the estate?"

"He's alone with the girl."

Akayama laughed:

"Oh, you would do well not to underestimate my brother."

"I might not have, but it is Ryuu whose reputation with a sword precedes him, which, I'm sure you'll understand, leads me to ask you this: if you are Arata, what use will you be against him? They say he is unmatched."

"I do not need to equal his skills. Do you have a brother, Captain?"

"No."

"Then perhaps you wouldn't understand, but to best someone, it is often more important you know them well enough to understand their weaknesses than that you match their strengths." He waited, apparently trying to judge Takashi's reaction, and then held out his hands. "You'll cut these ropes? I have men stationed in the next town. Forty. More than enough, wouldn't you say, or has Ryuu really outdone himself?"

"You think I would release you just like that?"

"I came back to the mountain for a reason."

"And what was that?"

"Cut the ropes." The hands he held out towards Takashi were plagued with tremors. The soldier shook his head:

"You'll hold a sword like that, will you?"

Akayama's lips drew up into an ugly smile.

"They'll be still after a sip of wine."

"Don't kid yourself. You have soldiers? I'll believe that when I see it. For now, my own men think you're fit for doing little more than lying here and rotting."

Akayama only kept on smiling, the kind of smile that reminded Takashi of fleshless heads set on pikes over city walls.

"You don't realise we're on the same side yet. You asked me why I came here." He sat back on his heels, eyes on the bonds that held his wrists in place. "We have something in common, Captain Takashi. All samurai have masters."

"My lord is Matsuda of Hatano," said Takashi, narrowing his eyes.

"Mine is Akayama. Have you ever wanted to be your own master, though, Takashi-*san*?"

"I'd rather have food in my belly, thanks."

"Ha. Not everyone's cut out for it."

"My work is at least honourable. I serve Matsuda, and there my duty ends. Why would I help you do something as shameful as killing your own lord."

"Because my shame is your honour?" His eyes flashed. "That I can even say so shows you that neither word has meaning."

"Food in my belly and clothes on my back have meaning."

"So you admit there's no honour in it?"

"You sound like the girl."

"I taught her some things." He chuckled softly and shook his head. "If only it were so simple as killing my lord though. No, no. If I am to live and be free, and most men would not understand freedom if they held it in their hands, Captain…If I am to be free, I need to take back what he's stolen from me."

"What is that?"

"Who I am."

赤山

Stepping back into the room where his men waited, Takashi felt drained. He understood men who had been pushed to the very edge of their endurance, but there was something about Akayama that both compelled and sickened him.

Shuru, who had been leaning against the wall, straightened in the presence of his commander. Homura was seated at the table and only glanced up. Two more men were kneeling by the door and they barely paused in their conversation. Two others were absent.

"Sir, we asked around to see if anyone could give a physical description of both brothers," said Shuru. "It seems almost certain he is Arata."

"I know."

Takashi threw the keys to the cell into the centre of the table, if only to see Homura start. The latter looked up, his expression guarded:

"Sir?"

"You pay your respects to your superiors, Homura."

Carefully, a little too carefully, the younger man stood up and bowed in silence. He remained standing.

"Your orders, Sir?"

Takashi hesitated.

And just like that, it happened: his greatest fear, that the pause between words and the silence between his own heartbeats would take hold of him. He froze. Homura stared back in silent challenge. Shuru remained by the wall. The two kneeling men were engaged in a series of words and gestures, which to his suddenly locked mind, seemed to move in an eternal loop:

"—Can't be killed."

"She protects him."

"Other way round, she said."

"He protects her."

"Either way—"

"—Can't be killed."

He was, he realised, looking at an incomplete jigsaw. There had been six men assembled. Now there were just four.

"Where are the others?"

"They won't fight," said Homura, leaning with his palms flat against the table.

"They say he's the devil," said one of the men behind him. It was probably not meant to be heard, but finding the silence between the ebb and flow of words, it seemed suddenly to echo round the room. The conversation clattered to a halt. The man who had spoken looked up.

Takashi tried hard to take a breath, but his chest felt tight. He gripped the table as he spoke.

"Homura, you faced Akayama Ryuunaka in battle. Though he went by the name of Arata, he is nevertheless considered to be one of the best swordsmen this land has known. Homura, was he immortal?"

"No, Sir."

"Homura, was he a devil or a demon or a djinn?"

"No, Sir."

"What then, in fact, was he?"

"Flesh and blood," said Homura without even blinking. Takashi sucked in a breath, ready to let the relief overwhelm him, even as Homura spoke again: "Flesh and blood, sinew and bone, and fast. Unpredictable. Dangerous. Single-handedly he has killed twenty-two of our men and, if the woman's words are true, he may have no intention of stopping until we are all dead. Look around, Captain, we are four! It's not enough anymore." He slammed his hands down on the wood. "Your orders. Sir?"

"Stand down!" Takashi snarled.

"Your orders, Sir!"

"Stand down!"

"Your orders, Sir!"

"I said, stand down!"

"Your orders" –

Takashi flew at him. For once there were no swords, no honours, no rewards, no names to be made. He had once fought over scraps of meat on the street to keep from starving. This was no different. The satisfying crunch as his fist met Homura's jaw was enough. The others fell on him, pulling him back. There was blood running thick from between the younger man's lips. His black eyes glazed with shock as he crumpled backwards into the wall.

It took Takashi a moment to regain any semblance of self-control. When he did, his body felt like water and his fist ached fiendishly. He covered it with his other hand. "We are not four," he spat at the huddled figure of his officer as he shook the others off. "We are forty-four."

13. Snow Princess

Mei had never seen snow the like of which fell on the Red Mountain the winter before Takashi and his men came to end their world. The clouds came one night and, for weeks thereafter, the air was sharp as knives. There was no moon at night and barely a whisper of sunlight in the day. When the snow finally let up, it left behind a crystalline world caught in a single heartbeat.

The birds had fallen silent. The day had grown still.

Mei crossed the altered garden, leaving dark prints in her wake. She fancied that their existence up here had become barbaric. The road to Okiri was impassable now and, though they had food reserves, they had run short of good, dry firewood and had taken to using the local saplings. These burnt with acrid, black smoke that clogged her lungs and made her yearn for the crisp, white world outside. Some of the men had started to hunt. They gathered on the terraces each morning with bows and spears, looking like wild beasts, panting and stamping and filling the air with their silvery breaths. They considered themselves great warriors who bestowed, on the women of the household, thick hides from the beasts they killed. The women indulged such behaviour with praise and pride for their valiant protectors against the inclement weather. Their ruthless sincerity always made Mei want to smile.

She minded the cold no more than she minded the heat. Everybody seemed so serious about it and yet they missed the most extraordinary of things, like the blanket of autumn leaves that had remained untouched for weeks and was now frozen into a glinting tapestry of stained glass lozenges, or the perfect icicles that hung from branches in the orchard, as if the fruit trees had opened unforgiving jaws lined with white teeth. It was these that she had paused to admire when suddenly she had heard someone call her from the house and had turned to see who it was.

Arata had pulled back one of the screen doors, just a fraction, and was peering out. A little of the loose snow had landed in his dark hair. She noticed how elegantly it sat, so light that it was buoyant, and so frail that it began to melt even as she watched.

"Come inside, Mei."

He held the door open for her but closed it as soon as she was at his side. She was struck by a sudden glut of heat.

They had hung tapestries on three of the walls and a belching, dark fire burned in a pit in the centre of the room. Beside it, swathed in clothes and furs, Kyoko sat, her form all but obscured by the mound of clothing. Only her eyes peered out above a high collar and these were dark, almost black. So unlike the grey eyes inherited by the people of the mountain.

Arata brushed away the worst of the weather from Mei's shoulders and she looked down as dark patches of water began to form on the floorboards at her feet. "You're melting, Snow-princess."

"I'm sorry," Mei said.

Kyoko's silence and lidded gaze were not uncharacteristic, but never had Mei sensed them to be so full of unspoken words, like a ward held up against her husband's levity. And Arata was smiling and ebullient as ever.

"Mei, will you fetch us sake and heat it in the kitchens?" he asked. "The storeroom at the end of the hall. Do you know where that is?"

"Yes."

"Then thank you, Mei." He smiled.

It was in the western wing of the house, packed floor to ceiling with a part of the household's winter reserves: the richer part, since these were stored within easy reach of the masters should they want them. Sake, plum wine, dried herbs and spices. She sought about and finally located the ceramic bottles at the back of the store, on the highest shelf. Out of her reach.

She even tried, though knowing that it was no good. Her fingers tiptoed in the dust on the shelf-top, an inch away from her prize.

Flushed to have let Arata down over something so simple, she nearly forgot herself when she reached his chamber, and had inched the door open a crack before she recalled there were rules to follow here and manners to be observed. She dropped to her knees to complete the gesture, head down at the moment she would have seen fully into the room. But her haste had earned her the tail-end of their conversation: "—Because it's all in your mind; that's why."

Arata broke off. His tone softened at once: "Mei?"

"I couldn't reach," she said swallowing, suddenly not wanting to look up from the bow. She heard him shift and cross the floor; then the soft touch of his fingers between her shoulder-blades as he stepped past her out into the corridor.

"Come, come. I'll fetch it down for you. Then we can have respite from this awful weather."

As she rose to her feet she caught the sharp edge of Kyoko's gaze before the door slid shut.

People puzzled Mei sometimes. They danced to different rhythms. She saw, every day, the little deceptions that played out within the house; the lies that were told, mostly to shield feelings: flattery, placation. Even simpler were their glib answers to 'are you well' and 'how are you.' No one ever told the truth to such questions. And then there were the greater things, the lies that walked and stalked in the corridors.

Nothing was well with Kyoko and Arata. "Come now, come! He threw open the door to the storeroom, a conquering hero and, though she knew of his lies, she found herself smiling. She liked him and always had; her own small dreams had not abated. "It's not hard! Even little Mei could reach up there, I'd wager." And, at that, she laughed and covered her mouth with her sleeve.

Extraordinary, she thought suddenly, that he could seem so out of place in his own home. He was brash and bold, like the farm-hands who had helped her father with the harvest. Not a nobleman at all. And it was easy to forget, delightfully easy, on a cold, dull afternoon, who he was and who she was too. "I'll hold a light," he told her.

She tried for him. It was something like a game. He took the fur stole off of her shoulders and folded it across one arm and told her that she could reach better without its weight. And then it seemed she could. Her fingers danced across the smooth surfaces of each bottle. She was up on tiptoes. The kimono she wore, always bound tight as etiquette dictated, seemed to tighten still more as she stretched. When she stopped trying because they were still out of reach, it took her a moment to notice the way he was looking at her.

His eyes were full.

She didn't imagine it. His eyes were full of her.

She felt the laughter fall away all too quickly from her lips, like a line of poetry dropped, and when he gave no indication that he so much as noticed her change of mood, she crossed her arms over her chest. He blinked. "What is it? What are you thinking, Mei?" He filled the room with his own laughter, which was deep and rich, and told her to try again.

This time she was ungainly. She felt the pull of her gown, the way it dug into her collarbone. She felt his eyes like beads of perspiration on her neck, sliding down her shoulders, across her ribs, over her hips and, in that moment, she resented the woman, Harumi, who had helped her dress that morning and, with sweet gall, had told her how beautiful she looked. Shades of silver, threaded with violet. Her fingers fumbled. A bottle fell.

She felt the lash of cold liquid as it spilt; the crash as it broke apart. "Princess! You are soaked through!"

Her eyes were on the floor as he stepped through the starburst of smashed ceramic and clear wine. Then, just as he had with the snow on her shoulders, he started to brush carelessly at the wine spatters on her clothing. His hands were firmer this time though, and a little too careless.

"No," she said.

"If I let you return all wet through, you'll be chilled before the day is out, and I sent you here so I am responsible." And, with that, he went back to brushing down her front, then he crouched so that he was level with her waist. He pressed his face against her belly. "You smell sweet."

"My lord…"

"Have you lain with a man?"

She didn't understand at first. It was almost as if the words themselves slid away, but she was vividly aware of his lips moving against the lower part of her belly, pressing hard enough that she could feel him through two layers of silk and cotton. In her mind's eye, she saw herself catching both hands in his hair and yanking him away from her, but she didn't. She stood there as if this were the very thing she had come for. He kissed her through the dress and told her to stay still.

At first it was as if she lagged behind herself, just two paces away, watching through a lattice screen, as he slid his hands between the folds in the kimono and up between her legs. The touch was just different, awkward. His breathing grew heavy though and, with it, his motions deeper, harder. She caught up with herself as he started to hurt her, stumbling back, surprised that there had not been a wall behind her or something else holding her in place.

He was kneeling on the floor, looking nothing at all like the man she remembered, as if clarity could contort the reality she'd believed she was seeing. He could undo everything, her dreams and any sense of certainty she'd had. But it was with horror that she recognised, in the figure before her, the same instincts as the robbers who had struck the village the night her family died; the same hunger that she had seen in the faces of the boys who had taken Yumi's life. Just another thief. For all his pomp, no different from the wild dogs who stole livestock or beggars who would cut a purse.

"I am sorry I misled you," she said, stopping him by tugging the kimono back into place, and only then realising he had done nothing to force her. The silk would no longer lie right. The thought that someone might see it and know sickened her.

"Are you going to run away?" he asked.

"Do you think I am afraid of you?"

The challenge tumbled from her lips before she realised what she had said. When he stood up he seemed to tower over her. Deference rather than defiance, she realised, would serve her better. "I'm going to go. I won't tell anyone that you—you…I won't tell anyone."

She had always talked, always said the first thing in her head. Now she marvelled that her voice still seemed even and polite. She had a notion that this could fade just like a dream, until his hand caught a clump of hair from the back of his head. The pins came loose. It felt as if he would tear all the hair from her skull and still she was more aware of his wet breath against her ear:

"Tell them."

"Arata-*sama!*"

He shoved her back against the shelves and more things began to fall around her.

She wasn't afraid though.

His hands were all over her body, pulling at her clothes. Still she kept on saying his name as if to appeal to something deep inside him. It was ridiculous, the thought stuck out like a rusty nail. The two of them were absurd, laughable. So ugly. Yes, what they were doing was ugly. She had entrusted too many dreams to him and, never having known them, he betrayed them.

"I think you're afraid," he said. "It's nice; it's good. Don't you get sick of being–perfect? This"–he tore the front of her kimono and gazed hungrily at what he'd done–"Is important. It lives; it breathes; it dies." He looked up from her body. "You don't even know what I'm saying, do you?"

Grey eyes. Like Ryuu's. Like her own. Eyes that had always danced though. From the outside, he had everything: more freedom than Ryuu was afforded; the perfect wife, home, family. So why when she looked into his eyes did she see him, just like Ryuu, standing on the edge of that cliff. The difference was that, at the last, Ryuu had stepped back.

"I'm sorry," she said very softly. "I can't help you."

He stared at her, then touched her face. It was the strangest caress. Fierce, as if he could erase her features. His thumb pressed her lower lip.

"And I thought you were stupid," he said.

"Please, Arata-*sama*." She appealed to something she thought she saw in him and he leaned in to her, whispering:

"It won't help you to think about it. It just hurts the more."

"It doesn't hurt," she murmured.

"Don't you feel anything?" His voice was hoarse, his body pinning hers awkwardly.

"I don't know."

"You don't know?"

"Differently," she confessed, wondering how and why they were still talking. He nuzzled into her neck. She felt his hand beneath her clothes now, at the base of her spine, bending her back just a little. "Differently. Because I don't get scared or angry or happy just at one time. Rather all together. And I can't separate it out." The words kept tumbling into his silence. She didn't know why; only that, in telling him, in giving them to him, it was one less thing he could take. He grunted as he tugged his *hakama* loose and let them fall to the ground. All at once the sense of his skin against hers was like an ocean of heat, his weight making it hard for her to breathe.

"Now?" he asked.

"Please don't." His thumb slid beneath her chin, tilting her head back. The angles were wrong now. She couldn't move and the muscles in her back were aching; couldn't even see him, folded back on herself this way. But she could feel him where their hips met. And his breathing, coarsening.

"This isn't anything to you then," he husked. "This is empty. Meaningless. You feel nothing."

She felt pain. And then, impossibly, his grip tightened further until it seemed she was cocooned in his body and the folds of her gown, and he chose a rhythm and a motion that tore into her. "You–feel–nothing."

She felt everything.

Though, since she had never been certain if the sensations that overwhelmed her at any given time were good or bad, glad or despairing, she went along with them, just as the day never cared that it was bright, though it was, and the night didn't realise it was dark. But he was wrong if he thought she was empty.

The pain, which was both physical and like colours in her mind, tightened itself into tears that came scratching out of her eyes. He put his hands over her ears and pressed his thumbs down over her eyelids and then it was worse because she was in a strange, underwater world where all that remained was sensation. And he was inside her; right through her. The pressure on her head tightened.

After a seeming eternity, he released her head and pressed his arm across her throat. Apparently forgetting her, he came as she choked. When he let her go altogether, she fell to her knees gasping, feeling transparent.

He was quick to dress again. She was all arms and legs and a sudden loss of weightlessness. Messy. Like leftovers. "You talk a lot, Princess. Are you done with talking?" He watched her trying to stand. "Are you angry yet? That's real. Go and get dressed up again. We can start from the beginning. I want you to feel something."

"No."

"No?"

"No, you don't." Gingerly she turned her back on him and started to dress. He remained, watching her from the doorway.

"I don't what?"

"Want me to feel anything. You're the one who's scared. You're the one who—" Something ploughed into her side, knocking her down. Then he kicked her in the stomach.

It was only one punch, one kick, but she didn't get up. He had broken something inside her and she heard, only distantly, his anger spitting words about how she had spoken back and should have stayed silent. She had never been good at that. Mostly, she thought, she understood people quite well, but people didn't want to be understood. When she was truthful, they said that she was cold or naïve or simply stupid. She knew she was different. She knew enough to know that a lot of women in her position might weep or call for help or try to find someone, but for a long time she did none of these things, but waited until he was gone, and then waited longer, until the pain let up. That meant, she guessed, that she would heal well enough in time, and, dressing as best she could, she left the house and stepped out into the grounds.

It was snowing and everything was white. He had made her forget the season altogether. The sudden, iron cold came as a shock, but a welcome one. She started to walk and, as she walked, she seemed to come awake, until she realised that she knew where she was going.

She went down to the orchard on the edge of the terraces, to the spot where she had overheard Kyoko and Ryuu in the spring. The tree beneath which she'd sat had died that autumn and now it was a gnarled black trunk. Several of the branches had snapped off in the bitter ice. It would never offer her shelter again or pour down its blossoms in her lap, so she moved on to where she had meant to go.

This was the very place Ryuu had stood.

It was true, and perhaps a shameful truth, that she had had feelings for them both, Arata and Ryuu. But she understood guilt and shame with no more clarity than other emotions, so she had not let it trouble her before. She had known only that she was happy here and that, when she had seen Ryuu, standing thus before the valley, she had felt a great pain run through her in realising that he sought an ending to all of this. From that moment on, she had known she was tied to the house. She didn't know why. She had no words for it. But she knew she couldn't leave.

Only now she thought perhaps she understood. Arata was the one who had already stepped off of the cliff. There was nothing she could do for him. She wished that she could. She had been grateful to him once, but she would hate him now. In that, she realised, she had no choice.

But Ryuu could still be saved.

She closed her eyes and imagined how he had felt. The wind whipped her face. The snowflakes were kinder, more gentle. She was not afraid of heights or of falling. Until today she wasn't sure she'd been afraid of anything. Now though, she thought she might be.

Go and get dressed up again, he had said. *We can start from the beginning.* The seasons came in cycles. He would want her again. The next time, she promised herself, she would be silent.

14. The World we Made

"I'm happy," Mei said suddenly.

The summer day beat down on them. Time had come to a standstill. Counting heartbeats. Mei was seated with her back against Ryuu's chest, his legs to either side of her. Birds circled in the sky and the colours of the valley blended in an end-of-day heat haze. "That's what I'm thinking," she said. "I am happy."

"Mei, you're always happy. You sing when others would weep."

"But right now, I mean. Is that strange?"

"Happy isn't strange." He shifted slightly, relinquishing his hold on her and, after a moment, she felt his fingers combing through her hair. "You know, I think I've grown accustomed to your strangeness anyway," he said.

"Is that good?"

"Hm, you still manage to surprise me though. I would miss it if you didn't."

"One day I might not."

"One day," he said, and the end of the sentence went unspoken because, like a barb, the truth remained brutal; it could only be a couple of days before Takashi mustered the forces he needed. "One day," he said, more forcefully, "We will go and see the village in which Mei was born."

"I think there is little left there that I would remember."

"But I would like to learn more about you."

"You know the important things."

"I know you sing poorly, you hate books, like flowers, even go barefoot in the rain. You belong out here. I think you're more a part of this – a part of the mountain – than I am."

"This is your home though."

"It's yours too, isn't it?"

"Yes, but—" she turned and the curls that he had braided into her hair fell down around her face "—But it's you. You're the one who belongs here. Your family have always lived—"

"You are my family, Mei." She stared at him for a long time, then turned back about and leant against him, her eyes on the valley. "The only one I remember anyway," he said quietly, as if he had surprised himself with the statement and wasn't certain if he could or should take it back. He had surprised her. "If anything happens, Mei—"

"We're dreaming," she interrupted. "This whole summer. None of it has been real."

He hesitated, then tried again:

"It's just that, if anything were to happen—"

"Nothing can happen to you while you're asleep. Dreams can't hurt you."

"I love you."

They sat like that until the whole landscape had faded to amber. Birdsong vied with the crickets.

Ryuu shifted suddenly. In her mind, she had always thought of him as Ryuu. "There was something I meant to give you," he said. She turned to watch him.

He had, in recent days, found a single kestrel feather, striped grey and black, and had tied it into his hair so that it hung to one side of his face. When first she'd seen it, she had burst into laughter and, as she would have expected of him, he'd taken great offence, as if her reaction were a slight. The truth was, the man she had once known as Ryuu would never have harboured such affectations. And yet it suited him. As time had passed, she'd seen the changes in him; they were the very ones he had accused her of. For the first time, he was letting the mountain creep into his spirit. This was his home; it always had been. But free of accounts and tallies, reputations and rules, the wild landscape permeated them both. And he had become something more than he had been, something unconstrained, yes, but more real too.

She had, in a fleeting moment long ago, thought that she loved him when he had saved her from the bandits who had killed Yumi. Then she had wondered if the same ebb and pull that had kept her on the estate, even after Arata, the real Arata, had torn apart her world, could have been love. Now she suspected love was neither of those things.

She felt something else now, and she knew that it was something dangerous. It was too sure, too immediate, too selfish in its will to survive and too hapless in its willingness to sacrifice. It made her want to stay here forever, even if Takashi sent his men. Death did not frighten her anymore because every part of her being would remain trapped here, in a single incandescent summer.

If she died, she thought, she would come back here. Again and again.

Ryuu was at her side again, offering her a small, cloth-wrapped parcel. "Well, it isn't much of a gift, for a lady I mean." He chuckled to himself as he thought of something and added, "Or even for one such as Mei."

"You suggest I am not much of a lady?" She snatched it out of his hands and he leant back, grinning at her affront. "What do you know of ladies anyway?"

"I read books, you know. They are full of princesses."

"Why waste your time on such things?"

"Because the heroes conquer and justice prevails, people fall in love and win against the odds." He watched her closely as she opened the little bundle.

Shaking it out, it took her a moment to realise what he had given her, and then she stiffened.

It was a knife: a very small knife with a ceramic hilt and violets of amethyst inlay. It was more ornament than weapon and yet she felt the warmth drain out of the summer's day as if someone had suddenly shown her that the colours and shapes of their bright afternoon were nothing more than the cardboard scenery of a travelling theatre. "It is easier for you to carry than a dagger and I'll wager it was made for a woman…What?" He looked up, noticing at last the change that had come over her. "What, Mei? You're not squeamish. Are you telling me you would balk at using this?"

"No. It was…Yes, I am certain this was a woman's knife." She wrapped it up again and slipped it inside her sleeve. He stared at her long and hard.

"I have upset you."

"You reminded me. That's all."

"Of what?"

"Of our circumstances."

"You know I would never let anyone hurt you." When she didn't respond, he shifted and rose to his feet, stepping around her to shoulder the drawstring bag in which he carried his sword for training. Then he crouched down and touched her cheek. "Can you do one thing, Mei? Can you believe in me? Foolishly, please. Irrationally." He kissed her forehead. "Believe that I am capable of anything."

赤山

It had been a difficult winter.

The seclusion enforced by the snow delayed Arata's trip to the governorate in Edo, where he was to represent the household in a plea for more arms. Always the lawlessness in the valley worsened but, at times like these, it went unchecked by the household who were, by now, an island in a storm.

Every morning, Harumi lit the fires in the servants' quarters, while the younger members of the household rushed over the bridge to the house to tend to their masters' needs. Then, when everything was up and running and clattering along, she would come to Mei's room to dress her and comb her hair. It was something she had done from the very beginning. That it was special treatment was something Mei had chosen not to see. She had liked the dresses, the bright fabrics, the attentions of the servants.

That morning was no different save that, when Harumi arrived, she was already seated on the bed in a thin *juban,* brushing the night's tangles from her hair.

"How many times have I told you not to try to dress yourself, you silly creature?"

The older woman coaxed Mei up to stand before the mirror. She chose a heavy silk kimono. "You haven't got an eye for these things." She fussed and brushed. Bright clothes again. Harumi fetched a sash, tugged it about her waist and made a tight, efficient knot.

Mei gasped, winced and almost folded forward. Her hands went to her side. "Child?" cried Harumi. "You look as white as clean linen. Are you well?"

"Yes. I—I just…"

It was no use. The pain in her side was making it hard to stand.

Harumi moved to help:

"Let me see."

"No, it isn't necessary."

"What have you done?" The older woman untied the outer sash, then that of the *juban* before tugging the undergarment down from Mei's shoulders. Mei had never suffered any modesty with Harumi before, but on this occasion she gazed straight ahead as the old woman ran a hand down her ribs and over the unsightly purple bruise on her side. There was an instant in which Mei was certain there would be questions. Then Harumi pressed more firmly and she gave a thin whimper. "That hurts?" she asked, somewhat unnecessarily by Mei's reckoning. She nodded. "Trust you to injure yourself when we'll have no recourse to a doctor for at least another fortnight." She hesitated. Again, the space for a question, but she didn't ask it. "I'll get Yuri to take a look at it. He's no physician, but he knows what he knows."

"No, please."

"I'm not requesting your permission. Lie down on your front." Mei moved over to the pallet. "He's a decent sort anyway, even though I know you think he's fierce. Lie down. There." Mei lay on her front with her head resting on her arms while Harumi arranged a blanket over the lower half of her body and gave her a second to wrap around her front. When she was covered, but still lying there like a piece of meat, Harumi went to find the old swordsman.

Her mind had been a welcome blank since the day before and now, instead of dwelling on what had happened, she had spent her energy on worrying about how to hide the evidence that Arata had left. That she had failed, even in this, felt like a humiliation almost as great as the first. Though she knew that was absurd, she kept her face buried in the pillows and didn't look up as they returned.

Oddly, neither Harumi nor Yuri demanded her attentiveness. Perhaps something went unspoken between them. She felt the swordsman's hand on her side, gentle at first. He felt around the bruise, then touched it lightly. Then pressed more deeply so that her body betrayed her with a tremor, and she heard him murmur an apology.

He had his hand flat on her back.

"Breathe deeply," he said, and she did so.

"What is it?" asked Harumi, sounding concerned.

"It could be she's cracked a rib or two or it could just be bruising. Since she's having no trouble breathing, it would be wise simply for her to rest. Mei?" She didn't look up. "Do you want herbs for the pain?"

"No."

"I'll bring you some anyway. You might change your mind."

"She'll be alright?" asked Harumi.

"Oh yes. A few week's at most. No permanent damage," he said brightly as he left.

"He's a good man," Harumi said after a time. "He'll be leaving us, you know, after the snows have gone. The masters no longer need him to teach them. Ryuu said he would always have a place here, but he has opted to go." Mei wiped her eyes and turned a little so that she could see Harumi as the latter continued. "Now, you're going to tell me who did that to you, aren't you? I'll not have it. Not in my household. And the matter is firmly my responsibility once you give me the name, so don't go feeling like you need to protect anybody."

"Arata-*sama*," she said, very softly. Harumi's light touches stopped.

"What?"

"It was Arata-*sama*."

Now the touch was withdrawn altogether and the older woman stood up. Her voice too had changed; it had become hard, almost angry:

"Why? What did you say to him?"

"I didn't—"

"Did you anger him?"

Mei shifted and sat up, still clutching the blankets to her front. She looked straight ahead of her. "Does it surprise you?" Harumi was asking. "All these years, he's had an eye on you. What did you think he wanted? And with his wife being so cold…" With a sigh, the old woman crouched down and slipped two fingers beneath Mei's chin, forcing her to look up. "You don't know what you've got. What I would not give to have been you and have had men of his calibre fawn after me. You could stand to lose a little of your pride, Child." Her gesture took in Mei and the substance of her shame. "This is not beneath you. There have been women like you in every generation of this family." Harumi's eyes returned to the bruises on her side and belly. "Make it as easy for him as you can," she advised. "You're a sweet girl, Mei, but you do say the things people don't want to hear."

And with that she had gone to fetch looser clothes for her and Mei had remained, holding the blankets across her belly. For the first time, she knew that it had all been real. And she saw herself through their eyes.

Knowing that she would have to dance to whatever rhythm the world granted her, in time she would find some way to live with that.

赤山

Ryuu was sleeping. The summer fragrances drifted in through the window and Mei sat, as she so often had, on the ledge that overlooked the orchard, listening to the soft sounds of the night and remembering.

If the day were a song then the night was a whisper. The birds were gone; the crickets too, but there remained the night creatures scurrying close to the ground and the intermittent laughing howls of foxes. She had grown so used to them that she had forgotten how human their voices sounded until she listened, really listened.

Why was Takashi waiting? In the day it felt like a glorious reprise and the time she had with Ryuu was like a dream. But at night it seemed more like a slow torture.

The moon was bright tonight and its slanting light illuminated her own body and the tips of the trees in the orchard, but it also fell on the sleeping form of the man she loved and softened his features until it seemed to her that they were both foolishly young, their bodies coloured silver, grey and white. Like glass. Yes, both of them like glass and brittle in the face of what must come.

She stared at the little knife he had given her. He wasn't to know that it was the first gift she had ever received from him. She wanted to treasure it, but she couldn't escape the sense of foreboding that had settled over her when she had seen it.

Since he had woken and become, to all but her, a man named Arata, Mei had believed she was going against her own nature in this deception. All through her life she had sought the lead from others: from her parents, then from the household. She had gone where fate had borne her, had laboured under the inevitable changes and cycles, the comings and goings and returns. She was what the world had moulded her to be.

And then one day, with a single lie, she had started to remake that world, steering her own fate: the one thing she had told Ryuu he could not do.

Then this.

The little knife was elegant, more suited to a woman's hand than a man's. Knowing what she did of its past then, was it possible that the same world she dreamed she had mastered and reined into her own accord was whispering back to her? Had it given her the very path she was meant to take in the form of his gift? A reminder that she was not here to make her own choices.

Or his.

15. Two Brothers

Though winter was coming to an end, nothing could keep the icy chill from the air. Not even from the *dojo* where two men, dressed and padded in the armour of *kendo*, circled one another like articulated wolves before one, with little ado, stepped forward and swung at the other's head. *Bokken* met *bokken*. There was a percussive exchange then a heavy thud as one of the wooden swords struck home. Its unfortunate target let out a grunt of pain and fell, clutching at his leg. His opponent merely stepped back, watching him.

The latter fashioned a crawling limp to the edge of the hall and propped himself up on the dais, removing his helmet from a head of dark, rust-coloured hair come loose of its binding.

"You're tense, Ryuu. Your mind is elsewhere," said the man still standing. His opponent grunted an agreement. "I'm sure Arata will return with the arms we need."

"No you're not," Said Ryuu.

Yuri removed his helmet and a clip from his hair so that it fell about his face in its usual fashion. He was a tall man and imposing even without his mastery of the sword. He crossed the width of the hall in a few paces and dropped the bamboo helmet next to Ryuu.

"You're too old to be churlish with me," he admonished him.

"You are right that I'm distracted."

Yuri sniffed and moved past him, glancing at the window of the *dojo*.

"You are not immortal, Ryuu, and nor is this House. Why do you do this to yourself if you do not trust him. Why worry night and day if he will return?"

"He is good with people, *Sensei*."

"When he chooses to be."

Ryuu stood up, testing his weight. Yuri had never gone easy on him.

"If I do not entrust him with tasks then he will fritter away his time on drink and women. Ow." Yuri chuckled and glanced at him:

"Painful?"

"I must trust him," Ryuu said, purposefully ignoring him.

"From what I have seen of the number of times you have been forced to save face on his account—"

"I regret nothing and would do the same for you."

Yuri fell silent at the finality of the statement. But it wasn't just that. The words would have more import for him now. Tomorrow he was leaving for Okiri and thereafter neither he nor Ryuu knew for sure. Though there would be opportunities for letters to be exchanged, it was hard to be certain how these times would play out. There were fewer places for swordmasters in the world, especially when the shogunate enforced peace amongst the clans.

The older man bowed.

"I would never ask it of you, my lord."

"I know. That is why I wanted to give you something."

Exaggerating his limp a little for the sake of his mentor, Ryuu crossed to his pile of possessions and sifted through it, until he found a small box wrapped in silk cloth. He held it out for the swordsman. "It doesn't look like much, but I understand the jade is centuries old and from overseas," Ryuu explained as Yuri took out a carved jade seal the deep green of a forest pool. "It's been in this family for generations. I give it to you because it is probably the single most valuable item on this estate and I could not find something of worth equal to the service you have given me." He cleared his throat, suddenly self-conscious. "You will find buyers on the coast. People around here will likely have no understanding of its value."

"You know I cannot accept this."

"You might acquire a freehold, Yuri-*sensei*. Make of yourself a landed gentleman." Yuri's dark eyes studied his face:

"And is that what we aspire to now?"

"These are strange times. People may think our lifestyle is barbaric out here, but I think we are lucky. If the rumours are true and the government is rotting at its core then at least here, on the edge of their world, we will be the last to fall. We can hold to our ideals a little longer than the rest." Ryuu sighed and crouched again as he started to unlace his armour. "In the end, what little power we possess will come down, not to titles and reputations, but to the wealth we own and the friends we have made."

Yuri was quiet. Ryuu laid aside the pieces of armour and placed them in a silk bag, then sat back on the dais, looping his hair into a knot at the back of his head.

"I haven't heard you talk this way before, Ryuu-*sama*."

"I'm not much of a poet."

"On the contrary"—Yuri smiled wolfishly—"I think you would be if you didn't lack for patience. More seriously though, there is a special quality in people who carry on living when their world has come to nothing. These 'ideals' you speak of, are they strong enough to carry you through?"

Ryuu shook his head, smiling suddenly at himself:

"I don't know. I've read of them in stories; stories of great warriors, like yourself."

As Yuri began to remove his own armour, Ryuu stood up with one of the *bokken* and started to spin it nimbly between his fingers, now and again breaking to cut the air. Back. Forth. The low whoosh of the wooden blade was very different to the sound of metal. "I can dream."

"Indeed you can and, for what it's worth, Master, I believe you would make a fine warrior if fate called for it."

"Hm." Ryuu stopped by the window. There were horses coming into the yard, Arata's black gelding leading at a trot. "They are here. Pray you don't tell my brother I talk like a fool when given rein, will you?"

"I will not." Yuri chuckled.

It felt as if times were changing.

Stepping out of the *dojo,* Ryuu gathered his *hakama* to climb quickly to where his men were dismounting. Arata remained on horseback, issuing instructions to the last and, in the slipstream of people moving around the horses, there was a sudden ripple as Ryuu broke into their number and several men remembered themselves enough to bow. Arata dismounted then, his form made bulky by a leather greatcoat.

"Do we have them?" Ryuu asked.

"The weapons? No, they will not send guns." Arata saw the flash of anger in his brother's eyes and clasped his shoulder. "Come inside." He smiled beguilingly at the servants who were gathering on the bridge and terraces. All at once the two men were hastening towards the house, side by side.

Arata was like a whirlwind and Ryuu was one of the few people who could keep up with him when he was passionate. That energy was something they both shared. "Ten men are all they would spare for us. They have given us only ten," Arata was saying, bowing his head so that only his brother would hear as they passed the servants on the bridge.

"Ten?" demanded Ryuu. "I can fetch ten men this afternoon from Okiri who would match their stock! We need weapons not men."

"They say that if we want guns, then we have to send them our own people for training."

"What people? What training?"

"Round up some bastards from Okiri, Ryuu, and send them for training if you must, but the authorities are not going to trust us with firearms. I told the governor there are criminals in the valley already who carry them, but in their eyes we too are little more than criminals, and the governor is hoarding the weapons he already possesses. Hello! Hello, Harumi-*san!*" He bowed flamboyantly as their housekeeper pulled back the screen door. "Where is Kyoko? Where is my wife?"

"She has stayed in her quarters, my lord."

Ryuu was speaking angrily:

"Sending ten men is an insult. The money was for weapons. Do they not realise that ten men will do nothing to touch upon the problems in the valley?"

"Would it not be proper for a woman to greet her husband?" Arata continued, ignoring him with the proficiency afforded only by a sibling.

"Harumi-*san,*" said Ryuu, at last taking heed, "Would you fetch me some wine and bring nourishment for Arata-*san* after his long time on the road?"

"Oh, I have brought back some fine wine, Brother!"

"Enough, Arata!" Ryuu hissed as soon as Harumi was out of earshot.

"Alright, you are angry." He wove through the doorway and into the main room ahead of Ryuu, and the breadth of the chamber at least meant his words no longer needed to churn in the confines of the corridor. Whatever room the two brothers were in, they seemed to expand to fill the space. "But it is not I who have angered you," Arata continued, moving so that the fire pit was between them. "You are angry with the shogunate."

"Do we have orders?"

"To keep the peace."

"With ten men? How? It is an insult. Ten men are ten bullets to the criminals in these parts."

Arata sat down heavily beside the fire, still ignoring his brother's frustration, and yawned against the back of his hand. He looked like a wolf curled up behind the flames, and then more like a man as he began to shed the heavy layers of clothing he had worn for the ride. The servant who arrived with the wine and food collected these up without a word as Ryuu too settled beside the fire, which soon made perspiration bead on his forehead. He drank deeply, watching the flames.

"I have had a week to mull it over," Arata said. "You know there are factions, for the emperor and against. For the shogun and against. Every man is at each other's throat, though not openly. And there's poverty, more than in Okiri."

"Why?"

Arata shrugged:

"Money is spent on arming the factions. The *ronin*, if they are not joining one side or another, spend their time abusing the merchant classes who are quietly growing rich and, because they are rich, Brother, they do not care."

"Was all in order with the payment of our trade duties?"

"Of course. My brother's work is scrupulous."

They drank in silence for a time. The fire flickered between them. Ryuu considered the strange feeling that had come over him as he left the *dojo:* that times were changing and that here, on the edge of it all, they might be forced to watch a tide roll out across the land. He did not feel like he was alone. In such a household, it was almost impossible to feel alone and yet he knew of the troubles in the valley and, if the government chose, they could bind his hands and make him no more than a puppet.

"What do you think?" he asked suddenly. "What do you think if I go myself to the valley this spring and raise an army – a standing guard for the farmsteads? We can play their game; if there are guns being sold through Okiri then we can acquire them as easily as the criminals, and what we don't need we send back to the shogunate so they can see what we are facing out here."

Arata, now sprawled on the cushions beside the fire, watched him with his cheek resting against his fist:

"I think, at the very least, it will be an interesting year."

"My lords."

Both men looked up as the screen door slid back to reveal Yuri kneeling in the half-dark of the corridor.

After a moment, he rose and crossed to Ryuu, bowing again and, this time, directing his obeisance towards Arata. Ryuu understood:

"It is tomorrow, Arata. Our oldest friend leaves us."

"Not a friend, my lord," Yuri said, straightening. "I was honoured to be your teacher."

"A friend, I assure you." Ryuu handed him a cup. "Now you must drink with us."

"No, my lord. Do not think me ungrateful, but I came here for one thing and one thing alone." With that, he pulled the lacquered box out of his sleeve and pushed it across the floor to Ryuu who only stared, his cup half-raised to his mouth. "My gratitude knows no bounds, my lord, but I cannot accept this gift. You see, what you said was right: it is not titles or reputation that define us. But you were wrong in one respect." He looked up. "I do not believe that it is wealth either. No, nor friendship. Friendship is a common thing, but there are deeper bonds that link us together even when we are far apart. I do not need the certainties nor the guarantees of your wealth. I already know who I am because I see myself in your eyes, my lord. I see my years and your own." He held his gaze until Ryuu nodded and picked up the box. The younger man smiled and wondered if his old tutor saw the tears that pricked at the corners of his eyes, even as he laughed dismissively:

"I would not insult you with trifles, Old Man."

Yuri smiled. Unable to hold his gaze any longer, Ryuu turned away. The fire crackled. He heard his old mentor dismiss himself and then the hiss and thud of the screen door drawn to.

"What's in the box?" asked Arata.

"Nothing of consequence. It's a seal, an heirloom that I thought might see him some way to acquiring property and land, but he has refused."

"Why is that?"

"I don't know." Ryuu smiled sadly across the fire and Arata stretched:

"Speaking of gifts, I bought some furs for the house, since I grew tired of the ones we were forced to stare at all winter. I bought wine for us. And, for Kyoko, I've found the daintiest knife you've ever seen."

"You think it wise to gift your wife a knife?"

"Ha! You're funny."

"Seriously though, what kind of gift is that?" Ryuu found himself grinning as he poured another cup of wine and watched the flames reflected in its surface. "Women prefer jewellery, gowns—"

"Ah. Ah, my brother, when did you last lie with a woman?"

Ryuu chuckled.

"I do not have to, to know what pleases them!"

"Oh, because you have read about it in your books?" Arata teased him. Ryuu shook his head and toasted his brother with good grace as he swallowed a mouthful of sake. Arata continued with a wry smile:

"When I can lecture you on swordplay, Ryuu, then you can lecture me on women."

"I bow to your wisdom, *Sensei*."

"Kyoko said she was afraid, all through the winter when the men were out hunting, that wolves would attack the house, you see. So she asked me: was there any weapon she could carry? I wear a sword, don't I? Women like to feel—equal."

"So she intends to defend us against wolves?"

"I told you, Brother. "Arata's eyes glittered. "It's going to be an interesting year."

赤山

Ryuu awoke, disorientated by the scents of summer and an open window. Mei was no longer at his side, but his head was pounding. An acute sense of loss permeated the room, as if a curtain had been drawn back, but what it was he had lost and how, he couldn't recall.

Pieces of a dream.

He sat up and dropped his head into his hands, waiting for the sensation to be overridden by reason. And, after a moment, it did begin to lose its power, but there remained the image of a man, a fiction from his dream. Except he was certain this man had been his brother.

More extraordinary was the tug of affection he felt towards someone he had effectively never met. Despair pricked him again. This time because he could recall a house full of people, of familiar voices. He had never been lonely with Mei. She was like sunlight in this world and yet, tonight, he found himself unsure, as if she were the dream and this part of him, which he was chasing now into a void, was the reality he had forsaken to keep her at his side.

Yet she too had been a part of that world. Four years since their marriage. Why couldn't he reclaim even a glimpse of that?

Why didn't he believe in it?

The screen door slid back and, all at once, he felt a flood of relief that she was here to take the edge of his despair and dull it once again.

She walked across the room to the window and climbed onto the ledge.

He blinked.

At her side, held as if she were ready to draw it, was one of the swords from the *dojo*. He was almost convinced that she would stream out of the window to fight an invisible foe, but as he watched she only leaned out as far as she could into the orchard beyond and appeared to stow the weapon in the branches of the nearest tree.

"Mei?"

The effect of his voice was a sudden shiver through her frame. Sleek and white in her nightclothes, she turned towards him, caught in the manner of a criminal. "What are you doing?"

"Hiding it…"

He rubbed his mouth:

"That's a new game."

She seemed to be at a loss to explain herself and, all at once, he felt slightly giddy. "Do you think, Mei, that I would notice if you were mad? I haven't passed so much as the time of day with anyone else for more than a month. You know, the more I think about it," he said, standing up to look at her work, "The more I think we might both be and I wouldn't even know it." He peered out into the orchard. There was, indeed, a katana hanging in the latticework of branches. The absurdity of that made him want to laugh.

"Do you mean that?" she asked, serious.

He put an arm around her shoulders and kissed her brow by way of an answer:

"What do you think, Fool?"

"I was thinking that, when Takashi comes, he will disarm you first if he can. He knows you rely on the sword too much. So let me make it so that, wherever you go, you will not be helpless, Arata."

"Don't. Mei, we can work this out another time." He held her more tightly and felt the flutter of her heartbeat.

"I don't think he will hurt me," she said.

"How can you know that?"

"Because I know him," she said quietly.

"No. What you and he...You—you don't know him, Mei."

She pressed her face against his chest and they stood that way for a time as the moon passed behind the mountain and the darkness became complete. "We can talk about this in the morning. Your hair is wet."

"I told you, I'll make it so you can't be helpless."

"Were you in the grounds? Oh, Mei"—he grimaced—"Is there anything left in the armoury?" She didn't answer. Then a shiver of laughter caught him as he realised it didn't matter. The swords, the house, the grounds; none of it mattered. And somehow, it reassured him to think that she had sequestered talismans across the estate like charms to protect him.

Or were they offerings? Such that there would be no spirits on the mountain that could not understand their intention.

Yes, he thought, it would be better that way. Let every spirit and that of the mountain stand here with them. For once, the empty house did not feel so empty.

16. A Silk Peacock in the Rain

It was the end of spring. The air was sweet and damp. The world though, had grown gritty and full of noise.

Mei did not know how things had come to a head. It was not that they had piled up, one upon another, until she could bear no more; it was not as if anything had changed from that first afternoon in mid-winter. She should have grown accustomed to her role by now, but it wasn't like that. It was as if she were still looking for a way to rationalise it.

She was a simple creature in many ways and her nature erred always towards lightness, and so it was as if her very constitution set snares for her when, each time Arata called on her, she found herself believing, this time, it would be easier. This time.

And Harumi used the word 'love' so carelessly.

If he desired her, Harumi said, then he loved her. If he sought her, he loved her. At first Mei tried to listen; such a notion sat more merrily with her dreams. But if this was love, then it was as ugly and confused as the first time they had come together.

To her, Arata seemed filled with poison. Whether she was quiet or forced herself to talk, or even tried to distract him, he always saw through her exploits and recognised them for what they were: bids for freedom. And, to each, he responded with the same bald apathy. If she tried to look through his eyes, the woman she saw was as empty, blank and dry as parchment. If she looked too hard, she knew, she would start to believe it too.

But where the rest was blank and empty, the bruises at least left colour on her body. And that was why it had become a ritual to check herself over each morning before the mirror, almost as if she required proof she still existed. He never left a mark on her face. If he left them on her wrists, she would wear gowns with long sleeves, and the only one who ever knew was Harumi who had become diligent about keeping her privacy while she dressed.

Gradually, it seemed to Mei, the world sped up, or she slowed down, until she was moving through water. That was how it came to a head. Not one thing piled upon another. No final straw. Just a sense of drowning.

When Arata left for Edo, she might have felt relieved, but any sense of freedom was smothered by the knowledge he would return. The night before he was expected, she sat in the dining room with the servants as she always had, day after day and night after night, and all at once she could not move. A bowl of food sat steaming in front of her. All around, people chattered as if nothing was wrong.

It was all wrong. Everything. Not a word, not a morsel, was real. And yet none of them saw it. Not one.

"Eat your food, Mei. It'll do you no good – no good at all – to grow thin."

As she stood up, she overturned the bowl. At last she could move again. And, in moving, she started to run; she hitched up her skirts and fled in between the seated servants. She had, in her mind, that she would run forever, until she collapsed or died or ran out of earth to run on.

As it was though, she reached the ornamental bridge and caught herself on the balustrade as if it were a shipwreck in a storm. The scent of winter was still fresh in the old beams. There was something real here, at least, something earthy and old. She gasped as a hand touched her back. Turned. And, when he reached out for her, she balled her fist to strike him.

Yuri was gentle, but his hand quickly covered her own before the blow could find any impetus. She was shocked; she had never struck anybody, let alone without first checking who he was. The old swordsman's hand was warm and dry.

"Good," he said, surprising her. "I thought you had lost any will to fight." He straightened to stand beside her, leaning on the balustrade. It was a clear night and the lights of the valley were ruddy, earthbound constellations. Mei did not get up at once, but remained seated with her back against the railings, at his feet. She rubbed her hand. "I'm leaving this place in two days' time," he said. "Why don't you come with me?" At that, she looked up and held his gaze for a long time. "I am not like him, if that is what you're thinking."

"No…I didn't…"

She didn't know this man. He was and always had been a part of the house, but his very existence had seemed to move on a different plane from her own. He kept an ancient tradition of service, but not the service she had become accustomed to, that of men and women raised in the residence who would never know any other life; his service rather arose from something deeper: a binding of his own spirit to the people and the land, or so it had always seemed to her.

"It might be possible to find you a place in Okiri. I know it may not be what you…That is, I think there are better places than this," he said, surprising her anew by stumbling. When she still didn't answer though, he sighed and bowed. "I am sorry. I have said too much." He turned away.

"Wait," she said.

As he looked back at her, she found her voice again: "Thank you."

Not for the offer, but for taking the moment to believe there had been anything to say at all, for imagining she still had dignity enough that it was worth preserving.

He shrugged. It was an oddly casual gesture:

"Will you stay then?"

"I can't really answer that."

"The choice is yours."

She stood up carefully and brushed at her gown, taking her time so as to get her thoughts in order. She wanted to be truthful, but at the same time, she had never told anyone the truth for fear that her tale, in the bald light of recent events, might shrivel and die before he understood it.

"I owe my life to Ryuunaka-*sama,* from a long time ago. I was attacked, along with a friend, when we were children. She was killed and I hid. We were out in the countryside at the time, just where the mountain road comes down to the valley, and this stranger…All finely dressed, he came from nowhere…"

"I thought it was Arata-*sama* who liberated your village."

"He did, but this was many years before that."

"Ryuu has never spoken of it."

"To him, perhaps, it was a very small thing. I do not know if he remembers—"

"Do you think, if he did, that it would change things?" He was studying her hard, his brows knitted. "Do you think that he would choose to protect you over his brother, if he knew?" She was shaking her head desperately; he hadn't understood at all. "Mei, he is not a cruel man, but he is bound by duties you do not understand, and he cannot act alone. He has sacrificed much to protect Arata, and he will sacrifice more if need be. And he does not – no, he cannot care – about you."

All at once she had stepped forward and placed her hands flat against his chest, at the point where his *kosode* overlapped, and the skin above his heart was bare. The gesture silenced him. She let her head fall against the linen. It was strange; a few months ago, she would never have dreamt of this: the impropriety and the invitation.

But she wasn't afraid somehow and, after a moment, he put his arms around her gently, having checked that they were not being watched.

It was as if everyone here saw only the surface and no amount of explanation would make him understand: things happened for a reason, she thought; they had to. And the world had borne her into this dance with Ryuu for a purpose. But if there was one thing that she had learnt, it was that a touch could stem the tide of questions, even within her own mind. "Mei," he said at last. "No-one can see us this way. Least of all him." He stepped back from her, looking shaken. "I cannot help you."

It was strange, that finality. His gesture, as he turned away, with one hand lifted, palm out, looked almost as if he would ward against her.

It was strange power she had, she realised, to quiet someone with no more than a touch. And it struck her suddenly that it might be for this that Arata came to her so often.

赤山

"I brought you wine," Arata said.

One way to survive was simply this: to become only that which could be seen. Only the surface.

She was beautiful. The fine silk that pooled around her body was dark gold. If Arata had any interest in what she wore, he never showed it, but Harumi insisted on splendour and Mei had come to appreciate that, in such things, she could at least hide a little of herself.

Tonight, Arata had been courteous. A ceramic flask was set before her. He allowed her this one indulgence always: to drink as much as she desired. Tonight was no different and, while he watched her, she drank all that she could stand, two hands wrapped around the flask.

She felt at once sleepy.

He had stopped her before she finished and had taken it to his own lips, but she was suddenly so tired she could barely lift her eyes to his face. She let her head nod into his hand as he cupped her cheek, and a swell of emotion lifted her, so unfamiliar that briefly she wondered if it were really her own. "Mei?" She tried to look up and found the colours were vivid in a manner she had never noticed before. So bright. The sheets, the cushions: each looked as if it were covered in weals of fluorescent moss. Arata seemed different too: less monstrous. More ordinary.

When he took her in his arms, her body seemed malleable and alive in a way it had not been for months. She didn't hear what he said; the words seemed to echo strangely and all that she could see, smell and touch seemed to expand and contract, expand and contract, like a heartbeat.

When he kissed her, she returned the kiss fiercely. This time, she felt nothing of the force he used to hold her. His will and her own coalesced into a single motion that seemed to cradle them both in the minutes that passed as he made love to her. Perhaps minutes. Perhaps hours. She lost track of time too. Everything had become as wax, melting in the heat and seeping into itself. Time. Place. Person. Sometime later, a smack stung her face. Heavy but open-handed. Enough that she took a breath. The mouthful of air seemed to creep across every part of her being. She'd been asleep but not asleep, both absent and present. In the last, overcome with such desire, or was it ecstasy, that their bodies had seemed to stand in the way of a single, final culmination in which neither of them existed without the other. He slapped her again and she moaned. He swore, his voice slurred as if with drink. She had become aware that she couldn't move. Not as she ordinarily would. Her whole body seemed to be pinned to the floor, not by his weight but by something invisible. And he looked odd.

The sense of flowing, of pulsing, was receding. The room was still a whirl of colour, but she was starting to focus on him. She had never thought that he, of all people, would be a point of calm in the midst of a storm, yet caught by a sudden wave of fear she wanted desperately to reach for him and couldn't. What had happened? What had changed?

He held her shoulders and his skin was clammy. She could see the sweat on his cheeks, the wildness in his eyes, a thin line of saliva from the corner of his mouth. "Mei?"

"Where are we?" she asked, or tried to ask. It came out as a slur and she realised her mouth felt like paper. Heat was rolling off of him. He lifted her so that she was sitting now, balled up against his body. Her head hung against his chest behind which his lungs seemed to work as loud and hard as bellows. She tried to get her thoughts in order. Not least, she had to remember who she was, who he was, that she hated him, and that there was a world beyond the violence of colour in this room. "Arata," she managed, "What did you do?"

"You're different when you want me…" He tried to kiss her. She began to smack him across the face and temple until he let her go and rolled away. Remembering herself a little, she remained seated, legs sprawled, weight on her hands, and she tipped her head back.

There was a lingering sense of pleasure, of hurtling through a black morass and of burning amidst those colours, but it was fading. The sense of motion remained: nauseating, jarring with her other senses, which now made themselves known. She was too hot. The room smelt of him and of sweat. Lights too bright. She kept her eyes half shut as she tried to stand, groping like a blind man and wobbling like a foal on its first steps. What had he done? He just lay on the futon, his eyes darker and wider than she remembered, his face half hidden in a pillow. Teeth bared in a smile.

"What was in the wine?" she asked, pressing each word out with care.

"...Thought I gave you too much, but look—look—you're fine."

She wasn't certain about that. While he lay there, eyes shut and smiling like a child, she sought about for her clothes. Finding nothing, she settled for taking a sheet from the bed and wrapping it about her torso for a little modesty, but as she turned towards the door, she noticed a table and, on the table, a small knife with an ivory handle inlaid with amethyst.

She looked back at Arata. His eyes were closed and it seemed he slept.

Some of the noise and motion on the periphery of her thoughts ceased and all around, it seemed to her, there fell a sudden silence in which her breathing and his became the whispered halves of a conversation. And a choice.

She moved closer to the table. However much her present reality spiralled and balked, she told herself, there would be days after this. There would be mornings, noons and afternoons. There would be question marks and explanations. It would not be simple.

But this part would be over.

He would never touch her again. He would never strike her.

Her hand closed over the hilt. Over the thought. The silence rushed in her ears, a cascade of white noise.

"Do it." At first she thought the voice was in her own head. When it spoke again though, she realised she could turn towards it and time again seemed to slow, becoming sticky at the edges. A small figure stood in the doorway; she seemed to carry a little of the corridor's darkness into the room with her. A scarf from her hair now hung around her neck, ruffled up so that it covered her mouth and nose, and a heavy fall of dark hair obscured the rest, so that all Mei saw with any clarity, were her eyes. It was as if all the colour and the life were gone from them.

If Mei had never known Kyoko, she would have believed this to be an apparition; not a living being. But it was the strange determination in that gaze, a sense of inevitable purpose, that held Mei now. Her grip on the knife tightened. It was as if this woman, this frail, sweet woman, who had always been so silent, so desperate, could exert an influence over her that she was powerless to resist.

The decision had already been made. She was only the hand that held the knife. A second sweeping sense of helplessness broke over her. Even in this, why had it not been her choice? "Do it," said Kyoko.

"No." Her voice wavered as she replaced the knife where it had been. She repeated it in a whisper like a mantra, stepping away from the table. "No, no." And then she fled, jostling Kyoko in the doorway and finding herself surprised that the woman had any solidity. The corridor was cold, making her recall that she wore nothing but a sheet torn from the bed.

Thereafter she had a sense of losing herself in the labyrinth of white paper halls. Her mind was sluggish, full of holes. But somehow she found her way back to her own quarters.

She woke sporadically in the night. At first it was because she felt ill, but then it was to filaments of memory. She had desired Arata. Somehow he had tricked her into a greater betrayal than his others. He had altered her senses, stolen the final piece of her volition and turned her own body against her. And yet, as sickening as that deception was, in the early hours of the morning, other thoughts crawled back to her: horror at what she had contemplated and, within that, a deep and searing shame.

Several times, she woke believing she had killed him.

But it was only in the hour before dawn that she found herself able to separate the dreams from reality. In the windings of her own guilt she had let her mind drift away from the very thing that should have been foremost in her mind: Kyoko had wanted him dead.

赤山

"Mei? What's wrong? Are you well?"

Several of the servants tried to stop her as she ran over the decking then down the path, almost tripping over her skirts.

She knew that she was running to Arata. She didn't know if anything she did now could change his fate, or whether it would just be far better for her to stay away, but in the end, it shocked her to realise, she wanted to save his life. Over the bridge and up across the terraces. She slipped past one of the maids to run barefoot down the corridor. The servant swore at her. She turned, catching a brief glimpse of the woman's angry face before she ran full pelt into something warm but as solid as stone. Stumbling back, she took a sharp breath.

Ryuu's face was a picture of disapproval, but his voice was even:

"Who are you and what are you doing running slipshod in my house?"

All at once, she recalled herself: not the Mei who had stood contemplating murder or the Mei who had been betrayed time and again by his brother, but herself, plain and simple and prone to a ripe red blush that bloomed suddenly as she realised she had barely hesitated to pull on her clothes, and they sat ungainly and loose on her this morning. Her hair too was unbrushed, no doubt bearing testament to her every motion the night before, and he would see, must see, that she had been intoxicated.

"My lord." She bowed. "I came looking for…" Arata? No, that would be dangerous.

"But who are you?"

She glanced up shyly, suddenly aware that it was the first time he had asked her.

"Mei, my lord."

"Mei?"

"Yes."

"That's it?"

"Yes, my lord."

A very tiny smile played at the corners of his mouth.

"I have seen you. You are our guest, are you not?" She stared at him, forgetting herself. He stared back. It was the most strange and unlikely thing. "You belong to one of my men?"

"No, I don't think so."

"It is something that you should know so," he said, and she had to check that he was joking because he seemed no less sincere. She looked away. "You seem distressed though. Who were you looking for?"

"For Kyoko," she lied.

"Oh, you are with Kyoko. She is at breakfast with her husband."

"Is she?" She looked up.

"That surprises you?"

"No. I…I don't know. Are they both well?"

Now he reached for her. A hand on her shoulder.

She stiffened. He noticed and removed it.

"I am sorry," he said.

She tried to brush it off with a shake of the head, a step backwards. She didn't know whether to feel relieved or confused at his news. She knew she should show neither to him, but it was too late now and she had already given away too much. His initial disapproval had turned to a breed of searching curiosity, as if he was unused to having such creatures as her charge into his quiet world.

"I had the most extraordinary and terrible dream," she said after a beat and his face became a little more serious.

"Should it set your mind at rest, I am certain they would not resent an interruption."

"No, it's quite alright. It's only a dream after all."

"As long as you are satisfied." He frowned then.

"My lord?"

"Perhaps consider, the next time you need to check upon your dreams, that curiosity does not have to outweigh propriety." It was barely a reprimand, but she flushed nonetheless and tugged at the gown she wore as if to hide the hasty knots she had made. Not before she saw that same glimmer of a smile though. Was he laughing at her?

"Thank you, my lord."

"Mei," he said. Just another little tug, as if he could not quite resist pulling her back. "One more thing: do you know why it is customary to take off your shoes before you enter the house?"

She blinked, not quite understanding. She had come barefoot from the servants' quarters, so he could not chide her for failing to remove her shoes. He motioned towards the corridor. "It should not bear explanation." A glance back and she noticed, for the first time, a line of damp footsteps on the wooden floor.

"My lord," she said again. Any other words had vanished and, this time, she was sure she heard him chuckle.

He called upon a servant to clean up after her.

She remained doubled over in a bow until he passed her then. It was easier that way, and she waited a long time, until she was completely sure he was gone, before daring to straighten.

It was so strange. He was so strange. Was he angry? It hadn't seemed like anger. Why, when so much else had happened, was it he who filled her with questions? Collecting up her skirts and feeling somewhat comforted that the night's events had remained just that, she turned and walked back the way she had come, past the scowling maidservant.

赤山

Ryuu watched her from the window. He must remember to ask Kyoko about her eccentric companion. It was good that she had someone though; she had seemed so unhappy of late, and that girl seemed to have spirit enough that she could distract anyone from their grievances. He could see Mei now, picking her way back across the terraces with her skirts hitched up and her calves showing. For someone who was obviously of standing, if the quality of her attire was to be believed, she was surprisingly dishevelled, like a silk peacock that had been caught in a storm.

He smiled at the thought. Or like the storm itself.

He had seen her a few times, he thought, but had never stopped to notice her. The women who stayed on the estate were most often the wives of his men, polite and often unseen.

Somehow he had the distinct impression that she was nobody's wife.

Yes, he would have to ask Kyoko about this Mei.

17. Beneath a Still Blue Sky

A woman's scream rent the air.

Mei saw one of the maidservants burst out of the copse on the far side of the estate and run full tilt towards the house. Ryuu emerged. She all but ran into him, catching hold of both his arms as she relayed a message Mei couldn't hear, and it was as if her distress transferred to him because he pushed her aside and started to sprint towards the woods.

Mei was on her feet. She had never seen that expression before.

The maidservant carried on into the house, shouting. Mei looked between them and then hastened after Ryuu.

The first of the summer's warmth was creeping into the woodland. She ran, naturally fleet and with a grace, when she was outside, that she never could maintain within the bounds of the house. Curiosity though, rather than urgency, made her give chase.

She was still one of the first to arrive and it was a strange scene that greeted her.

On this side of the estate there was a rock formation that had always drawn the eye. A large boulder had, once long ago, worked itself loose of the mountain and tumbled down the sheer cliff. By chance alone, it had become wedged between the rock-face and a natural tower of stone that otherwise should have stood, needle-like and alone. The boulder formed a natural promontory, but had ruined and left impassable an extant footpath, which had once wrapped itself around the cliff. So precarious was the fallen rock that it looked as if a single touch could cause it to tumble the rest of the way down into the valley below. Yet beyond it, the exposed top of the stone spire was flat as an altar, as if the gods had prepared a stage from which to worship the rising and falling of the sun.

Mei had explored every inch of the estate. She knew every broken path. She knew the spire and the stone. She had never tried to reach them.

She liked a sense of heights, but the bridge and the trees and the forest were her domain. Not that plateau, open to the sky and surrounded by a drop on all sides so precipitous that only eagles should yield to its temptation. There was something blasphemous about passing beyond that fallen boulder. Reckless, and defiant in a way that she had never been.

Ryuu had stopped and was staring up at the rock. Beside him, on hands and knees in a posture of supplication, was Arata. And, above them both, kneeling on the altar, was Kyoko.

She had died up there, beneath the blistering sky

At first Mei had thought she was threatening to jump and that Arata was begging her not to. The idea terrified Mei. Even the thought of that free-fall; the valley floor so far away that it would take forever. But as she reached the two men, she realised that everything she had seen at first was wrong. There was no freefall. There never would be. Kyoko had taken her own life and left her body and her blood where no one could reach them.

Ryuu's eyes were locked on the woman's silhouette against the sky, the back of his hand pressed so hard against his mouth that his lips were already white beneath his knuckles.

As Mei watched, he approached the path up to the boulder. It was inches wide, worn away even where it had not been torn apart by rock falls. He dug his hands into the vegetation in the cliff and tested his weight against it.

And hesitated, his fingers tangled in moss and vines.

His feet were splayed on the wider portions of the path. It was then that she saw a shiver run through him. Something happened. Something changed. And, all at once, she realised what she was seeing: he couldn't move. Right there, in front of a gathering crowd, she understood his body had frozen without his volition.

Mei approached him through the long grass, ignoring the servants who were arriving and gawping. She kept walking until she was just an inch from the drop and another step away from beginning the path's ascent. Ryuu had barely managed a yard of the precipitous trail. Without thinking, she reached out. He didn't look up. Didn't turn towards her. Yet after a moment, his hand fell heavily into her own and his grip grazed the bones in her fingers. After a moment's hesitation, he stumbled back onto the grass.

He let go at once, lurching past her.

She didn't move. Just stared at the points where his feet had been on the trail, balanced above the sheer fall.

Harumi approached them and spoke quietly to Ryuu:

"Who is going to get her down?"

"It's impossible," said someone nearby. Mei let her eyes follow the broken path up to the shadow of the boulder. "Kyoko is so slight. That's how she managed it."

"Kimiyuki! Kimi!" Harumi called forward the skinny boy who helped in the stables. His face was grey. "You have to go up there, Child."

"Look at him!"

"Well, you go!" spat Harumi at the man who had grasped Kimiyuki by the shoulder.

"You send a grown man on that trail and it will crumble beneath him!"

"So send the child!"

"I've never tried climbing something like that," the boy said uncertainly.

"He's too young, Harumi-*san*."

"I'll do it," said Mei.

There were a number gathered now. Everyone in the household was staring and pointing. Ryuu was bending over as if he was ill, his hands on his knees; Arata was still kneeling. And all those close enough to have heard were looking at her.

"You?" demanded Harumi.

"I can climb up there."

"And carry a woman's body?"

She nodded.

"I used to help my father measure out the *koku* at harvest. I can carry at least my own weight, I know. And if Kimi can help me…"

"But it's dangerous."

Mei glanced at her, not really understanding:

"But someone will have to."

"But you—you're just—"

"She's Kyoko's friend," said Ryuu. His skin was colourless, his breathing sharp. Harumi stared at him and then at Mei.

"My lord"–Harumi lowered her voice–"She may be light enough for the path to hold, but is she strong enough?"

"She says that she is."

"And she would have to stomach it."

"Mei," he said sharply. "Are you squeamish?"

She shook her head and he nodded. "Let her go."

"Ryuu-*sama*," Harumi began, and he turned on her, raising his voice for the first time in Mei's memory:

"That path will not hold for you or I! We either try or we leave the body! Do you want to see it every day?"

There wasn't really a moment when they acquiesced. Mei would, in time, remember loosening the kimono she wore and tying up the sleeves, so her arms were bare like those of a child ready to go out climbing trees. As for her dress, she let one of the men use a knife to cut from a point above her knee down to the hem so as there could be no restriction on her movements. And then, with more clarity, she would remember the climb.

It was the end of *uzuki* and the ground was damp. Mud and grit had collected on the narrow way. Kimiyuki went up ahead, but stopped halfway and let her pass him. Thereafter she kept one hand on his thin shoulder. He would not stop looking at the drop. For Mei though, it was the same instinct with which she climbed trees or followed new paths she found in the mountains. She was as much at home here as she was anywhere on the estate.

As she drew closer though, the boulder grew in size. By the time she had reached it, she could see no way around. Its surface, and the altar of stone beyond, were bathed in sunlight, yet how to climb to either eluded her. From the ground it had looked to be perhaps half the size of a man, a ball of rock that had come bouncing down in some long-forgotten fury. Not so when she found herself pressed against it, contemplating the end of the path. It was as wide as three men and shaped in such a way that it grew wider above her head before it grew narrower.

"Don't try," Kimiyuki breathed. He had halted at a point some three paces behind her where the path still retained its full breadth.

Without looking down, she reached out over her head with both hands and took hold of the rock at its widest point.

For a dizzying instant, she was angled in such a way that her toes were still on the path, with no traction at all, and the sheer drop to the valley was behind her.

When she lifted her feet, the centre of her balance shifted and her legs swung out over the drop.

The fear within her made her want to scrabble and clutch. She knew that would only make it worse though. She had found fair handholds; she had to trust that she was strong enough to pull herself up.

She waited until her body stopped swinging, the rocking pressure on her arms lessening, then she curled up her legs until she could feel her knees against her belly. There was still nothing beneath her. Her fingers, taking the whole weight of her body, started to tingle and lose sensation. She tried to pull herself up, finding handholds, one after another, in the red stone.

When she felt the rock at last beneath her knees, she went slithering on her belly across the stone. And lay there.

The crushing blue of the sky above her. The weight of red rock beneath. The sun on her arms and face.

This is what Kyoko had felt.

She sat up and crawled across the boulder.

Mei did not look back. On the tip of the world, there were only the two of them.

The young woman had knelt out here with all the vastness of the mountain and the valley and the sky, and she had cut her throat from left to right. There was blood on the bright plateau.

Mei crossed to where she still knelt. The girl's eyes were closed; her lips were grey. All down her front, the life from her body had stained the fabric black and a pool in her lap was still wet, reflecting the sunlight like a dark mirror.

But Mei did not feel horror. Maybe that would come later, like the shadow left behind after staring at a bright light. Maybe, in time, she would suffer for this and regret, but she did not feel horror. Not now. She felt pity.

Still clutched in Kyoko's hand was the knife she had used to take her life: the miniature blade with the ivory hilt. Strange that it had been something they had briefly shared. The one time that Kyoko had ever spoken directly to her.

Ignoring the blood, Mei took the blade and sequestered it in her collar before crouching as if she would speak to the corpse. She put her arms around the dead woman and shifted in such a way that she could take her weight on her back. That alone would not suffice though. It was not like carrying bags of rice. After a moment, Mei untied one of her sleeves and used the cord to bind Kyoko's wrists so that her arms were wrapped around Mei's body.

As she did so, she allowed herself just one concession to curiosity, sliding back the sleeve of the dead woman's kimono to the elbow. For her own part, Mei knew that not a week went past that Arata did not leave some mark on her arm; he had a grip that could dig into her like wire. But Kyoko's arm was unblemished. And it was in that moment that Mei realised, even if she searched forever, she would find no bruises on the woman's body.

赤山

The hardest part was getting the corpse from the boulder to the path. Because the rock overhung though, Mei could lower Kyoko's body to Kimiyuki, who inched up the trail to take the burden. In an ungainly fashion, he dragged the corpse a short distance until there was enough space for Mei too to lower herself to the path.

They took the weight between them. Their descent was slower. The combined weight, even spread between the two of them, loosened stone and grit from the trail. She marvelled that the clattering, as it fell, went on forever, one stone dislodging another.

Men relieved them of the body even before they reached the grass. Kimiyuki staggered forward and, with little ado, vomited up the morning meal.

Mei felt a little dizzy.

"My poor girl!" Tears streamed from Harumi's eyes. She put her hands on either side of Mei's face and Mei, who had never been her poor girl or anyone's, fought a desire to push her away. "It's so terrible! My poor, poor girl!"

Ryuu was watching them. As Mei's focus was diverted towards the *daimyo*, Harumi's affections seemed to dwindle. No amount of raucous sympathy, it seemed, would force her own distress upon Mei. Letting her be, she drifted back into the gathering crowd. Ryuu stared at Mei.

"You are fearless," he said, and it sounded more like an accusation than a compliment. She understood that she was meant to feel horror then, but all that she could think of was the pale, perfect skin of Kyoko's forearm and how it must have felt to be alone up there. Whatever she had believed of Arata, there was still a chance that she understood only a fraction of him.

赤山

The house was plunged into silence. Messengers went back and forth to Okiri. By the third night, it was clear to all present that their world had been altered.

In Mei's memory, Ryuu had never entered the servants' quarters. Their two domains had never crossed. Up at the house, a balance had been carefully maintained all these long years. Kyoko and Arata, for all their differences, had been a unit, a family. If the house had had a heart then, from the outside at least, that was what they had been. They had been the face too that Akayama had shown to the world. Ryuu ran the estate, wrote the letters, kept the tallies and paid his men, but he was content to stay behind the scenes in all these things. And so it had always been. For all their faults, and despite Arata's deceptions, there had been a balance.

With Kyoko's death, the world tilted.

"The master wants to see you." No, he had never come to the servants' quarters, so Mei assumed that it was Arata and prepared herself as best she could, though Harumi did not attend her tonight as she ordinarily did.

When she went to meet him, he was seated at a table in the anteroom. Ryuu, not Arata, and they were not alone, but several other of the servants had been called to join them. Still there was something wrong with this scene. Ryuu's usual energy was lacking. He leant his chin on his hand and, with his other, rolled a coin between his fingers, an oddly intricate motion that, by its repetition and exactitude, after several seconds, felt strangely obsessive. Mei watched him for a moment. Then he sat straight and the coin stopped. His eyes drifted over the assembled servants. None present knew if an official meeting had been called, so they ranged around in varying states of self-awareness.

"We have sent messengers to the Shirakawa," he said at length, referring to Kyoko's family. "But it will take them too long to travel here. We shall bury her on the estate, tomorrow. It would be unwise to wait." Mei glanced about. Several faces plainly demonstrated their owners were uncomfortable. It did not help Ryuu's cause that he sounded like he was speaking his thoughts aloud, unfiltered from his mind to his lips. "So this was an unfortunate incident to which you were all witnesses. The records in Okiri will show her death was an accident. There is no need for the details to leave this estate." The coin started turning again nimbly between the fingers of his left hand.

A balance, yes. Yuri had been a part of that and he had left now too. With Kyoko gone, so was the indistinct promise of family. They were just two brothers alone now in the vast and ornate house, orphaned of what might have been.

Ryuu talked for a short time, but it all amounted to one thing: within the bounds of integrity, they should not speak of this ever. He thanked them. "I will talk with Harumi and Mei now," he said.

The servants began to troop out. Mei felt her face grow hot. While Harumi took a seat, she remained standing, and Ryuu frowned up at her. "You look different." She stepped down and went to the table. She had not attended to her make-up, but she realised that this was probably the first time he had seen her in the flamboyant silks she reserved for Arata. "You are quite the creature of many colours," he said. "Where were you born?"

"In the valley, my lord."

"Local. I should have known…Your eyes." He was thoughtful a moment, looking between the two of them. Then he frowned. "I had hoped to ask you about Kyoko – whether her actions, her demeanour – ever suggested she would do this."

"Oh no, my lord," answered Harumi without hesitation and Mei was relieved she hadn't had to open her mouth. She felt like glass, as if all her emotions and intentions were visible beneath her skin. These sentiments crawling in her guts.

"Did she ever speak to you of Arata? Did she seem to resent him?"

"No, my lord." Harumi again. He winced a little at the speed with which she answered.

"Mei? What about you?"

She was careful:

"He was always good to her, my lord."

"She took her life to spite him, you see. He might have stopped her, but she knew he wouldn't follow her up that path. So she made him watch. Can you even imagine what that felt like?" Mei listened and felt herself grow cold. So Kyoko had given Arata a choice. It was strangely calculated of her. He could have been under no illusion that the fault was his own, but she found herself wondering what form shame or guilt might take with Akayama Arata. "She intended to destroy him," Ryuu said and Mei felt the pain in his voice.

It was so much easier to imagine that the people in this world who were good and kind would not love so easily that which was cruel.

"I am sorry, my lord," she said.

"It is not your fault," he said, rising gracefully from the table. Both she and Harumi stood and bowed.

Perhaps she imagined it, but it seemed to her that his eyes lingered on her as he left.

18. A Teller of Stories

"You are most popular tonight," said Harumi as she scraped a comb through Mei's hair and looped it up into a knot, which in the mirror, made a soft curl at the back of her head.

"Lord Ryuu–*sama* wanted only to understand my part in this," she said softly. The summons had come from Arata half an hour later. Usually she dreaded having to face him, but tonight was different. The image of his brother was still strong in her mind, sitting at the table in the servants' quarters with the coin turning over and over in his palm. Tonight she could feel no deeper emotion than the one she had seen behind his eyes. So it would not do to fear. Her fear was such a slight thing by comparison.

"You serve them. That's all. You do as he says and keep your head down. There's no blame to be meted out. Now then"—Harumi turned to her—"Some *oshiroi* and powder for your face—"

"There's no need tonight."

"Of course there is. He will expect you to—"

"I said there's no need."

The stout woman stepped back, her lips pursed.

"I don't know why even now you refuse him." She took the white wax from a stand beside the mirror and, as Mei watched, she began to mix it with water to form paint for her face. The delicate trails began to dissolve. Briefly, it was all Mei could see.

She could feel a heat rising inside her. It came from everywhere and nowhere and it painted the room from the inside out. She lunged for the clay bowl. Her knuckles struck it hard enough to knock it from Harumi's hands. White paint spilt across the floor and it shattered.

Harumi slapped her hard across the cheek. Mei raised her fist.

And hesitated.

Harumi was just another part of the kaleidoscope of lies. Somewhere, in all of this, Mei suspected, the old woman had lost herself, the same way the others had, the ones who glanced aside when they saw her dressed up so finely and visiting their master's quarters; the ones who now talked behind raised hands and gandered at the ripples stirred by Kyoko's death.

Mei stared at her fist. It had not been in her nature to fight before she had been with him. It had not been in her nature to hit or kick or bite. He had altered her. She had flown too close to his fire without ever noticing how it forged her and remade her. Kyoko had never stood a chance.

Mei's own wings had started to burn up long ago.

Harumi gathered up the wax and brushes. Mei watched her, feeling her anger like sparks thrown up from a blaze.

"Forgive me," Mei said.

"We are all a little hot in the head, I think, after everything we've seen—"

"No. Forgive me. I am not going to him tonight."

赤山

For the fourth time, Ryuu read the missive. It was curt and direct, requiring of him only a single signature and yet it was everything he cared about, written in a tight, deliberate script. His brother, the house, the estate and the sacrifices he had made to be here; none of these things were named and somehow that was worse. The demand was for coin and stipends. They had reduced everything of value to this, a line of figures, purposefully designed to ruin him, and here, a florid seal: Takashi Isamu, in the name of the *daimyo* of Matsuda.

He did not know this Takashi. The man could be anyone: a samurai seeking to make a name for himself or a mercenary bought for a price. The Matsuda though were close to the shogunate.

The Akayama, three hundred years ago had picked the wrong side in a war. It was a fracture no amount of replastering could conceal. The shogun, who had then been no more than a warlord, had marked the clans who opposed him as *tozama,* outsiders. As a status, it should have lost all meaning over time, but the past had a way of lingering in places like this. Favour still fell on others in court: the Matsuda, the Shirakawa. But Akayama had been strong, controlling the trade routes and the post towns through the mountains, and Okiri, for all its faults, had been loyal and fruitful.

Akayama was rich in wealth if not in favour, while Kyoko's clan had been golden in the eyes of the shogunate, yet had frittered away everything of substance. In secret, they had turned to the money-lenders in the city.

That was why, if on the surface, the marriage had been one of fantasy and decadence, beneath the facade, it had sealed an alliance. The Shirakawa delivered the Akayama into the shogun's favour; the Akayama in turn delivered the Shirakawa from their debts. It was an alliance which now lay in tatters.

Nothing linked this letter to Shirakawa Kyoko, but then again nothing would. There were no blood feuds in this time of peace. There was no revenge and little left of honour. It would come dressed up in the colours of coin and exchange.

Ryuu did not have the money that they now asked for, and they knew that.

It was a choice he was being given: bleed the land with taxation and risk an uprising, give up everything of value and leave the estate in the hands of the lenders, or remain and face the enemy.

But an enemy riding in the name of the government? How could he stand up to his own lord?

"Ryuunaka–*sama*?"

He looked up. A boy had pushed aside the white curtain that divided Ryuu's room and now he knelt. He was of samurai–stock, sent to the house for training to learn the values of both war and servitude. It was a timely reminder that Ryuu had his own men to fall back on if necessary. "Ryuunaka–*sama*, there is a woman here for you."

"A woman?"

The boy managed a blush that started in his cheeks and crept along his face and neck, piquing Ryuu's curiosity. "Please. Send her in."

He weighed the papers down with a stone and turned just as the curtain was drawn aside once more and Mei stepped into the brightly-lit space. He blinked. Already she had dropped into a bow. Someone, he noticed, had pinned up her hair. It seemed a strange thing to have done at this time of night, but then everything seemed strange, and he had just now discovered that, much to his surprise, he felt an odd sense of anticipation in her presence. "Is something wrong?" He gestured for the boy to fetch them drinks. The curtain swung back into place and they were suddenly alone. She didn't move from her obeisance. "Mei?"

"I'm sorry."

"For what?"

"I came here to tell you–to tell you—" Her breathing was fast in the silence.

"It's alright," he heard himself say and her head came up just a little, her eyes resting on him briefly before she renewed her focus on the floor.

"It is important that you know that, since the winter, your brother has asked for me often, my lord. Sometimes nightly."

He must have released his breath because he coughed suddenly and she looked up. "I'm sorry, my Lord."

It took him a moment to remake his expression. Perhaps his most pertinent emotion was shock. Not at Arata. God alone knew his brother was enough of an idiot for this, but the girl? She was everything that Arata was not. She was bright and full, a breath of fresh air in a space haunted by formality, and he had noticed her. He had stopped and smiled because she was something new in this staid world. A knife twisted in his stomach. Why her? Of all the women Arata might have taken, why her?

But it was more than that, wasn't it? In light of Kyoko's death, her confession was a shouldering of blame. Strange that she would come to him. It was possible, just possible, that presenting her to the Shirakawa would blunt their haste for revenge. A scapegoat for his brother's sins. Except it wouldn't feel like justice. That he entertained the idea, even for a moment, made him sick to the stomach. And anyway, there was something about the way she had phrased the admission....

"You are his lover?"

She didn't answer. Still he could hear her breathing, fast and frightened, and he started when he heard the door to his chambers slide back and, an instant later, the boy slipped through the curtain, bearing a tray of tea.

"What are the circumstances," Ryuu asked carefully, "Of your arrangement? Does he pay you?"

A tremor ran through her.

Perhaps it was an insult.

The truth was, Ryuu was a little out of his depth. The boy poured them both tea, blissfully ignorant of the conversation, and then removed himself again. Ryuu put the cup to his lips, hiding what he could of the heat in his cheeks. Matters of this nature had always been Arata's domain and he could have relied on his brother to trample all over his embarrassment. Unfortunately though he was alone with her. "I'm sorry. That was coarse of me."

"No. It is not a matter of compensation," she said carefully. Her fingers were delicate around the teacup. He found himself watching her smallest finger tapping out an unheard rhythm against the ceramic design. "I don't believe we ever came to an arrangement."

"No, sometimes these things…you might not." He frowned. When he looked up again, she was watching him.

"I thought you would be angry."

"Ashamed." He saw her surprise and cleared his throat. "I should have known. I knew what he did in Okiri. Did Kyoko—did she know about you?" She nodded, eyes brightening a little and, whatever she was feeling, he realised he felt it too. He had been holding on so tightly he had failed to notice that, since Kyoko's death he'd barely exchanged a word with Arata. It was not coincidence; it was the vast question left unasked; it was the apportioning of blame. And all at once he thought he understood why Mei had needed to come here tonight. "I know," he said. "It is on my conscience too."

"I didn't mean—"

"I know," he said.

She stared at him. Then she reached over to pour their tea and he watched her, because he could. "Is my brother in love with you?"

She froze at that. He couldn't blame her. It was clumsy; he was almost inclined to follow it with another apology, but she had already sat back on her heels, her eyes down.

"Harumi believes so, yes—"

"Oh no, that is not what I asked. You are not in love with my brother"–she looked up at that–"So then is he in love with you?"

"It depends upon what my lord means by love."

He was silent for a long time, finding the directness of the question suddenly thrown back at him. If she were just a woman guesting in his house then no doubt their conversation would be unacceptable, but she was not. She had already crossed a line.

All around him, the woodcuts and paintings that decorated his chambers stared down at him, silent witnesses to their strange exchange. Warriors in bands of ivory armour; women lounging beneath blossom–heavy trees. Each one like a door opening his house onto other worlds and ages. At last he shook his head.

"I don't know. Something for poets and painters I think," and he had already risen to his feet and crossed to the window, closing it against the night. He didn't really need her answer. It would not change things. Indeed, he was beginning to suspect it would make things more complicated.

He was thinking back to the day they had found Kyoko, to the way they had sent her up ahead of the men to bear the body down. Mei had tied up the sleeves of her gown, leaving her arms bare to the shoulder. Even now he could recall dark bruises above her elbow. It hadn't meant anything. People bruised. He had seen and thought nothing, but he had noticed enough that he recalled it now and wished he didn't.

"What are your pictures?" she asked timidly and he realised that she had been glancing around while he had been lost in thought.

"Which? There are so many." He smiled a little. It was an extravagance. He might have filled the whole house with them, but then people would have talked and called him an eccentric, so he had kept them for his private quarters and they were crowded in, a thousand times and places vying for attention. He liked to be alone in here with the stories from his youth, and perhaps it was eccentricity, but he hid it well enough. "Most are ancient. The paintings were my father's. I had the woodcuts commissioned in Kyoto and brought over the mountains."

"Are they emperors?" She rose to her feet. It was, Ryuu realised, genuine curiosity.

"A few became emperors. They're warriors, and courtesans."

"This one." He came to stand beside her. A warrior, brandishing a sword, reared on horseback. A demon sprang out from behind a bush stuffed with red berries, its face a caricature of greed. "A monster."

"An *oni*. It steals the man's soul until the sun goddess takes pity and steals it back for him."

"Why would she do that?"

"I don't know. The story doesn't say."

Mei's smile was one lacking in self–awareness. She seemed entranced and he almost had to shake himself to recall where and what he was. "You like tales then?"

"Tales. Hm. When people tell them, but not books. Not just words on a page. Once it's set down in writing, something's lost. But before that, you can change things." She reached out and touched the tips of her fingers to the woodcut.

"Would you–change things?"

She was silent for a long time, the smile fading slowly. It had taken him courage to ask that. It was as much an admission as a question.

"I always thought I should have been good at making stories," she said. She turned to him. Her eyes were a little brighter than before and he realised, with shame, that she was offering him a way out. She had not asked him for help, but the least he could do was explain why he could not give it.

"It may be best for you if you leave the estate. If it came to it, I would not take your word over my brother's." He hesitated, realising there was room for a more exacting truth, and he spoke gently. "I mean, if we were challenged publicly. He is still my blood. My family. We could not afford–I could not afford to move against him and, for that reason, I cannot protect you." She didn't answer. Another doubt crept into his mind. "If you want coin for your discretion—" A sharp glance. Either she was angry at the suggestion or it was not enough."You know, don't you, that in reporting him, you would make enemies of both of us?"

"I did not come here to threaten you, my Lord. Though I envy you that your own honour can be bought back for coins."

The retort was like a knife in the gut and for a moment he was lost for words, forced again to reassess the woman standing before him. The statement could not be more pertinent, though she could not possibly know the choice he faced with the Shirakawa. He stepped back and briefly his thoughts must have shown on his face because when he met her eyes again, the cold was gone and she seemed troubled that he had reacted so.

No longer trusting himself, he suggested again that she leave and this time there was no hesitation. She gathered her skirts and bowed. Not low. Perhaps she knew that her departure was now more important to him than formality. He watched her turn away.

And realised that he was never going to see her again.

"Mei." She stopped, cheeks flushed and eyes bright with sentiments she would keep to herself until she was out of his presence. "Do one thing for me," he said, his voice softer now. "When you are far from here, will you make a story for me? Give it a different ending to this one. Make my brother and I just a little better than we are."

"Yes, of course," she said. And now she smiled and he realised he had been waiting on her forgiveness. "And I shall make it so magnificent you shall wish that it were true."

赤山

Upon stepping out onto the terraces, Mei sensed that she had left a part of herself behind in that room. It was the part of her that Arata had claimed long ago when she had let him into her dreams. It was the part that Ryuu had saved from drowning that day. It was piece after piece of her that had crept into their world and lay nestled in the crags and cliffs of the Red Mountain, and though she knew that there were towns and fields and cities and lives beyond the valley, she did not believe in them.

These pieces of herself would remain, she thought, tangled up and hidden: on the terraces, in the bedrooms, in amongst the trees and the gardens and the rocks. If she never returned, she thought, she would try not to begrudge them that.

19. The Lord of the Mountain

Ryuu tugged back the blinds and sunlight flooded the room. Soon it would be summer. The sky outside was a vibrant blue and the miniature orchard behind his brother's quarters quivered with crowds of birds and humming insects. He had cleared the room of empty ceramic flasks as he spoke of the Shirakawa and Matsuda, but the smell of wine was still strong, as if Arata had tried to polish the old wooden beams with it and had kneaded it into the fabric of the house. When he turned, his brother was sitting up on the futon, blinking. Ryuu had prepared himself but still he was shocked at his appearance: his skin was waxy and his eyes sunken. They were close enough in age that there was often little to choose between them, but it seemed, in recent weeks, years had mauled his brother's body. There were white sores on his lips, and his hands, resting against the sheets, would not stop moving.

Ryuu could reprimand him, but it would do no good at all. His most effective measure had been in refusing him wine two days ago. It had not been hard; he had drunk through all their reserves and no more deliveries were due from Okiri for a month. He wondered if Arata had heard one word he had said. He turned back to the orchard, and was surprised when his brother spoke:

"Our mistake was in thinking we were ever more than pawns." The words were slurred but certainly coherent. Despite himself, Ryuu was relieved and turned back towards him as he continued. "What are you going to do?"

"I–I think I will need to go away for a time."

"To Matsuda or Shirakawa?"

"Shirakawa."

"Let me go."

Ryuu looked at the sky, deep blue and peaceful. The mountain settled into its seasonal rhythms, oblivious of the small dramas that played out on its peaks and plateaux.

"I need you here and sober to lead the rest of my men if I have not returned when the Matsuda come."

"How many are you taking?"

"No more than five I think."

Arata grunted and, out of the corner of his eye, Ryuu saw him seeking around for a flask and turning his nose up at the cup of fresh water he'd left for him.

"You don't know the roads as well as I do," Arata said. "When was the last time you were in Edo? For the martial tournaments? How do you intend to pay Shirakawa?"

"The jade seal Yuri refused."

"Do you think they'll accept it? Isn't the point in their naming an unaffordable price so that they have an excuse to come for us anyway?" He shifted and rose to his feet with a groan. "And it's the Matsuda we should be paying if you go along with their charade. Shirakawa intends to distance himself from this."

"Yes, he does."

Arata joined him at the window, still blinking and rubbing at his eyes and cheeks with a heavy hand. He stifled a yawn.

"Pay the Matsuda. It might not solve anything, but Shirakawa will be forced to go along with it. You call their bluff. Show them we have resources too. They'll think twice about coming up with more lies."

"It's all lies," Ryuu said quietly and Arata grunted agreement.

"Take more men if you go to Shirakawa. If they refuse—"

"They won't refuse."

"Of course they'll refuse. They think Kyoko was without blemish and, whatever they believe of me, you are *daimyo*. They will use you to set an example if they can." He was staring hard at Ryuu now. "I don't like your expression, Brother."

"Don't try to understand, Arata. It will do no good at all."

"No." A light of awareness dawned in Arata's eyes and he stepped away, animate with a sudden energy. "No, no, no. There is nothing noble in giving yourself up to them, Ryuu!" He turned in a half circle, like an animal finding itself caged. "Why? When we can afford the payment? Think of what you have done for me." He went back and took hold of his brother's arm. "Think, Ryuu. I live because you paid the bastards who cheated me, and you always said, it is better that way…What's different now?"

"She said…" Ryuu shook his head. It felt like many things were crashing in on him. He hadn't even known he'd made the decision until now. Arata clung to his arm, reminding him of the small boy who, decades before, had clung to him when their father had come looking to discipline them. "We're buying into our own lies, Arata."

Arata stared at him, his emotions unguarded:

"Who told you so? Kyoko?"

"Mei."

Arata shoved him backwards and he almost laughed at his brother's anger. It felt as insubstantial as gentle snowfall. For the first time, he was seeing things clearly.

"Why did you listen to her?" Arata growled.

"She saw someone I used to be." Arata pushed him again and he caught himself against the window sill, marvelling a little at the younger man's ferocity.

Ryuu had always been the thoughtful one though; Arata simply acted and reacted, incapable of comprehending why he felt the things he did. To many, he was volatile, unfathomable. To Ryuu, he was just a man. There was only so long anyone could be buffeted from one place to another by their passions before they started fighting back, and that had always been Arata's way: to face the unknown like a cornered beast. There was no finesse in him.

Wildly he stared at Ryuu, his hands tightening into fists, looking for all the world as if he wanted only an excuse to strike him.

"She turned Kyoko against me!" he barked. "Did she get to you too?"

Ryuu said nothing. He was seated in the window now, could feel casts of sunlight, warm bars across his back. The room looked old and uncared for. "What is this person she saw in you, Ryuu? A man who resigns himself, admits defeat? Does everything she touches wither and die?"

"She made me want to live."

"You think Shirakawa will let you live?"

Ryuu bowed his head, letting his eyes fall closed and finding tears beneath that his brother couldn't see. He didn't know anymore. The only thing that had made any kind of sense since Kyoko's death had been his conversation with a woman who had come from nowhere, burned briefly and vanished once again. It was as if he had been someone, but only by the light of her eyes. The old stories had made sense, for just one night.

You couldn't buy honour. She had told him that much. His duty was to the house, the family. But with Arata's words trampling on his certainty, the rest was falling back again into a mire. "She gets inside your head," Arata said. "Listen, Ryuu, I will take the seal to Matsuda. See if they dare accuse us again."

Tension ran through Ryuu like a bolt of lightning, and his fingers dug into his knees.

"It doesn't change anything!" he shouted; it wasn't at Arata; it was at everything. It was at the woman who had gone. "Don't you understand?"

"What needs to change, Brother? What needs to change?" Arata dropped down on one knee, his hands still on Ryuu's arm, pawing at him. Ryuu looked at him and blinked as if seeing an apparition in the chamber, hanging on his robe.

"You."

Arata's eyes hardened.

As Ryuu continued though, his words gained strength: "I'm not covering up for us anymore. Not for you. Not for me. That girl, she didn't deserve what you did to her." Arata stepped back from him. "Nor did Kyoko. She asked for my help and I told her no. Because of you. Because I was trying to protect you, and all this time, Arata, I've been looking in the wrong direction. I've been thinking that you could love the things I love…"

"She did. She got inside your head."

"When she told me I thought it was extraordinary; my brother had found someone who made him willing to risk everything, sacrifice everything. That's what I thought!" Ryuu shook his head, eyes bright as they came to rest on his brother, "And then I realised that no, just like everything else, you sought some way to control her. I know you, Brother. I know what you did to her." Unblinking, he held Arata in his eyes. "I wanted you to be happy and then I remembered one time you seemed truly happy: you'd raised your sword aloft to kill a criminal, one of the thieves brought up from the valley, and I remember thinking: how could this make him happy? There is no joy in it, no honour, no pleasure. And then I realised, you had finally found someone who could not escape you."

Arata stared back at him.

"Is that what you think of me?" he asked at length. Ryuu looked away. "Are you going to report me? For a village girl? You'd be the laughing stock of the courts!" When he had no response, he gripped Ryuu's shoulder and shook him hard: "Answer! Is that what you think of me!"

"Were it true, it would make of me a poor excuse for a brother." He looked down at Arata's hand on his shoulder. "If I hated you, Arata, then what allies would I have left in this world?"

The younger man let go as suddenly as he had grasped him.

"None. Then you should not say such things." Arata turned away to begin pacing again. "What would make you say such things? I've never seen you this way, Ryuu. What is wrong with you?"

He couldn't say. It was a pain wedged somewhere between his heart and his stomach, pressing down on him with the weight of the mountain itself and, for a long time, he couldn't even speak. Just minutes earlier he had been intent on giving himself up to Shirakawa. Perhaps Shirakawa would find some way to kill him. His fate had not been his consideration, but, were he to die at their hands as redress for Kyoko, at least he would die free.

The worst thing was opening his eyes and finding bars that had always been there, but which he had never seen before. He watched Arata pacing. It had been an illusion. From the very beginning, an illusion. He had believed his father and his retainers when they had said he was lord and *daimyo*, yet all this time, the truth had been there in front of him.

He gave his money to Arata; he gave his men to Arata; he sent Arata out to act in his name amongst the samurai. And when Shirakawa had asked if the family were eligible, he had given a wife to Arata, and a future. He had made so many excuses: had wanted to make him responsible, had wanted to make him happy, had wanted to keep him reputable.

But look at things from another angle and the lord of Akayama was not Ryuunaka.

For more than a decade now, he had served his brother. Quietly. Methodically. And without complaint.

Without a word, Ryuu rose to his feet. Arata watched him:

"What do you intend to do?"

"I don't know," Ryuu said as he reached the door. "Changing things though. You were right; it was a foolish idea."

赤山

They had run out of time. Somehow Ryuu knew that Arata would be the first to act. It no longer even surprised him—

"Your brother, my Lord—"

—When hoof beats sounded in the courtyard.

"I know. How many men did he take?"

Was it so strange to imagine that, with the house split, their warriors would start to choose sides.

"Fifteen, my Lord."

"If you can ride, you are with me."

"But what are you going to—?"

"With me!"

His whole life up until that moment felt prescribed. The victim of somebody else's plan. With or without him, it would play out today.

And as he rode out of the courtyard, he glimpsed a face in the crowd, in amongst the servants. A woman's. Pale. Eyes full of the sunlight.

Then was it possible that Mei had returned? He passed by so quickly though that he might simply have imagined her. Either way, his heart sank; he had somehow hoped she would be far away if things had to end with bloodshed.

Arata had worked out that the jade seal was the key. It was worth more than the price the Matsuda had been tasked with exhorting from them, so whoever held it could barter, not just for their own life but for the lives of all those in the house.

It was the beginning of June and violently hot, and salt collected on the horses' sides as they rode, a whirlwind through the stone channel. The familiar dust of the mountain coated Ryuu's hair and face until every inch of his bare skin was the same red as the rocks through which they rode.

He only knew that there would be an end. To his own cowardice. To his indecision, to weeks of turning problems around and around in his head until he thought that they were eating out the inside of his mind. And now this. An end to it all.

He struck the first of the men from behind. Easy enough. He hadn't known them. These were Arata's disciples from Edo and he had killed before on sojourns in the valley. Always face to face. He had been taught that way, though perhaps there were some days when it was just as effective to stab a man in the back.

His own samurai rode into Arata's men like a wolf-pack, following their master's lead with swords drawn.

Death was swift where they could loose it without a fight. And then all who remained in the pass were face to face and eye to eye and, all around, a cacophony of metal.

Ryuu might, in time, wonder if it could have been less brutal. If it was his brother who had begun it or if, in the end, it was him.

Through the melee, Ryuu found him, still riding, as if he would leave all the bloodshed behind. As if he was immune. As Ryuu caught up, Arata turned and spat at him:

"Have you lost your mind?"

"Maybe!" Ryuu thrust his fist into Arata's saddle bag and, taking a handful of the leather, tore it with all his strength. The horse skittered sideways. A profusion of water flasks and leather gourds came streaming from inside. "Where is it?"

"You can keep your damned seal!"

With Ryuu riding behind and on his left, Arata loosed his katana and, keeping his right hand on the reins, stabbed backwards. It was easily avoided. But it was a warning.

"Do you intend to fight me?" Ryuu snarled, and there was genuine fear in Arata's eyes as he glanced back over his shoulder.

At least he could still frighten him.

As important to Ryuu as the steel in his sword and the speed of his reflexes was his ability to become someone else when he fought. He had learnt early on, in instants of shameful hesitation, that as himself, as Ryuu, he could not kill. It was something that Yuri had never understood about him. Whether weakness or delicacy, he knew only that he abhorred the instant of death, that he saw himself in their pleading, disenchanted eyes and knew there was nothing honourable or glorious to come. The final cut was always that of an executioner, whether in the midst of battle or as a mercy at its close, but it was therefore a disgrace. Even in the valley where the spectre of kill or be killed was a harsh truth, Yuri had repeatedly saved Ryuu's life and berated him his hesitations. So he had learnt.

There was a plateau, a place where he was distant from all of this, with horizons as broad as the sky and the colour of steel. He left his thoughts there when he fought, and the separation of mind from body was as liberating as taking flight. But it was a place without right or good, or pleasure or disgust. Killing became a series of motions, which, when performed well, brought aesthetic satisfaction.

He had earned his reputation in martial tournaments held between the clans, but had proven it to himself in curbing the raids on the valley's farmsteads. There he had found himself to be a wholly effective murderer. "Fight me, Brother!" he hollered at Arata who had slammed his heels into his horse's flanks. Ryuu loosened his sword with his thumb.

Perhaps Arata had waited for that small sound or even a motion in the corner of his eye because he suddenly sawed back on the reins. The horse staggered and reared.

Arata threw himself clear, stumbling as he landed. He turned to face his brother who had ridden on past him. And now he drew his sword, transiently torn between confrontation and escape.

Ryuu, blade drawn and controlling his mount one-handed, wheeled back towards his brother and approached unhurriedly.

"Enough, Ryuu! You killed men back there." Arata shambled backwards and Ryuu let the horse, snorting and champing, follow him, until he was all but trapped against the rock wall. "I should not have taken your soldiers. I understand!"

Ryuu lifted his blade slowly until the very tip touched his brother's throat. Arata stood there, his lips moving silently.

After several seconds in which neither man moved, Arata reached out with his left hand and, palm over the blunt spine of Ryuu's blade, moved it sideways and down, away from his body. Betrayal and anger flickered in his eyes. "Why did you come after me? I would pay the Matsuda and save your house and your name."

Ryuu blinked, seeming to come back to himself, glancing around. They had proceeded further into the canyon than the rest of his men and were alone.

"What's left to be saved is unrecognisable."

"The Shirakawa will kill you if you give yourself up, Brother. I am returning the favour you did me in paying for my life." He glanced back the way they had come. The pass had fallen silent. Ryuu imagined their soldiers, men who had shared quarters, fighting one another to the death on a sunny afternoon.

"I'm going to take back the seal and then you will leave the estate, Arata."

"To go where?"

"Anywhere." Ryuu sheathed his sword and dismounted. "For once, I don't want to know where you go or what you do." He turned towards Arata's horse, eyeing the torn saddlebags. By the gold lozenges that littered the ground like confetti it would seem that Arata had raided the coffers too. But asking his soldiers to choose between them had been the greater crime.

"You have no allies, Ryuunaka," Arata hissed.

Ryuu began to sift through the saddlebags. The seal was small but, he suspected, Arata would not have left it loose, so he was searching either for a box or a parcel wrapped in cloth. He winced as his hand touched broken glass. A bottle must have been shattered during their wild ride. Carefully, he removed a large shard and was about to throw it away when he caught sight of a silhouetted reflection, its arms raised.

It was a split second. Arata struck downwards with the pommel of his sword, a blunt blow to the back of the neck. It should have knocked him out, but Ryuu was reaching for his sword now. Arata's pommel impacted the muscle in his shoulder, doing no more than buying Arata the time to comprehend his mistake.

Then Ryuu swung at him.

Arata dodged and cut down. Ryuu had pushed close and now felt his brother's sword feather–light across his cheek. It stung like venom. He was closer than he should be. Closer than Yuri would have advised. He used his own to thrust Arata's blade upwards and back, making him stumble.

Already, Ryuu saw desperation on Arata's face, but his own mind was shutting down. He fought to kill; they even said so in the tournaments. Expect no quarter from Akayama. There was no emotion; only technique. The simple one-two of the movements. Step to the left.

Parry.

But, through a haze of learning, discipline, and analysis, the words of his teachers etched into his mind, he started to notice the manner in which Arata held his sword. The younger man's left hand was low on the hilt. Nothing unusual in itself, but, every time he lunged, he corrected himself, as if to cover up something at the base of the katana. As if he meant to protect it.

In thinking about it, Ryuu found himself moving in ways that would again and again force Arata to adjust his grip. It was like dancing with someone who changed every third step. Fascinating. And with each readjustment, he vindicated what Ryuu believed he had seen. Closer still. Until just the bases of the blades met, the ringing metal blows dipping to a low whine, the brothers' breaths coming hard and fast over the sounds of the scuffle. Their faces just inches apart. At least, he thought, in the end, they could look each other in the eye. Arata didn't see him switch to fighting one handed. They were so close now it barely mattered. Force and anger turned them on the spot. He only noticed when Ryuu's hand closed over his own and pushed his katana backwards from the hilt. The blunt back of Arata's own blade, followed by the sharp edge of Ryuu's, struck him, shearing a sliver of skin and muscle from Arata's cheek.

He fell, bellowing, and Ryuu fell with him, engaged now in an entirely different fight.

He was trying to wrest the katana from his brother's hands. In so doing, Ryuu let his own weapon go. Screaming, hollering so that the sound rebounded from the walls of the pass, Arata was like a spoilt child trying to hold onto a toy. A child with half its face torn away. And Ryuu was clawing at the bound hilt of his katana, his fingers already slick with blood and sweat.

When it came loose, Ryuu snarled at his victory. He stumbled back from his brother who just lay there, railing at the sky.

Ryuu held the katana hilt to his ear and shook it. It rattled.

With sticky fingers he started to unscrew the hilt and, as soon as it was loose, he shook the little jade seal into his fingers and glanced up in triumph at his brother.

He was gone.

Ryuu didn't know when Arata had stopped roaring. He had been feverishly intent on the sword and his prize.

He slipped the seal back inside the hilt and rescrewed it, then glanced around. The pass was empty. Even Arata's horse seemed to be gone. He wondered if he was starting to lose his mind. The sudden silence of the empty road filled him with a foolish dread that perhaps he might have fought an apparition. Even the sounds of distant fighting had fallen away and it was hard to gauge whether he had not lost his way and wandered into a soundless dream.

Yet when hell returned, it came from above.

Arata must have climbed up onto the rocks running parallel to the road. He fell suddenly. In a face awash with blood, his eyes remained untouched, like searchlights. His sword was a line of silver filling Ryuu's vision.

It struck the side of his head, knocking him backwards. The sound was more deafening than the pain. And Arata's weight, in the same instant, crushed the breath out of him.

There was blood in his eyes.

He could hear himself breathing, could feel himself struggling out from under his brother, wiping the blood from his hair. He could see Arata staring at him. Struggling to his feet like a drowning man torn free of the ocean, Ryuu noticed he already held one katana, the one that had belonged to his brother. While Arata stood unmoving, he collected the other blood–stained weapon Arata had dropped in his fall.

So now he had both, and the blood was blurring his vision again, and his head had started to throb like a demon.

"Ryuu…"

He ignored his brother's voice. The distancing effect of the fight was wearing away. He had never intended to kill Arata, nor even hurt him. So long as he had the jade seal in his own possession, his brother could go.

All he needed to do now was return to the house.

No–one stopped him. As he mounted, he shakily slipped Arata's sword into his belt and tied the other to his saddle. He hunched a little as he rode. The pain in his head was immense.

The mountain pass was darker, the sun having moved from its zenith. He passed dead soldiers whose blood left black stains on a suddenly grey landscape.

Had it always been this dark?

He reached up to touch the wound in his head. He was lucky that Arata had chosen to strike him with only the flat of the blade. Beneath the swollen skin and morass of blood though, he found something hard. A sliver of bone. And then the pain blinded him.

He was nearly at the end of the pass. Riding into the sunlight, he could no longer see the landscape. Etching it onto a white sheet, someone had missed out important details like the road, the bridge, the house.

He hadn't been lucky, he thought. He hadn't been lucky at all.

His last memory was of how very bright the sky had become, as if he had ridden into the sun.

20. Demons and a Burning Garden

They camped in the shadow of the pass, Takashi Isamu and his men and Akayama Arata and his. It felt odd to be this close. The way the soldiers had talked on the long ride, you might have thought they were taking on some mythical enemy. Takashi's had been quick to spread the rumour of a demon and a witch on the Red Mountain, but with nearly fifty men under joint command, there was little doubt now as to which way the tide would turn. Morale was high, if spiced with an appetite for the supernatural. The stuff of legends. Whatever fate might bring tomorrow, every man here would return as the hero in his own tale, having slain a dragon and challenged the devil.

Only Takashi found himself unable to muster any enthusiasm for the task ahead. There were two people on Akayama. Just two. There was nothing to take pride in here tonight; he alone could not partake of the camaraderie because he understood exactly the kind of cowardice that would lead an army against one man and one woman on the edge of civilisation.

Arata had joined him this evening.

He had watched the young lord throughout their long ride and had been impressed at first by the change in him. He rode at the head of his men with the air of a conquering hero, displaying conviction and courage that even Takashi could see were luminous. There was no question as to why people followed him.

Astonishingly, his appearance had changed little from that of the man, beaten and bound in a cell in Okiri's garrison. His hair was still loose, his eyes a little wild, a rime of unkempt stubble across his chin; but these things, which had seemed evidence back then of an unsettled mind, were transformed by the light of day into the trappings of a rebellious spirit. If there were devils on the mountain, he was one of the more glorious.

He was, amongst other things though, entirely at the mercy of liquor and little, Takashi guessed, could or would change that. He was the kind of sot who functioned only when he was drinking and he did so, throughout the day, from a flask in his saddle–bag and then with the men at night, as if he himself was unaware of his condition. This evening, as he had settled himself down amidst the makeshift nestings of their weapons, saddles, bags and tack, Takashi had asked him bluntly:

"Are you drunk?"

"I hope so."

Takashi watched him. His hands were perfectly steady as he removed his sword from its sheath and began to oil the blade, letting the tip bob inches from the campfire flames. The scent of clove oil intensified in the heat; the effect was intoxicating but not unpleasant. "The last time I was sober, I saw my wife die," Arata said simply, his focus on the blade. "Now, am I telling you that to stop you questioning me or do you ever wonder if I have a heart of sorts, Takashi–*san*?"

The old swordsman didn't answer, but he watched the fire as Arata finished with the blade and retrieved a flask from inside his *kosode*. When the man was drinking again, he chose another tack for conversation:

"Your sword has seen a few decades. Was it passed down within your family?"

"No. Indeed this one"–he patted the weapon–"Is just something I picked up from a man who claimed it had a thirst for blood. My brother stole my own. I intend to retrieve it from him tomorrow." He gave a wolfish grin and Takashi frowned.

"Is your brother worthy of the reputation that precedes him?"

"Is he...Worthy?" The question made Arata unexpectedly thoughtful. Takashi watched him stare dog-eyed into the fire for several heartbeats before he said: "The last time I saw my brother was here, in this gorge, and I had killed him."

"So to his list of accolades we must add 'risen from the dead?'"

"Hm," said Arata, chewing his lower lip and nodding: "He's a stubborn bastard."

"If stubbornness granted life eternal then my father would be lecturing me right now, Akayama–*san*."

Arata chuckled and then spoke with sudden lucidity:

"Ryuu is an extraordinary swordsman. He has skill; he has discipline and perseverance because he dedicated himself to the art many years ago and cultivated his talent day after day. He has the finesse of a poet because he always was one at heart, but the part that he will hide from you to the very last is this, Takashi–*san*: when it comes down to it he can smooth over his own conscience and feel not a thing as he draws your blood. He can be as heartless and as vicious as the devil. Never let him trick you into thinking otherwise." He took a long draught of wine. "He is no match for us, but don't face him alone. I won't. And as for any man that underestimates him, well, let their blood paint the mountain lest its colour fade." He started to laugh.

Takashi didn't trust him. He did not enjoy being led by a man he didn't trust and yet there was something about him that drew you in. He was beguiling in the least likely sense of the word, and a very difficult man to dislike outright. That night, Takashi did not sleep.

赤山

Mei ran over the ornamental bridge, tap–tapping in her sandals, her eyes on her feet and on the ancient boards, which whined softly at her passage. Only as she reached the other side did she look up, smiling as she went:

"See, Arata, see!"

He caught her about the waist, almost as if pulling her into a dance, and then she was still, her back against his chest, both of them staring at the bridge. The last few days had been good. They'd been filled with a purpose and an optimism he thought he had forgotten. "Will you try?" she asked.

"You know, despite what you take me for, I think I have a little sense." He kissed her head and she gave a deep chuckle, which faded as a cloud drifted over the sun.

"It's such an old bridge. It seems sad. How many people do you think those dragons have watched come and go from the house?"

"I don't know, Mei–*san*. Maybe none since they're carved of wood."

"Idiot. They're the guardians here. Why do you think they've agreed to do this?" When he didn't answer, she turned and grinned up at him, perfectly self–aware.

Ever since he had asked her to be a little more ordinary, she had been for the most part, obedient. In the last week though, she had started showing another side to herself.

He might have called it whimsy, but it was more than that. She saw the world from different angles and his entreaties for anything more banal were now being met with open challenges. She was trying to catch him off–guard.

In truth, he might not have been surprised if she'd named every dragon on the bridge and engaged them in conversations while he slept. So long as she followed up such oddities with a smile, they bordered on charming. If she didn't do that, he might one day accept she had lost her mind, but whenever he pondered that possibility, he was forced to conclude there were probably worse places to get lost. "What next?" she asked, bouncing on the balls of her feet.

"Next, I need to practise with my sword. It's been two days. Do you want me to be rusty when they come?" He laughed when she pouted. They had become quite the pair. She never wore her hair up these days and her gowns were only neat for the first few hours of the day before she started hitching them up to more easily navigate the paths of the mountain. Today, he thought, she was more beautiful than ever. Back when he had woken weeks before he had thought her quite plain: her attire simple, her hair bound, her gestures and voice adjusted to suit the unwritten rules of his household. Today she was dressed in a loose yellow kimono of fine silk and her hair, which the sun had lately stained a reddish brown at the tips, lay untamed across her shoulders. When she spoke, when she moved, she was entirely unaware of any of the things he saw in her, that she touched something deep within him. "You can watch if you wish."

"When I was young, the farm boys in the village used to strip to the waist and pretend to be famous warriors, brandishing staves made out of our neighbours' broken fencing, and the girls used to stand around like swooning ladies as if they might be saved by heroes from their dull existence."

"Were you one of the girls?" he asked, letting her go so that he could collect a long-bow he had left on the side of the path. He could no longer risk moving about the estate without it.

"No, I used to think it was far more fun to take a branch myself and knock the legs out from underneath the proudest boys." She ran her hands back through her hair, smiling: "Don't imagine you're so beautiful I need to watch you swat flies for the next two hours."

"I wasn't! And anyway, it'll be a while before I can get the image of you stripped to the waist and beating farm boys out of my head." He gave her a mischievous grin and turned towards the terraces.

"Arata..." He looked back, expecting some kind of reprimand and was surprised when he saw her head was tilted downwards, her eyes dark with sincerity or concern, or something of each: "Before you go..."

"Swatting flies."

"Hm." Her lips quirked a little at that. "I wanted to ask you if you dreamed last night."

"If I dreamed?"

"You wept," she said, watching him. "I was awake and I think you were asleep and dreaming."

"I have bad dreams sometimes," he admitted. "You don't need to...Please don't–"

"Would you tell me if you remembered?"

He stared at her. That uncanny ability to cut through to the truth. Was it really so obvious?

"I wish I did. They're nightmares really. Sometimes I'm fighting; sometimes there are strangers all around. Mei, I forget them the moment I wake." She studied his face almost as if she suspected he might be lying. " You know how, when you die, you are reborn – maybe as a person, maybe as a hummingbird or a snow monkey?" He smiled and touched her cheek. "Like that. They're not me. I don't know if they will be or if some day they'll make sense but"–she leaned into his touch–"If I had one wish, it would be that you–that you cherish me as I am now. I don't know if I can ever go back to being that man, though I know – I do know – that it is he whom you married and not me. I am jealous of him."

She put her head on one side, looking almost amused:

"Why, Arata–*san*, did you not just wish for your memories back?"

Before he could tell her that yes, that made more sense, a sound rent the air. It was a little like a bell, a little like a cymbal, clear and distant. He saw Mei's eyes widen, her lips part.

A few days ago they had rigged up a device on the rocks above the pass: a steel tray strung between two posts with a wooden spoon poised above it and from this, a thin thread running straight across the road. Mei's idea. Anyone coming through the pass would be unlikely to notice such a tiny thing, but once disturbed, the spoon would fall against the tray, making a sound like a warning bell long before they might have had a chance to hear hoof beats.

"It could be nothing," he said. But it didn't feel like it. Clear and bright and marring the quiet of the afternoon.

It had been a game. Climbing up there, setting it in place. All of it a game to fill their minds. That and the plans they had made.

Now, facing the possibility that each must be set in motion, the heady optimism of the past few days shattered. The weight of the sky bore down on him. It would have been easier simply to face them, to fight one on one. Nothing so elaborate as the things she had asked him to do. He realised he had his hands on Mei's shoulders. "Don't..."

"I told you, he will not kill me." She snatched his hand, kissed his fingers and, just like that, turned and started to run back the way she had come, darting across the bridge.

He wanted her to have said more. He wanted to reassure her that they would be alright, or tell her he was in love with her, or even tell her good-bye: some acknowledgement that they had come this far. If Takashi was coming through the pass, then this, all of this, would be decided before nightfall.

But she had gone without a word. And willing the numbness from his hands, he crouched, took a deep breath, and strung the bow.

赤山

Mei knew they would have one opportunity, and one alone, to split the horsemen. The fewer Ryuu had to fight at any one time, the more chance he would have of killing them, but still she had not been prepared for the numbers that emerged from the pass like a black tide. The ground thrummed with their hoof beats.

She ran towards them.

Ryuu had detested this plan, her plan. She was the one who made all the plans. Ryuu had had such a look in his eyes these last few days, as if he was hoping to stand in the midst of a storm and let it tear him apart, and all she could think was that she would never forgive him if he didn't fight to the bitter end, not with honour or virtue, but by the very skin of his teeth, clawing, brawling, biting, tearing. Death, she had decided, was not noble. She would never forgive him if he chose it. And it was by sheer stubbornness that she had corralled him into this strategy. Because he was the target; he was the threat. In order to make them follow her then, she had to make herself easier to catch.

Not that she was planning to be caught.

She paused only briefly. Some of the horsemen had slowed as they left the road, but on seeing her, they slammed their heels into their mounts' sides and at that, she ran. Down across the courtyard and into the orchard, as far as the cliff–edge where Ryuu had once stood contemplating Kyoko's words. She didn't look back. For this to work, they had to trust one another. And she trusted him. She told herself, she trusted him.

A heavy scent hung in the long grasses beneath the trees. If the horsemen had looked closely as they slowed their mounts to wade into the tangled undergrowth, they might have seen the dark stains splashed across the roots. The orchard smelt acrid and unnatural, a perfume so strong that Mei was certain they would notice.

Feeling like a ghost, she began to walk along the cliff-edge, away from the house. She sensed, rather than saw, the horsemen spreading out through the trees, and concentrated on her footing. This close to the edge even she had to be careful. It was all a part of the illusion, of course. She had suspected Takashi did not want her dead and his soldiers' hesitation was confirmation. They were afraid she would jump.

Still keeping her eyes down, she reached the edge of the orchard and the path running down to the waterfall. The terrible smell was behind her. She could breathe again and she stopped, pausing where she stood to utter one word under her breath. "Now."

And as if he had heard her, the whine of Ryuu's arrow filled the air. The horses shuffled in the long grass as their riders shifted to follow the missile's course, but they were already too late.

Mei took a deep breath and started to run again. The arrow thudded into the ground a few feet behind her.

There was a crackle, the smell of smoke. A sudden roar as the oil–drenched grass ignited, and the cherry trees went up like flares. And from where she was, she could feel the wall of heat at her back. The men began to scream.

Ryuu was blinkered in his reliance on the sword. There were so many other weapons on the mountain; there were so many ways to kill.

She darted straight out across the path and into the bamboo thicket beside the *dojo*.

It would be a fool's errand to send horses in amongst the broken stems and, as she had known they would, those who still pursued her reined in on the path. She kept going. Slower now. Picking her way through the strange geometry of green. The bamboo had always been a secret, inhospitable world. Away from the path, the sounds of dying men and burning gardens were suddenly muffled. Damp hung in the air. Birds fluted between the higher shoots, and her own breath hissed in and out as her body reminded her of her exertion.

Don't look back. Keep going.

She concentrated on the broken stems. She couldn't risk an injury now. The men might have boots and knives to hack through the undergrowth, but she had balance and silence on her side.

Behind one of the tallest clusters, she dropped down on her knees. There was space enough here for her to hide and there were three long spears of bamboo sequestered in the heart of the plant. She stared at them.

Of course, it had been a fine enough plan when she had come up with it. Go to ground here, defend herself if necessary, then when she was free to do so, descend the rest of the way, down past the waterfall and across a make-shift bridge of saplings to the broken path that wound around the mountain. It was the plan she had explained to Ryuu many weeks ago beside the waterfall. She was to heave the bridge of saplings in behind her, thus leaving herself marooned on the outcropping, safe from the swordsmen. He would come for her when it was over. A fine enough plan.

But looking at the freshly-sharpened spears, she felt sick to the stomach. It was one thing to believe you could kill; another to do so. She wasn't squeamish. She just wasn't like Ryuu. She'd never had anyone show her how to use a sword, had never felt the resistance in another's body. How much force would it need? She took the first spear and rested the butt in her lap, leaning her cheek against the smooth green as she listened. The forest was a trickster. There were soft sounds everywhere.

She listened instead for rhythms.

She hadn't expected them to follow her here. This hideout had been a last resort, but she had known, the moment she had seen their numbers in the pass, that she would have to come here. There were easily enough men to chase her and plenty more to go after Ryuu.

A woodpecker clattered somewhere, making her start.

Leaves fell down and settled on her shoulders and in her hair. There was a tear on her cheek, already a warm stripe of moisture. Funny because she associated tears with pity, but this one had come from nowhere and it was treacherous in its willingness to mourn.

Something shuffled in the undergrowth.

She straightened, hardly daring to breathe. Her hands had started to sweat, warming the bamboo in her hands. It was not a gun or a sword and the truth was that all she had now was the element of surprise.

Two men were approaching, glimpsed between the green lines. There had been more, she thought. Two might mean many things: that they already knew her hiding place or that the others waited on the path. Either way, they expected it to be easy. She'd be damned before she gave them easy.

Delicately, she removed one sandal and planted her foot atop a young shoot. It had been broken, leaving a flat enough tip that she could balance her weight upon it. Stepping up, she was now at least a foot above where they would expect her and that, at least, played to her advantage.

They rounded the cluster of bamboo at the same moment. She lunged towards the first man.

It was uncalculated in the end. The spear sunk into his shoulder. At least she thought it did. It caught on something. Remained upright, standing in his arm like some kind of abhorrent decoration. He roared in pain.

The other man caught her around the waist and she struggled and twisted in his grip so that she'd turned her body to face him when she jammed her thumbs into his eyes, wincing as they sunk back into his skull and his scream became a high-pitched keen. He clawed blindly at his sword, releasing her.

She was running again.

She felt a sense of elation as she reached the road, but it lasted only as long as the illusion that she was alone.

They collided with her from the side, heavy shadows, pushing her from the path as she stumbled and a powerful blow fell across her shoulders. She'd barely registered the first before it came again, driving her into the mud. She covered her head. The rich, deep smells of the earth were in her nose, on her lips. A third strike across her belly knocked the breath from her.

She lay gasping.

A sword, no, a sword still sheathed in its scabbard, now rested with its tip on her sternum. A soldier stood panting above her. She wrapped one hand around the *saya* and the motion made him increase the pressure on her chest tenfold until that alone made her fingers loose and sensationless. Her vision blurred and she was aware only distantly of the men who joined her attacker.

She did know that the knife Ryuu had given her was gone. She had kept it in her collar since he'd gifted it to her, despite knowing what she did of its past, and now that the familiar weight was absent she felt a wave of despair. Whatever happened, he couldn't know that they had captured her. He couldn't know that he had failed.

赤山

"You cowards!" Takashi hollered at the horsemen who had wheeled back towards the pass. "He is one man!"

He and Arata had reined in beneath the shadow of the cliffs just as the scene had descended into chaos. Too many soldiers were fleeing from the flames. Worse still were the unfortunates who came stumbling from the blaze, transformed into human torches. He had seen several throw themselves from the cliff as they burned. And any who went to help found themselves within range of a constant stream of arrows. These same men who had cajoled one another with stories of devils and ghosts had believed their own words and seen them brought to life.

Arata took it all in with a lingering smile on his lips.

"This is going to be interesting," he told Takashi. The older man just stared at him.

"Did you know he would do this?"

"I thought him capable, but I never realised he would discover that for himself. I told you. Never underestimate him. I used to believe he was on my side." He urged his horse forward, onto the bridge between the two halves of the estate.

The arrows were originating from the edge of a copse on the far side. Looking closely, it appeared a simple mortar wall had been constructed there, no doubt for the very purpose of giving a bowman the advantage; the site overlooked both the courtyard and the orchard. Takashi was torn briefly between following and trying to rally his men, but Arata proceeded with a compelling inevitability, and Takashi turned towards Shuru and Homura who had followed him into the lee of the cliffs. They were the last two men under his sole command. The rest, who fell in behind them, were Arata's soldiers. "With me," he said, and detested himself as his voice wavered over the words.

He realised, even as he urged his mount onto the bridge, that it was strange Ryuu did not turn his arrows on them. The *daimyo* had enough targets in the orchard and the courtyard, it was true, but it was those horsemen who processed across the bridge who now posed the greater threat.

Takashi discovered, halfway across, why they had been spared.

His own horse had fallen into step behind Arata's. The young commander rode close to the cliff; it was something Takashi had noticed, that he avoided heights where possible, and so both horses had hugged the near-side of the bridge, where a series of struts held it fast against the rock. The other horsemen came two by two.

Takashi heard a sound then that he had only ever heard once before in his life. In the forest as a child, an ancient tree that must have stood for a century or longer, had been a lair of sorts for him, with imaginary halls and caverns between its interlacing roots. One day, as he had played, he'd heard a sound like groaning thunder, and one of the vast branches had peeled itself free of the trunk. Slowly at first. Then splintering, tearing.

This was the sound. First a whining groan, then an agonised splintering as fully half the bridge began to rip itself loose. Arata slammed his heels into his horse's flanks. Takashi would have done the same had his animal not slipped. Behind him, to his right, he realised, the bridge was gone. He could see shapes falling, his own world tilting. He felt the horse beneath him scramble for its life and knew that he was helpless. Its hooves scraped on the wood, its hindquarters dipping. Then finding purchase. Then he at least was on the still extant part of the bridge, the part closest to the cliff. To his right, all the balustrades had fallen, and the ends of the old beams hung, like torn teeth, snagging out over the drop.

He urged his now jittery animal off of the bridge, thinking that at least half of Ryuu's plan had failed. Enough of the bridge remained that riders could cross single file. Then he realised it was probably meant to be that way. To have demolished the whole thing would have left Ryuu stranded. It had been just one more way to thin their numbers.

He looked behind him at those who remained on the bridge. Shuru and Homura were not among them. It would have been hard to explain to Arata what that meant, but the young nobleman, whose expression was implacable as ever, seemed to understand. He saw the hunger in Takashi's eyes.

"Alive," Arata said.

And Takashi knew he meant that Ryuu was to be captured, not killed, but in that moment, the word seemed too apt, as if Arata knew, and how could he possibly know, that for the first time in years, in a haze of anger and intent, Takashi felt just that. Alive.

He'd had Akayama Ryuu prone before him eight weeks ago and had neither understood what he was seeing nor had the courage to end the life of a dying man. As he approached now, Takashi could not deny that this was the same man, though altered. He had something of his brother about him. There were similarities in their looks, but it went deeper than that. If Arata was a demon then Ryuu was a god within his domain. His skin, a burnt umber, was the same colour as the mountain. His hair, too, at its tips, had been lightened to warm reds and browns by the sunlight, as if he had spent every day since his wakening out here on the terraces and in the gardens, infused over time by the mountain's spirits. And if Takashi was in any doubt as to who or what he was fighting, the focus in Ryuu's eyes should have doused his uncertainty.

The horsemen had reined in. As Takashi watched, Ryuu set down the bow stepped forward, sword low, as it would be in the first stance of a duel or tournament. Then, slowly, as if inviting them, he spread his arms wide, his smile that of the devil. "Alive," said Arata again.

Takashi raised his sword above his head.

His roar was wordless, but it was enough for the horsemen behind him. They streamed past, a tide of bright flanks and tails, clattering, rasping leather armour and thunder, cutting the lawns with their hooves. Muscles that severed the earth.

Takashi had never seen anyone fight the way he did.

It was not the way Ryuu moved; it was the lack of forethought. It was as if he saw every choice his enemy made before they made it. Long before they realised their intentions, he was there. There was a deadly beauty in that. Takashi felt it. Like that of a predator in the full throes of the hunt, of a forest fire, of a skeleton stripped by flies and decay and left behind in the perfect semblance of life. It was the beauty of this world in its totality, filled with every colour from frivolity to violence to death in all its forms. It moved the human soul to terror but raised it too beyond impermanence.

And like nature, which was capable of pulling forth life from death, Takashi realised, there was an efficiency in his motions, which meant not one was wasted. He did not unhorse the men. There was no need if he could strike them as they rode. It seemed to Takashi that he waited for one, just one, in the furore, ducking the blades and blows of others in a stream of motion that looked haphazard. His eyes would follow a single man until, as if by chance, he would be brought into a sudden and deadly confrontation with his target. The soldier would fall. He would move onto the next.

Takashi had ridden to the edge of the fray. All at once he realised that there were now more men dead or dying than fighting in the whirlwind. Not all were courageous either. Several had either fled or were hanging back, perhaps as much out of incredulity as cowardice. Takashi saw Arata wheel away from the fight and canter back towards the bridge and felt a wave of disgust that the young noble would run. Until he realised why.

Arata dismounted at the bridge.

Three men were crossing, two of whom were contending with a prisoner. Mei was fighting them as best she could, but even from here it was clear she would have no chance of escape. As Arata dismounted and approached, she ceased her struggle. Indeed the life seemed to go out of her and her knees buckled. The men alone kept her on her feet. A brief exchange of words and they handed her over to Arata.

Takashi turned back to the fight. There was blood on Ryuu's face and shoulder, but whether his own or someone else's, he had no way of knowing. Those grey eyes focused on him though, and he felt his body sing with a deadly hunger. Today, Takashi Isamu would fight for his life and for the lives of all those who had ever meant anything to him. He did not wait, but, as Ryuu skirmished with an injured soldier, he dismounted and drew his sword.

Do not face him alone, Arata had said. He no longer cared.

Ryuu bared his teeth and there was blood in his mouth too.

"Takashi…"

"Just the same. Have you had enough yet? You must be in pain." This close, he could see that most of the blood was Ryuu's own. He was not immortal, but if any of those blows were fatal, he was as yet unaware that he was dead. Takashi let his own wild hatred show in a grimace and the whites of his eyes: "You are finished, Akayama!"

"Not until it's done!"

Dead or not, Ryuu struck with the same savage grace as ever, and Takashi was reminded of Inuko's words as he had lain dying in Okiri. There was something wrong with this man.

His decisions did not register in his eyes. In fact, Takashi suspected, those same grey eyes were clouded with unimaginable pain. It was only this dislocate between body and mind that allowed him to go on. Still there was no let up. Takashi grunted again and again as he was forced to parry. Every time he thought he had a strike, Ryuu found a weakness to exploit: in his stance, in his grip. He had never felt so full of openings.

"Ryuu!" That was Arata's voice. It elicited no reaction in his brother and, Takashi realised, he was going to lose if this continued. He was sliding backwards in the pounded mud, his boots growing heavy with it.

"Brother!" A glimmer of recognition. Takashi tried to act, but Ryuu's blade moved too fast and he could not avoid it in time. A line appeared through his shirt, and filled immediately with scarlet. Ryuu sneered and raised his sword again as Arata shouted, "I will kill her, Brother!"

A change.

Ryuu turned at the threat. Takashi was aware of the sudden pause. Aware of Arata behind him, holding a knife to the girl's throat. The captain struck without thinking. Instinct and experience. If he had chosen it, he could have taken Ryuu's head.

Alive, Arata had said.

He stopped the blade at Ryuu's throat. The *daimyo* stiffened, but never took his eyes from Mei. Had he let the blade carry on clean through, Takashi realised, Ryuu still would not have taken his eyes off Mei.

"Get on your knees," Takashi said roughly.

He didn't do so immediately. Mei was already kneeling at Arata's feet, her whole demeanour one of apology. Despite the knife, her chin was down. From where Takashi stood he could see her lips pressed together in a thin, flat line. "Get down on your knees, Akayama." This time, Ryuu did, and closed his eyes. The swift end he so clearly expected would have satisfied Takashi. "Let me kill him."

"I need something off him," said Arata.

"Be quick."

"You take the girl."

He pushed Mei towards Takashi and crouched down before his brother, moving to take Ryuu's weapon from his hand. He examined it. Ryuu watched him with lidded eyes as Arata shook his head and plunged the sword downwards into the mud just out of arm's reach. "You took my sword, Ryuu."

"Is that what this is about?" snarled Takashi.

"No, he knows what this is about."

But Takashi found himself looking closely at the man at his sword–tip. He thought his demeanour had changed. Expecting death, Ryuu had closed his eyes and waited, but as his brother had addressed him, he had opened them again, distant and unfocused at first, but gradually, gradually, they had filled with an emotion. It looked a little like fear, but no, what was it that Inuko had said?

He was lost. That was it. He looked like someone who had lost his way. "You know, don't you, Ryuu?" Arata growled. Yet Ryuu's eyes fell away from his brother, coming to rest on the girl. And as Takashi watched, their eyes met. And there was no doubting the fear in her eyes.

"Mei," Ryuu said, "What have you done?"

21. Wildflowers

Arata pushed Mei into the room ahead of him. She was trembling from head to foot. The change in Ryuu had been complete, from one moment to the next, he had been paralysed. At first stiff with disbelief, then empty. An emptiness she hadn't seen in weeks. Not since he had first woken.

He had recognised Arata. It had pained her to witness one further change: Ryuu had begun to seek his brother's trust. He'd begun to explain what Mei had told him, had begun to beg Arata for details, for forgiveness, for understanding. But his brother had refused to believe him. Mei had been forced to watch Arata strike him several times with heavy punches that left his nose and lips more bloodied than before.

At no time did Ryuu resist his brother. His eyes were wide and blank throughout.

When Arata finally stopped, he left Ryuu belly down in the mud.

She'd scrambled forward then. The lawn had been churned into a mire by men and horses, yet Takashi had let her go. Clumsy, she had reached him, at which a tremor of life had taken hold of him and he had shoved her away. The rest blurred.

At one point Arata had knelt down beside her. Ryuu had been bent double and on his knees in the mud, and Arata had whispered into her ear:

"Did you intend to take every piece of his dignity before you let him die?"

She had known, had always known, what she was risking. One day, she'd believed, he would remember himself and, sometimes, in her fantasies, he forgave her the lies. In others, he left her. It had never once occurred to her that the truth she had kept hidden would be the one weapon that could fell him more effectively than any sword. And she had never foreseen it might be wielded by Arata.

She looked around the room they had brought her to. She hadn't been here since a dim evening a world away, when she and Ryuu had spoken freely for the first time, and he had shown her these same woodcuts, pictures that now gazed out at her from every surface and every wall with wistful, dreaming eyes.

She hadn't come here and only now did she realise why.

Because he lived, she had never thought to mourn him. Because he had been in danger, she had tried to help, and she had done things wrong. Oh, so many things! But somehow, she had believed she was saving him, that there was something to be saved. Now, looking around at the artworks he had collected and commissioned in life, she felt something wither inside her.

She had been fooling herself. All that remained was an after–image of a man and, as much as she had captured it and held it to the light, it had never regained its form. The Ryuu she had known, the one who had seemed at times fierce, at times teasing, at times arrogant;

the one who had stood on that cliff–edge and closed his eyes, and whom she had pledged she would save; he had been stolen from her long weeks ago. And the man that she was cursed to love now was thin, almost transparent. Only the trail of a comet.

She looked at the woodcuts. Ochre coloured warriors bleached into cherry wood raised their swords and rode into battle on fan–tailed ponies.

Courtesans lay dripping blossoms on eternal sunny afternoons.

Stories.

Mei covered her mouth with both her hands to stifle a howl of grief as she turned round on the spot, finding herself surrounded on all sides by pieces of his imagination. She fell forward onto her knees, closing her eyes, but it was all still there when she opened them.

There was a weight on her chest and she could feel her breaths coughing against her hands. Still she could not afford to let herself weep. She was listening, listening for some sound that would tell her when they killed him.

Arata returned after a time. He was no longer carrying a sword, but now had a flintlock jammed into the back of his obi. He closed the door behind him, staring at her, and she staggered to her feet.

"Don't touch me! Don't you ever touch me!" Her voice had barbs. It no longer sounded like her own.

He said nothing but moved over to the drawers and cupboards and writing desks. He started to rifle through them. And after a long time, he addressed her, his manner almost civilised:

"I'm looking for a seal. You may have seen it. It is carved of green jade."

She rubbed a hand across her face. He was searching with too much efficiency for this to be a game.

"What do you need it for?"

"It shouldn't concern you." He pulled out one drawer and emptied it onto the floor. It pleased her that he was probably not going to find anything he needed here. Neither she nor Ryuu had been into this room for weeks. Thinly she asked:

"Where is Ryuu?"

"In my chamber." He looked up. "He has begged Takashi to let him end his own life."

"You're lying!"

"Why would I need to lie? You think there is anything left for him?"

"I hate you!" She wanted to tear at his face with her bare hands, reduce him to nothing more than flesh and viscera, but her own skin crawled in his presence and a mixture of fear and revulsion kept her pressed up against the wall, as far from him as she could be in the small space.

He finished going through the desks on this side of the curtain and glanced up.

"This place is a prison, isn't it, Mei? It gets into your soul."

"Let me see him!"

"Why would he want to see you? You destroyed him." He upended another drawer onto the floor. "I don't even recognise that man."

A dry sob escaped her and he glanced up, going very still where he stood crouched over the contents of the cupboards. "My cold princess! Did the summer come too late for you? By the time you realised even your own heart could thaw, had you already fed him your poison?"

"You're the one who's poison!"

"You used to sound convincing, Mei. Now you just sound scared." He continued to watch her, a glimmer of fascination in his eyes. She recalled that expression from before, so that she knew his next words were designed to hurt, because she understood only too well how he loved to choose his victories. "I told him about you and I, of course."

She pressed the back of her forefinger into her mouth and bit down hard enough to make the pain eclipse all else. Still her breaths were catching in her throat. He had risen to his feet and had approached her as if witnessing her succumb to this was worthy of his full attention. "He tried to rationalise it; started to tell me some of the things you and he had done…Nothing we didn't share first, I told him." Her legs gave way beneath her and she slid down, curling up over a wave of sobbing.

His tone changed: "Why him, Mei? Why, after everything? You turned Kyoko against me. Now my brother. Everyone I cared about…"

"It wasn't me!" she moaned. "It was you. It was always you. You came here to kill your brother. What does that make you?"

"I came here to finish what he started. He put me out of this house!" he snarled. "He took away everything I was!"

"He loved you. Why else is he listening to you, even now? Ask yourself that, Arata. He couldn't remember anything but he knew you as soon as he saw you!"

"He is a shadow over all of my life. Beyond this estate, Mei, my name is a curse. It does not matter if I am skilled in a trade or can wield a blade, they will not employ a samurai. Am I to live a lie forever, take another name, pretend he never wronged me? No. When the house falls, I am free."

"The House is fallen," she whispered.

"Not while he lives. He is the House."

She dropped her head into her arms again, feeling as if she was melting into herself. He just stood there while she cried.

After a time, she heard him move away to the other half of the chamber.

She could hear him sifting through papers on the writing desk. She lifted her head, seeing the white curtain that divided the room ripple in a faint breeze as her vision shifted in and out of focus between her tears; tears that turned the colours of the chamber to stained glass.

"You never answered my question," Arata said from behind the curtain. "A jade seal?"

"No," she murmured.

"If not the seal then perhaps you know where my sword is."

The swords! Her breathing hastened:

"He put them in the gardens."

Arata stopped and swiped the curtain back to stare at her:

"The gardens? Where in the gardens?"

"Different places so that he could use them to fight."

"You're lying. Not even my brother would be so stupid and, anyway, the summer's air would rot the blades."

"But we always knew we had only days."

He scowled.

"You know where they are?"

"Some but not all."

"Do you know where mine is?"

She swallowed.

"He said it was in the field of wild flowers."

"What?" He stepped back into the anteroom. "Where is that? In the grounds?"

"I don't know exactly. He didn't say."

Arata gave a bitter smile:

"He's the only one who knows then?"

And she nodded, wondering if he could hear her heart trying to beat out of her chest with hope.

赤山

Ryuu sat with his back against the wall and his chin on his chest. With his eyes closed, he could map the pains in his body: cuts on his arms, bruises on his face; he'd bitten down hard enough on his tongue that there was a lingering taste of blood. Had any of Takashi's soldiers inflicted a direct cut, he would be dead, but he had taken innumerable glancing blows, and their swords had left open wounds on the back of his forearm: shallow slices where he'd been forced to defend himself. At the time it had felt like they had been small sacrifices to make for his life. And hers. Now it felt as if he would sooner shed his skin like a snake than heal and be whole again. Arata's final blows had left his head ringing.

He had not expected pity.

Nor did he pity himself. But she had changed everything and thinking of it sickened him. How he had trusted so completely.

She was an illusion. She had come to the house, Arata had said, as a whore from the villages. She had seduced him. At the time, Arata had been married to a woman called Shirakawa Kyoko.

Kyoko. That was how Ryuu knew he was telling the truth. Unlike Mei who, he realised now, formed her stories after the fact, Arata spoke of things he already knew, discoveries he had made that Mei had explained away, but which, in his brother's picture, suddenly made sense. And the more he spoke, the more he undid her lies.

Mei's affair with Arata drove his wife to take her life.

There had been a reckoning and Arata had wanted Ryuu to send her away, but when it came down to it, in a past he could not remember, Ryuu had sided with Mei and turned against his brother. Arata had been left rootless, with only the clothes on his back. He had returned to take vengeance on Ryuu for the shame he had brought to him and to the household but, even that, it seemed, would no longer be possible.

"You fought me as you always did," Arata had said, crouching before him. "You fought me to kill me," his brother was saying, and Ryuu had felt the other man's presence like a force. Arata had a power over him, he realised, but he couldn't recall whether its force lay in affection or in fear. Arata had lifted the hair from the scar on his brow and spoken with regret: "I thought, in return, that I had killed you, Ryuu. Do you know how heavily that weighed on my conscience. Yet, in time, I heard you lived. You and the woman." He sat back on his heels and rubbed his mouth. "This house was mocked in the courts – a lord and a village woman refusing to show their faces? Do you know what they said of us? Of me, because I bear your name?"

"We were held against our will."

"No…No, no. Did she tell you that?"

Ryuu tried to recall, but his memory, even of the last six weeks, was suddenly muddy. When had Ibuko come to the house? It hadn't been that long after he woke. By then Takashi had been holding them hostage.

But no.

If Takashi and Arata had been together all this time then he'd had no reason to keep hostages. It had been Mei who'd explained Ibuko's motivations; Mei who had told him about Takashi. Hadn't it? Panicking, he realised he couldn't recall. Her lies had bled into the landscape, into the very foundations of the House, into the few weeks he had had, colouring everything.

"I don't remember."

"Of course they sent men in the end, Ryuu. What were we supposed to do. Six weeks and the House is the hands of a woman of no background, no family, no standing…And this is what she wanted!" Arata hissed in frustration and rose to his feet, jabbing his chest as he began to pace. "Exactly what she wanted! For you and I to be at one another's throats and the whole estate in her hands."

"How could this—how could this work in her favour?"

"She knew we would kill each other," he said, as if it were the most certain thing in the world.

"No." Despite himself, Ryuu was assailed by a sudden memory of her body flush against his own. She had seemed to burn against him at night; sometimes the only source of warmth he had ever known. And she had loved him.

But she had kept him here.

There had been a world beyond the estate; it had never really taken form in his head and yet now he was fiercely aware of how naïve he must have been. Had he left Akayama and ventured into Okiri, sooner or later he would have realised…

"Our line is ended," said Arata, ceasing to pace, and it seemed that despair overcame him because he slumped suddenly, his face turned away from Ryuu. "My only worth lies with your name, and we are come to this."

"Did you think I did this on purpose? I remember nothing, Arata! Nothing!"

"And what made you think you could continue on this estate alone? Your own pride? Your arrogance?"

Ryuu's breath caught as he realised how it would seem from the outside. He and Mei had cloistered themselves in this world. At very least, it was a flight of fancy, but over and above that, it was an oversight of his duties, the encroachment of his own ignorance. He had let her play him.

"I believed her."

Arata glanced at him.

"She has a way." Something in the way he spoke made Ryuu look up. Arata nodded towards the futon. "She is very…convincing."

For some time after that, Ryuu had only stared at his brother's back; the hunched shoulders, the unkempt hair. He had seen the similarities between them; in their features, in their gaits, in their gestures. He could not release himself from the sense that he was connected to this man by cords that wound deeper than even he understood, and the dissonance between them was unbearable. The knowledge that he had lain with Mei did not anger him; it only shaded in another part of the truth.

Arata had risen to his feet then: "I did not want to come here and kill you, Ryuu. I would have for the sake of this House, but this"—he had gestured to his brother—"Seeing you brought to this, by my hand, I cannot forgive myself. What honour is there in killing you now? A man who cannot recall his crime. And, for this, we are both condemned."

Ryuu had pressed the back of one hand to his mouth, almost as if he could stifle the sense he had of falling.

"I could take my own life, Arata," he had murmured.

Arata had glanced down at him appraisingly. It had surprised Ryuu to see that the suggestion did not elicit more emotion in his brother. There was almost the sense that Arata had waited for this.

"Is that what you want?" he'd asked.

Ryuu wasn't certain. He did know that he wasn't afraid and that such a gesture would clear the name of Akayama, but he wasn't certain of wanting anything anymore, or feeling anything clearly. It seemed he was back again, at the very beginning, staring out at an unknown world. Only this time it was not only his memories that were gone; he had run out of time too.

赤山

Takashi was kneeling in the hallway outside the room where they held Ryuu, cleaning his blade, oiling and gritting it. He didn't look up as Arata returned. He wasn't in the mood for the younger man's company, but Arata hesitated as he passed:

"Did you want the girl?"

Takashi looked up.

"Why are you asking me that?"

"I am no longer interested in her."

Takashi watched him continue on past Ryuu's chamber and stop on the edge of the light. There was no oil left in the stores so they'd been frugal with the lamps. The captain gripped a piece of rice paper in his teeth as he buffed the blade. He didn't know whether he would need to use it again tonight, but force of habit was strong.

"What do you think?" Arata asked after a long time. Takashi removed the folded paper and set it aside to replug the vial of oil. The question was not about Mei.

"I think it's dusk and we have to spend another night on this damned mountain."

"She said my sword is in a field full of wildflowers."

"Wildflowers?"

"The way she said it...She wants me to tell him. I can't help but think it's some kind of code between them." Takashi considered this and was willing to concede it was a possibility, but he had seen Ryuu's condition and doubted that even a full pardon would rouse the man from a stupor of indifference. The emptiness in his eyes had grown worse since Arata had visited him and, Takashi suspected, there was more to it than was apparent from the outside.

"What's so important about your sword?"

"You've seen the rest of this house. Everything of value is gone."

Takashi yawned behind his hand. He decided not to tell him about Mei's payment of fine silks and trinkets still stored in the coffers in Okiri.

"Here, I've cleaned up the blade you were using before."

"I told you. That's just something I picked up," said the younger man.

"It cuts. Take it."

With a scowl, Arata returned to where he was kneeling. Takashi studied him squarely as he stowed the sword on his hip. He was a cruel man. Of that there was no doubt. Effortlessly cruel. But he was also passionate and stupid and driven in a manner that made others want to follow in his wake. Takashi thought he might also be mad, but he wasn't entirely sure.

Certainly he was not dull. And it was the volatility of his nature, the way he approached all things with a kind of reckless abandon, oblivious to those about him, that made someone like Takashi, plodding dutiful Takashi, want to steer his course.

Maybe it was for that reason that men followed him, or found themselves sucked into his games. Not Takashi. He would be pleased to see the last of Akayama Arata and, in any case, they were in joint command now. One was not following the other.

Even if Takashi had spent the last half hour cleaning his sword for him.

"Who is watching Ryuu?" Arata asked.

"Two of your men. If you give him a knife he will gut himself and save us the trouble, I think. What did you say to him?"

The side of Arata's mouth quirked up as if he saw something amusing in the question.

"It would solve things, wouldn't it? I've never seen him like that before."

"Really?" said Takashi. "Will you let him?"

"For all that he might want that, I am not giving him any kind of weapon."

"You'd talk a man into that and then refuse?"

"Who said I talked him into it?"

Takashi decided not to answer. He wanted nothing more to do with either of them if truth be told. "You are still willing to kill him, I trust, after we are done? It was revenge you wanted, after all," said Arata.

"I will kill him, but, when it comes to revenge, I think you have done enough."

Arata gave a ghostly smile:

"Takashi Isamu is grown soft."

"Contrary to what you imagine killing to be, Arata–kun," he said, getting to his feet and replacing his own blade. "I have killed over a hundred men, and not one of those was out of revenge."

Arata leered:

"You must be very proud."

"I don't like you," Takashi said. Arata threw his head back and laughed. Then when he was composed again, he shot Takashi a handsome grin:

"Wildflowers!"

"What do you intend?"

赤山

Moonlight glinted off of the mud on the path. Ryuu's footsteps were uneven in the half dark, his muscles complaining at every step, though the pain from his previous exertions was nothing compared to the pounding in his head now, whether it was his own heartbeat or a phantom drum ushering in a dirge. He had exhausted himself in the previous fight and it was taking a heavier toll on him than he was prepared to admit. He shook himself and glanced back.

Behind him, the path that led up to the house was a ribbon of broken moonlight. He could see his brother's silhouette at the trail–head, one arm raised. Arata held a gun trained on the *daimyo*.

Apparently the younger man no longer trusted the paths of the estate, having watched his men burn to death in the cherry orchard and fall from the sabotaged bridge. Mei's strange little lie about Ryuu having hidden a sword amongst the wildflowers had unsettled him still further, so that now Ryuu, with his hands bound awkwardly behind him, was meant to demonstrate their way was clear.

Nothing made sense anymore, and nothing was familiar.

Even in this, her lie was senseless.

She had been the one to hide the swords, not him. Even if she had believed Arata would let him live a little longer for this, it only prolonged the inevitable.

"Keep going," Arata called. "I'll tell you when to stop."

The field of wildflowers.

It had taken him a moment at first to remember that Mei had said it was up above the waterfall. Back then, she had claimed that it was a place they had often visited together. Now the lie was like a fresh wound. Why there? It had seemed to be a message for him, but if she had meant it as such then her arrow had flown wide of its target. His mind was failing to make logical connections and she was the one who had reduced him to this after all. "Mei was," Arata had said, "Born without fear or a conscience," before he had gone on to explain who she was.

She had been, he thought, too sweet, too bright in this cold world. He had fallen in love with someone who had never existed.

Twenty-six years he had lost, in the blink of an eye, and yet they were nothing, nothing at all, compared to losing these six weeks.

This damned blood-beat in his head! He felt as if his skull was going to burst. "Stop there!" shouted Arata.

He had reached the edge of the bamboo thickets, the point at which trees began to blanket the climes. His toe caught on a stone. He staggered and nearly fell, and heard Arata's deep laughter as he descended the slope behind him. Ryuu turned:

"I told you there was nothing down here! We rigged the bridge and the gardens, nothing more! Why are you doing this, Arata?"

"I don't believe you. You and I seem to come to some arrangement, then I speak to the woman and she seems intent on getting a message to you. Wildflowers, Ryuu. What am I meant to think?"

"For god's sake!" He wanted to reach up and knead his pounding head, but the bindings on his wrists seemed to tighten even at the thought.

Takashi and several soldiers were coming down the slope behind Arata. Mei was with them. They had been going to leave her locked in the house until his brother, perhaps with certain foresight, had realised she might well be lying about the sword as well. Takashi held her by the wrist and she kept her head down.

Arata and his entourage paused about twenty paces from where Ryuu stood.

"You can go on!" Arata called to his brother.

But Ryuu had hesitated. Where he had stumbled, at his feet, was something that looked like a scrap of bone, but on closer inspection, was too perfect, too symmetrical, embossed with a winding, floral pattern. The knife! The one he had given her; she must have thrown it away.

But no, of course not. That was despair talking. Had she never loved him in any way, she still might have found some use for the weapon tonight. So she had dropped it in error as she'd run.

Yet nothing added up. Why had she let everything go this far when she must have always known how things would end? Why had she stayed?

Think.

A field of wildflowers.

She was trying to tell him something, surely. She'd always been good at making connections, wild connections but not impossible ones, and she must know how the memory of that afternoon would affect him. She'd said the field above the waterfall was the one place that was their own. He'd never even been there. It was just another lie, and if she had taken anyone to her precious field it had probably been Arata.

He stared at the miniature blade, his body going cold. It was there. That thought. It was wrong. Arata had never known about the field or the waterfall. The secret was still there between Mei and Ryuu. Was that what she was trying to tell him? That it didn't matter that it wasn't real? It was still theirs.

A small motion. It looked like he had stumbled again, but as he straightened, facing his brother, he had the knife in his hands behind him. He was shaking and that made it harder, but why was he afraid? He had nothing to lose; he had even asked them to let him die. Nothing had changed.

Nothing had changed. "What are you doing?" Arata shouted. "Why have you stopped?"

"It's right there. Just a little way on," he called back, his voice breaking over the syllables.

"So keep going!"

"No."

Ryuu cut through the bindings and stood there, trembling, a rhythm thundering in his temples. He kept his hands behind him.

He saw the decision in Arata's eyes an instant before it was made. His brother stared at him down the length of the gun.

And fired.

And the bullet went wide. Must have gone wide. He felt it skim his arm and realised he had a second chance and, knowing that, he fell.

赤山

Mei screamed. Takashi let her go to grasp Arata's arm:

"He was goading you!" the captain roared. "For god's sake, he was goading you!"

She streamed down the muddy path, sure-footed still despite the sense that she was being pulled towards him. She reached the body alone and fell on him, shocked at once to find him warm and breathing.

"Get up, get up!" he hissed. His eyes were open. Her hand hesitated on his cheek as she tried to understand what she thought she had seen and what her eyes now told her.

"Ryuu..."

"Let him think he killed me. I have the knife. Let him come."

"Ryuu"–She glanced behind her. Arata and Takashi were indeed approaching, Arata still holding the flintlock–"What if he—?"

"I can kill him. You just have to let me."

She stood up and scrambled back from him. Both commanders were about ten paces away now and she had no need to mend her face to show grief or shock. It was there, plain for them to see. Because she could see what Ryuu could not.

That he had reloaded the gun and intended to fire again.

Arata angled the gun down towards Ryuu's body and, without making any decision, she stepped forward.

This time the sound was so consuming that it was neither loud nor soft nor like any sound at all.

Something hard struck her side, knocking her backwards.

She took a breath in the sudden silence and a jagged pain raced up towards her ribs. When her legs gave way, Ryuu caught her. That was how she knew he must have finished the charade. "Mei? Mei!"

He sounded panicked. She saw blood, bright on her yellow kimono. It was on Ryuu's hand too as he tried to pull her own back to see the wound she had instinctively covered. She had thought that it would hurt more, but instead she was breathing faster, seeing clearer. The colours; the sound of his voice.

"It's alright," she said.

"—Not alright." He had turned his back on the others and now he was tearing at his own sleeves, bunching up the torn linen and pressing it against her side. She coughed, looked up and saw Arata standing a short distance away, still holding the gun.

What was supposed to happen now?

"They said your existence was charmed, Ryuu," said his brother. "But I didn't believe it until now." He threw away the now empty weapon and reached for his sword.

As Ryuu rose to his feet, he lifted Mei too. It took her a moment to find her balance, but she could stand. His arms were strong again; his eyes were clear and no longer empty as they flicked towards her.

"Can you walk? Can you run?" She nodded vigorously. "Then you remember the plan, don't you? You have to run, Mei."

She opened her mouth to protest: their plan had been for Takashi's soldiers, not Arata. And after all, perhaps Ryuu might need her. But some instinct within her told her that her part was done. Her life; his life. She'd completed the circle.

As Ryuu turned back to the commanders and the remaining soldiers, she stepped away from him, finding herself weightless.

He had told her to run.

She ran like she had never run before.

22. The Last Dance by Moonlight

As the soldiers closed in on Ryuu, his body responded as it always had. Only distantly was he aware of pushing himself beyond his limits. Muscle, sinew, the shallow wounds that opened anew. But this state of mind was not the cold silence that usually allowed him to fight. Instead his head was full of noise and motion. He had become indistinct, unfocused in the storm, but there remained will and emotion and purpose. He planted his feet in the mud, his intention filling the space between the soldiers and the path down which the woman fled. Arata did not wait to see his fate, but took a second path into the forest, towards the waterfall and Ryuu had to let him go as Takashi and the soldiers fanned out around him.

Perhaps Takashi recalled their first encounter because he held back. Three soldiers approached instead. Ryuu held the small knife in front of him like a candle, taking one step back to let them believe in his fear. It was all they needed, and all he needed was their over-confidence and never to be at the end of their blades. He could be out of their reach or, as he was now, suddenly far too close. The knife plunged into the nearest man's gut up to its hilt and slashed the chests of the other two. His breath was burning in his lungs. Somewhere off to his left, Takashi swore.

Two other men decided to live and fled.

When Ryuu stabbed another, this one mercifully quick to die, he reached for their sword and found Takashi's boot jammed down hard upon the blade. He staggered backwards, looked up and met the captain's eyes. There was a cool intensity in his gaze. The wild hunger for vengeance was gone. Takashi appraised Ryuu as a man might a beast.

"What the hell are you?" he said. Ryuu bared his teeth:

"I have no idea."

His name had been Arata.

He had lived for twenty-six years before waking to this vicious world, and in that time, he must have been somebody. For now though, he was just the product of one bright summer. But not an empty vessel. In the time he'd had, he had learned things, stupid, unimportant things: that he grew bored easily, that when he fought, he had a slight weakness on his right side, that he preferred sweet foods to savoury, that he trained better in the mornings but was capable of daydreaming whole afternoons away; that he had loved; that he could love. Whatever lies she had told him, they did not change that.

He was in love with someone. Perhaps it wasn't her, yet it had her shape, her face, her eyes, her lips.

He stumbled back into the forest and Takashi followed.

The ground quickly became too steep for them and both men found themselves more intent on their footing, on catching themselves in cradles of grey saplings, from which, if given enough advantage, they could launch an attack. It was a dance between the tree trunks, no longer on a flat plain, but descending, ever descending. Takashi was below him of a sudden, blade cutting through the thin trees, leaving fewer hand-holds for him. Clever. Ryuu grasped the knife's hilt now, stabbing down from above, letting himself fall like an avenging angel.

He fought in a dream.

Mind trained hard and fast upon the blank spaces, upon the insignificances of a life so briefly lived. And upon the clarity it took to kill. He saw his skill, his strikes, his energy, reflected in Takashi's face. He saw himself.

And he was good. Not just good, perhaps, but something out of the ordinary.

The captain had hesitated. Ryuu put his full strength behind the next thrust, expecting him to try and dodge, but it was only as he sprung downwards that he realised there was nowhere for Takashi to go. The darkness behind him was the edge of the mountain. And Ryuu himself had misjudged. Had he realised, no doubt, he would have struck with less force and Takashi's desperate slashes might have connected. As it was though, they collided, Takashi avoiding the knife as he tried to get past Ryuu, back into the relative safety of the forest. There was a moment in which neither man could have known if they were on the ground or in the sky, until Ryuu came down hard on hands and knees and Takashi just kept on slipping backwards through his grip. He reached for him. Why, he didn't know. Some instinct to preserve life, in the end, more powerful than that which made him take it. Ryuu caught him by the wrist, but only for a second before the leather glove he wore tore, and of a sudden he was holding nothing but a trail of ripped fabric.

He froze. Silence. The scrap of material came loose from between his fingers and started to float down like a petal until it too was lost in the dark, and still he couldn't move. In fact, he might never move again. The ravine tried to suck him down and, at the same time, it turned his muscles to stone.

Eventually he slithered backwards on his belly, away from the drop, and when he trusted himself to do so, got back up onto hands and knees and crawled in amongst the trees to catch his breath and wait for the sense of paralysis to pass. Mei had said he didn't like heights. She'd failed to mention he was rendered entirely helpless by them.

There were tears on his face. He lay with his back against the mountain, his whole body aching as it tried to convince him he had done enough. More than enough. He needed to rest.

But there would be time later and if there was no time later then he would have more than his share of rest in the next life. He stowed the knife in his collar, rose to his feet and began to climb back up to the path.

There were two places where he and Mei had relied on the precipitous nature of the mountain to be their weapon and their defence: one was the broken bridge; the second was the outcrop of ancient path, accessible only by lying bound saplings across the gap. At both these points they had debated how they would themselves be able to cross back.

In cutting through the bridge that had once linked the house to the servants' abode, Ryuu had been careful to leave enough of the structure that it could still carry two men side by side, or a rider on horseback. It had been wide enough that he'd not needed to see the drop beneath.

The same was not true of the old path. And that was why, in their plans, only Mei had needed to climb across the saplings, and wait for him until he called for her. That had been their plan; the one he had, in the end, asked her to keep to.

赤山

"Mei! Mei!"

Ryuu stood as close to the cliff–edge as he dared. He thought he could see her on the broken section of road, but all he could make out clearly in the moonlight was something pale that might or might not be the outline of a woman, or perhaps just a pile of stones against the rock–face. "Mei!"

He wondered if she had made it. Rain fell in a soft chorus on the grass. "Mei!"

But, of course, the saplings were on her side, so she had used them to cross the drop and had then pulled them up after her to prevent anyone from following. He felt a wave of relief. The silhouette was hers. Still she wasn't responding. "Mei!"

When she moved at last, it was in slow motion. Looking up, her face was ivory. She lurched forward and, with agonising slowness, began to shunt the makeshift bridge out across the gap, an act he watched with some trepidation. He reached for it only as it stubbed the long grass on his side of the drop. Then he held out his hand for her.

She didn't move.

Several heartbeats passed and she made a motion toward the bridge. It went uncompleted.

He was reminded of an animal caught in a snare; movements made empty by the tightening trap. She had reached out and fallen back, clutching the wound in her side. He felt suddenly sick. "I'm coming over," he said.

She didn't try and stop him, but he wished that she had. As he edged out onto the saplings, he felt them bend beneath his weight. A second step took him fully onto the makeshift crossing with just a few inches of wood between himself and the drop. The blood–beat began again in his head and he swayed where he stood, imagining himself sinking through the young trees. And suddenly that was all he could see: himself, falling through, lurching sideways, falling forever into darkness as the saplings splintered.

And dizzy, he dropped to his knees. The shadows seemed to spin slowly and rise to meet him. He felt the void licking at his hands, could see a black gulf spliced between the saplings, and his own hands, trembling, gripping.

He looked up. She was perhaps ten feet away, propped up against the cliff, her head tipped back and her body moving like a bellows with each breath.

Hand over hand, he felt his own breath join the motion as he found a rhythm his body would obey, his eyes held fast on her. One hand after another. His knee grazed the wood as he slid it forward. Once more. And once more again. And, as if there had been no challenge in it at all, he found suddenly that he was on hands and knees on solid stone, and she was there, within a hand's breadth.

"Mei…"

Panting, she smiled:

"I knew–you weren't–scared."

Her hand was clamped tightly over the patch of scarlet on her kimono. Black in this light, he could see that it was considerable, but could see no stains on the rocks around them. Try as she might though, she couldn't catch her breath. He reached her, putting all else out of his mind: who he was, who she was. For now it didn't matter.

"I need to see how bad it is," he said.

Taking her weight, he guided her down so that she lay on the old stone trail. Her breathing became a series of spiking gasps it pained him to hear.

"I'm sorry," she said, watching his face. "It hurts."

"I know." He tried to make his own voice steady. "You need to breathe more slowly though, alright?" She nodded, eyes frightened. "One, two…One…Two…" He began to count as he untied the sash of her kimono, careful not to brush the wound. Slowly the rhythm of her panting became more even.

He took her hand from the wound. The silk beneath was tacky with dried blood and he pulled the kimono aside as delicately as possible, then tried to make sense of what he was seeing.

Sword wounds were usually showy, their severity measured by their depth. With this though, it was impossible to tell. There was a small entry wound, almost unremarkable, with flecks of shrapnel dusting her belly. Most of the blood had clotted though; he could see little that was fresh. "It's not bleeding," he said, his voice breaking with relief. Her eyes were still wide and afraid. "That's good. That's good, Mei." He brushed her hair back from her face. "I'm not going to try and take the bullet out, alright? Because I don't know enough…But we're going to get help."

"Where's Arata?"

"I don't know."

"And Takashi?"

"He's dead."

If that meant anything to her, it didn't register on her face. He took a deep breath, turning to look back the way he had come. He could carry her, he knew, but Arata was still out there.

"Ryuu," she said, and he blinked at the name. It sounded strange when spoken tenderly. "I knew you wouldn't give up." She had reached up and, as her fingers brushed his cheek, he took her hand and held it, kissing her palm. It was clammy but real, tasting like salt and damp earth.

She closed her eyes again, and, as he watched, little silvers of tears formed beneath the lashes.

"There's something I don't understand," he said at length, giving her the time she needed to steady her breathing again: "Why did you stay, Mei? All this time."

"Because you had saved me."

He frowned, recalling:

"Meeting by the waterfall, and that poor girl dead?"

"That was always true," she whispered. "It's why I came back."

"Back?"

Her voice was so quiet he had to lean in to hear, his own body sheltering hers from the continuing rain.

"You said I should leave the estate. The day you rode out and fought with Arata, I came back to tell you…How we met."

"Why? What did it matter then?" He smiled, shaking his head, and running his fingers back through her hair. Her expression was achingly earnest.

"You blamed yourself for Kyoko's death. I wanted—I wanted you to know—that you had saved someone. Once," she said. "You saved me."

"Oh." He leant down, pressing his face against hers so that she couldn't see his tears. "Then all this time, we already knew each other?"

"Not really," she said, and he felt her fingers curl against his cheek: "You pulled me from the water; that was all." Even so, her touch was fond. "We never spoke. And, back then, you never even asked my name."

He pulled away and stared at her. Her grey eyes turning to smoke as they drifted in and out of focus. She was so different. So alone. Moreso now that he understood they were strangers. They had always been strangers.

"What's your name?" he asked her gently.

"Chimariko Mei."

"I'm Ryuu," he said. And this time the shine in her eyes overflowed into tears.

赤山

He didn't know how he managed to carry her back across that narrow bridge. Partly perhaps it was because her arms around his neck held him very tightly, and that gave him hope. Very little of her strength was gone. She encouraged him all across that dark abyss and never once did her belief in him falter.

"I need to find a sword, Mei."

"In the field above the waterfall."

"Arata went after that one."

"He won't find it. I hid it in a tree like the others, but I hung it flush against the trunk. He'll never find it in this light."

They stopped at the fork in the road. On the one hand, if Arata was there and armed they would be in trouble; on the other, if Ryuu himself continued without a weapon, he was putting himself at a significant disadvantage.

"Where are the other weapons?" he asked her.

"Back at the top of the trail, near the house, and in the orchard."

"Too far," he said. Taking a deep breath, he turned down the trail towards the waterfall.

赤山

Mei sat with her back to the rock, inches from the pouring water as he removed his shoes to climb. She was turning her knife over and over in her hands. He couldn't be sure, but he thought she was glad to have it back.

"Count three trees in from the edge of the falls and there's one branch that stretches out too far, like a hand," she said. "It's there."

"As much as this has been a fun game, we might keep the swords in the *dojo* next time." He took his weight on his hands and started to climb. "I'm sure Arata was glad you let him join in." He thought he heard her laugh.

It was still raining. Had she not said once that it never rained on the Red Mountain? It did so now. A wind was blowing too as he climbed, bringing with it the scent of a storm. Fortunately, it was not high. No more than twenty feet and he did it without looking down. He crawled up onto a rock at the head of the falls, stood up, stepped forward and immediately descended, ankle–deep into water. A gap opened in the clouds and he saw, for the first time in a drift of moonlight, the field of wildflowers.

The clearing was vast. A meadow. And some of it was flooded with the river that fed the falls, but every inch of it, including those parts that were waterlogged, was covered in red and white flowers.

Wisps of cloud passed across the moon and the landscape itself seemed to ripple and respond. Wherever they were caught in the ethereal light, the flowers were luminous, living beings, which bobbed and ducked away from passing shadows. He waded into the river and the flowers lapped against his calves, so it seemed to him that, all about him, from the banks and gentle slopes of the field, they watched.

The river was shallow and, as she had commanded him, he crossed, counted the trees and found the one with a branch that looked like a hand. Sure enough, bound by its *sageo* to the protruding limb was a sword that, even in the darkness, he could tell was of a fine quality. It turned gently in the breeze, a relic awaiting its custodian. And he had to climb onto a stone to reach it and unlace the bindings.

Stepping down with a grunt at the aches in his muscles, he took it, slid it into his belt, and prepared to return.

A figure stood at the top of the waterfall.

It took him a moment to realise it wasn't Mei.

Another shifting patch of moonlight. In it, Arata's face was calm, almost immaculately so.

As Ryuu watched, Arata started across the water, sending two silver tides out across the meadow.

Ryuu drew the new sword and stepped into the water.

But it was different this time. He knew it by the silence. Even their motions, the splashes and churning that should have been kicked up as they circled one another, seemed muted. Arata had always seemed desperate. But now Ryuu saw in him the same clarity with which he fought, when every movement became effortless, when every strike was little more than another step in a routine he had learned before birth. His consciousness hung outside of his body, on the edge of the moon–bright blade.

As it skimmed the surface of the water, taking the heads of flowers and tossing them into the falls.

Arata sprung back, his silhouette dripping darkness. Ryuu could see two steps ahead, his strikes and thrusts like lines of fire already carved onto the mind's eye. It was not difficult to avoid them, but he proved impossible to catch. Like Ryuu himself, he had become only the shadow behind the weapon, his body having no more substance than the wind. His soul in the arc of the blade.

Forced together by the need to reach each other, Ryuu imagined a dark column between them, invisible to the naked eye. It was into this intangible shield that his sword could reach, but there, the air seemed thick with energy and, try as he might, no cut of his would strike beyond. Arata too could not touch him. But they pushed at it; they squeezed it between them until the darkness was full of light and flashing blades and the thin, high sheen of steel on steel.

Mei had been at the base of the waterfall, Ryuu thought. Was it too much to imagine that Arata had let her be? There had been no scuffle. No cry. But then it seemed that he had left her world behind now.

Perhaps he had fallen with Takashi and all of this was but an after-image.

Arata stepped back. His voice seemed calm:
"Why will you never let me be?"
"Where is Mei?"
"I said, why will you never let me be?" He struck. Their swords met in a single, percussive note and he span away. "Why must you always be with me? Your name? This damned mountain? Why will I never be rid of it?"

"We are free, Brother. We are not who we were." Ryuu's *hakama* sloshed through the bobbing flowers. He felt dizzy, light with exhaustion.

"I have lived long enough to know I do not want to serve you or anyone, my lord."

"We all serve someone, or something."

"Who do you serve?" asked Arata.

Ryuu stepped up onto a rock. The hiss of the waterfall; its hollow ring on the rocks below.

"Do you hear it?"

"Hear what?"

"There is a rhythm the whole world dances to. When all our masters are gone, it still remains. Listen."

They were at the head of the falls. Twenty feet to the pool below. It was clear to him now, the noise, the hiss, the point where the calm black drift of the water through the flowers lost its form and dissolved inevitably into a white, ever-moving edge.

He looked over it and realised he wasn't afraid anymore.

His next cut forced Arata to sidestep closer to the drop.

Arata's eyes flickered towards the falls and a tremor ran through him. He made his first mistake.

Lunging away, he was suddenly closer to Ryuu. The base of Ryuu's blade sliced into his shoulder and, with a snarl of pain, Arata took the sudden breakdown of the space between them to reach out and throw both arms around his brother. Together they fell.

In the deep water, Ryuu's clothes were suddenly heavy. The weight in his muscles dragged him down. They were floundering suddenly. Ugly, clumsy creatures, on hands and knees now, their weapons lost in the fall.

He thought he saw one of the blades in the water, a line of moonlight, and he lurched towards it.

Behind him, he heard Arata splashing through the plunge-pool and, as his hand closed over the discarded weapon, there was the sound of wood being smashed against stone then pieces dropping into the water. As Ryuu turned he thought he saw Arata standing over him with a sword. Then he realised his brother had smashed his *saya*, knowing that the wood would splinter with the grain. Pieces of it bobbed on the surface of the river, but the shard he held was as long as his arm. With a roar, Ryuu, swept his blade towards the figure of his brother.

Arata had stepped forward. He made no move to parry or even avoid the thrust. His whole focus was on Ryuu. So that even as Ryuu's steel tore through him, he was still reaching, reaching with the ragged stave until the scene crashed in on itself. The crude spear plunged into Ryuu's thigh. Arata staggered backwards, a slough of black blood inking the moonlight as he fell with the blade through his chest.

Ryuu tried to tug the stave out of his leg. The pain was sudden and savage. Enough to distract him and make him miss the shadow that descended on him, claws round his throat, and shoved him down beneath the water.

His throat filled with darkness and cracked shafts of moonlight.

It was shallow, barely a foot of water, and yet he was falling. Forever falling.

Ryuu's hands closed on handfuls of mud and shale. Finding no purchase, he began to claw instead at his brother's hands: warm, heavy hands that just pushed him further down. The mud began to clot in his hair, against his skin, sucking and tugging at his body, then gradually folding around him in warm blankets.

His eyes filled with the dark. The world hung briefly between one breath and the next, then slid in upon him, a terrible, crushing weight.

It was in this darkness that he felt a series of percussive beats.

Then the surface of the water in a film across his face. It ran out from between his lips, chased by a muddy cough. He gasped.

Mei stood over him, looking crooked somehow, her body all angles hung with silk.

In the water to his right, Arata lay unmoving with a knife in his neck. Its inlaid hilt stuck out at such an angle that, as the next cloud passed, the moonlight caught in the ivory.

"Mei."

She looked at him. There was no hint of emotion on her face, no sign that she knew what she had done or that she felt anything if she did. She reached out for him and, after a moment, he took her hand and staggered to his feet, sending dark water sloughing over the corpse.

Chimariko Mei, Arata had said of her, had been born without fear or a conscience.

23. Encounter at Dawn

She said the wound in her side was bleeding again. At the base of the falls, she had crouched down waiting for the dizziness to pass.

He suspected it didn't. Her skin was waxy pale.

As he tied a crude tourniquet above the wound in his thigh he thought about what she had done in her condition just to save his meagre life. But thinking back on her expression as she had gazed at Arata's body, he wondered if it had really been for him that she had done it.

The rain sounded like cymbals in the forest all around. It mingled with the scent of river water in his clothes and hair. What had once been the gentle stroll of a summer's afternoon back to the house now seemed to him like the ascent of the tallest peak. He had no idea where to start, no idea if he could carry her or should even try while there was still a chance she could walk. If he preserved his own strength now perhaps he could help her later. But the thought of riding with his leg in tatters tugged at his own cowardice. He was already in pain. The sheer magnitude of the journey they needed to make was enough to make him want to curl up with her beneath the falls and never move again. "We should go," he said.

How they did it, he would never know. By turns she walked ahead of him like a ghost, or else she stopped and let him take her weight a while. By contrast, his own progress was slow but steady. The pain in his leg felt fresh with each step, but it didn't worsen.

While he went to fetch horses, she stood propped in the doorway to the stables. Still standing.

He didn't have to venture in very far to realise that there were no horses. And it was not hard to guess that some of the soldiers whose mounts had been killed in the skirmish had taken them, choosing to flee while they still had their lives.

He stood in the dark. In here, the air smelt of grass and damp and dust, echoes of a half–forgotten summer. He leant with his forehead against the wooden frame of one of the stalls and let the truth crash in on him: they couldn't leave. They had never been able to leave. The notion that they had ever had that freedom was the scratching of his imagination on the inside of a dream.

"It's burning," she said, staring at the house. He came to stand beside her.

"It's not burning, Mei. It's just the same as it ever was. The oil lamps will gutter in the end. It's just empty now."

"In my mind, it's burning."

He looked up to see the lights reflected in her pallor. She didn't look like Mei anymore. She looked like some time ago she had been tired and that this tiredness had sipped for a long time at her spirit. It struck him that she had been all spirit. Now that it was gone, she looked hollow, like a doll made of silk and paper.

"We need to walk," he said.

He lurched past her. Defiance moved him. Nothing else. The pain in his leg seemed to double, triple, at the thought of climbing the pass, but he could still feel anger at the injustice of it. She didn't follow him and he couldn't blame her.

He could go. He could fetch help. Though he might struggle to carry her with his leg this way, if he went ahead alone it could take him no more than a day…A day. He stopped. She was watching him from the door to the stables.

There were some things, he thought, that you couldn't leave behind. If it took him a day, it would be a day he could never get back. "Come with me," he said.

赤山

Their progress was slow. She said the pain felt different now. Certainly he could sense none of the strength in her that had previously reassured him. Only a slow burning fever. He chose not to see her face, the way she craned her neck as if straining for each breath. Lips so pale they looked like a single blossom fallen amidst the snow.

They were a little way into the gorge when she started to stumble. He had tried to take her weight. His own steps wavered, but whenever she lost her footing, he held her up and the pain in his leg reared, ugly and red. He heard himself gasp.

She no longer heard though. Her eyes were glazed; her feet found their own way, the motion mechanical.

"Mei," he said.

They stopped.

Dawn was creeping into the canyon, catching in the stone, roughening it with a light like charcoal. A sound was coming. At first he thought he had imagined it or that perhaps the first scraps of the day were playing tricks on him, but there it was again. A slow rhythm. If the mountain had a heartbeat...

Mei fell against him.

He caught her, held her. Waiting.

A man came through the gorge. He was a soldier, dressed in *hakama* and a heavy leather tunic. It took Ryuu a moment to recognise him because he was not accustomed to seeing ghosts. The man's eyes were as empty as Mei's had been. His hand trailed in a chestnut mare's reins as he led the horse. A sleepwalker who had stumbled into their world. Ryuu stared.

And after several more paces, Takashi stared back:

"You!" He stumbled forward. Now Ryuu saw that his hands were bloody, his nails torn, his fingertips black with dirt. As Ryuu watched, he scrabbled at his belt and pulled a gun from the folds of his obi. He was quite sure it was the gun Arata had discarded in the forest. Reloaded now. It shook. It hung in the air before them, testament to something neither of them understood. And it was this that passed between them: on the surface, the truth that a single bullet would earn Takashi the reward he had sought; beneath that, the uncertainty that was buried deep in the soldier's eyes; that he did not know why he was here, that he did not know why he held the weapon. That he would not know why he killed.

Takashi stepped forward.

Ryuu must have stirred because, clenched to his side, Mei gave a soft moan and opened her eyes. She reached for Ryuu and he gripped her tighter before he realised that the motion was an endeavour for her to take her own weight again. He was torn. There were things he should say, things that would feel right in this moment. He could beg for his life or he could laugh that it had come to this. Or he could look to Mei. Her eyes were wide and dark, her lips pursed and drawn down as if she wanted to tell him something. Suddenly he understood. She had always said Takashi would not kill her.

"Let me take her to Okiri," Ryuu said.

Another shudder ran through the captain, enough to make the gun rattle. If he fired now, Ryuu realised, he still might not hit them. But still he didn't back down. "I'm turning myself in!" barked Ryuu, desperation catching in his throat: "Once we're in Okiri! I'm not asking for anything more! My life is yours. Do you understand?"

Ryuu felt Mei struggle in his arms. He let her go and she managed two paces before she fell to her knees between the two men. For the first time, Takashi's eyes flickered away from Ryuu to the injured woman.

Her lips moved.

When at last she spoke though her voice was frail.

"If you let him live, I'll go with you."

Ryuu froze at the sound. The words should have been empty, except they weren't. There was a tenderness in them that he had not foreseen. He watched as something passed between the two of them and briefly he saw the way, with but a few words, she made a fork in their path. The captain contemplated a future in which she was with him. Her offer was neither an empty plea nor, entirely, a sacrifice.

He felt anger, the anger of one who longs to possess another. He felt it sated quickly by the realisation that she was not his. Had never been so. Even if he discovered that he loved her, that for now was down another fork in the road. "Let me go with you," Mei said dully. Then, almost to herself: "I would be only yours. Yours alone."

The gun seemed suddenly heavy in Takashi's hand, its weight pulling his aim down until it came level with Mei's head. Ryuu's breath caught in his throat with an audible hiss.

"No," said Takashi.

Something like a sob bubbled up in her throat, her words barely audible:

"Why not?"

And, with that, the soldier became animate. In a single motion, he dropped to his knees, discarding the gun at his side. The symmetry with which they faced each other was equalising.

"Because I am dishonourable," said Takashi, the words spilling out over themselves. "I could not be seen at your side." He had taken her hand, seeming to Ryuu to crush the delicate fingers. Then all at once, he had scooped her up in his arms and she was limp, as if the moments before had been an aberration or hallucination. The truth was this: her figure as pale as ice in the grey morning, and lifeless, the wind catching in folds of yellow silk. Her eyes had closed into two curves of black lashes. "Could you ride?" Takashi asked, acknowledging Ryuu for the first time, his gaze lingering on his leg and the makeshift tourniquet, which in the morning light, had faded to the colour of claret wine. Ryuu felt a surge of relief as he understood.

"Not fast enough," he confessed. Takashi seemed to hesitate. He looked ragged enough himself and he seemed to be deciding which of them would be best. Ryuu made the decision for him. "You have my leave. Please take her."

"Then," Takashi said, nodding in acknowledgement, "We will see you in Okiri."

He mounted, lifting Mei into the saddle with ease, so that he could hold her with one arm around her front. In that moment, as Takashi slammed his heels into the mare's sides, Mei's head had nodded forward, her hair across her face. If Ryuu had wished to commit her features to his memory, it was already too late. And even as the thought occurred to him, that it could be the last time he saw her alive, already they were gone.

He stared at her footprints in the dust, at the spot where she had knelt, at the gun lying discarded. The rain was still falling lightly. His part here though was done. He turned once to look back the way he had come. In his mind, the house still stood amidst the summer garden, in the cradle of the mountain.

He laid his hand on the hilt of the sword he wore, as if such a simple action could somehow moor him, and with one last glance, he set his mind firmly on the road ahead. He would not come back this way again.

赤山

"Come away."

Ryuu glanced up. He had been leaning on the railing of a deck that wound around an enclosed garden in the monastery. The air here smelt of rain and flowers. He had come to a different world and, even now, it felt as if the dust was still settling. There was too much for him to take in. People knew him here. The monks had bowed and called him Akayama–*sama* before he had opened his mouth. It was all too strange.

He did not consider himself, even now, a creature that would be given over too easily to despair, but nor did he fully understand how, from here, he was supposed to take another step. "Come away," said Takashi again. "You won't find peace here."

"Is there anywhere more peaceful? The quiet in these gardens will not be matched in town." He had caught but a glimpse of Okiri. While on the estate they had spoken of it as if it was nothing very splendid and common sense still told him that it was little more than a hamlet fed by a rich valley in the mountains. Yet there were more people in the streets than he had seen in his short piece of life: women, children, vendors calling out from stores that sold foods and water and spices he had never tasted. A whole world but a short ride from the house, and one of which he had no doubt once been a part. If he could be a part of it again, he didn't yet know, but he felt confused and excited and afraid.

"Don't stay here. This is a place where people come to die—"

"How can you say...?" Ryuu caught himself. There was a surgeon with Mei still tonight. He was not superstitious enough to believe a mention of death could procure it. Still he chewed his lower lip sourly.

"The smell of it lingers," Takashi said.

"Then go to the temple and pray for her."

They glanced at one another. Since a truce seemed to have been called, though by whom neither seemed quite sure, Ryuu had discovered he had no particular argument with the swordsman. At their basest, they were creatures of a similar stock.

Takashi was obviously coarse and not all that intelligent, Ryuu judged. For his own part, he had made it clear that, after some initial scepticism, he now considered Ryuu to be something of a puppy, incapable of judging what was best for himself. They'd traded insults from the moment when the young lord had limped into the grounds of the monastery and the monks had begun to tend him. He had wanted to see Mei, but none would let him. It was only Takashi who had deigned to shove him down in his chair and had proceeded to hold him there whilst a man worked on his leg. It felt much better now, but he was going to die before he admitted that.

The rain continued to fall.

There were other things they had in common of course, but they were hard to define and harder still to discuss. Each had lost everything and that had made it just a little harder for either to maintain their vendetta. And then of course there was Mei. Perhaps the less they examined common ground in that respect the better. Yet for now she was the unspoken foundation of their alliance. She would not be here were it not for them. But for Ryuu, the fear of her loss was coupled with the knowledge that he would have no-one. Takashi was now, by some twist of fate, his only link to this world.

Takashi seemed to sense something of this and was loath to leave the younger man.

Of a sudden, he reached out, took Ryuu's wrist, and stubbed a piece of paper into his palm:

"These are directions to the barracks, should you need them. Give my name at the gate. Don't give your own; do I need to tell you that?"

"No."

"Good. You're not as stupid as you look. There'll be a room waiting for you in the inn next door. My name again."

He stepped away. Ryuu felt the square edges of the folded parchment digging into his palm.

"Takashi–*san*?"

"Yes."

"Why?"

Takashi hesitated, then sighed and leant heavily on the railing. The rain caught on his sleeve:

"Her, I think." He looked thoughtfully at the garden. "When she visited, she told me not to fight. Didn't beg me. Just told me I didn't want to, like she could see right into my soul, and I hated that. I thought she was stupid not to see that I'd never have chosen this if there had been a choice. Who chooses this life?" The rain tap–tapped on the wooden awning above their heads and danced on the leaves in the garden. "But now I don't believe she meant 'Takashi, you don't want to'. I think she was trying to tell me 'Takashi, you don't have to.'"

Ryuu considered this.

"You ever think," he said, "That we hear the things we want to in what she says?"

Takashi chuckled drily:

"Maybe. Anyway, where I come from if you pit forty–four soldiers against one man, that man has run out of choices." Ryuu nodded slowly. "Tell me honestly, how many of the traps you set for us were of your own creation and how much of that was Mei's?"

"Mainly hers. She thinks in ways I'd never think. It's like she thinks round corners and, even if you'd suggested some of those things, I'd have said they were impossible, but she just sees straight through all the ways things can go wrong to how it could be. If it went right."

Takashi hesitated then stubbed a finger towards Ryuu:

"That's it. And it's people too. She has a gift. Not who they are, but who they could be. And most of the time that's the last thing you want to hear: who you could have been if you hadn't messed up every damn choice you ever made." Ryuu stared as the soldier scratched the stubble on his chin thoughtfully: "But, in the end, when it comes right down to it, it's good to know that someone saw it. It's good to know it's still there."

The thoughtfulness passed. He shrugged, looking suddenly weary. "I'll retire now, I think."

"Thank you," Ryuu said. He watched as the soldier waved off his gratitude. Then he waited until he was gone before he checked the list of directions Takashi had given him. He was ashamed to admit it would take him courage to leave the monastery and walk through busy streets.

There were, he thought, a lot of things that were going to take him courage.

24. Thirty Miles to the West

She was seated on a bench, from whence she could see a little stone bridge and, between the flowers, a pool of black lapping water. As Ryuu approached she neither moved nor looked up, her hands folded carefully in her lap. He noticed the small things: the way she wore her hair up. The kimono that was not so fine as the ones she had had back at the house, though it was of a heavy fabric as if, despite the heat, she still needed those layers to protect her. A smattering of make-up around her eyes. It should have gone unnoticed, but he had, he thought, become too accustomed to her.

It had been difficult to convince the monks that a meeting would be beneficial. Even now, he was aware of idol gossip. He had mistakenly given her name as Akayama on the first occasion, which had led to tongues wagging and a harsh reminder that, as much as none would dare to question him, there were rules to follow out here. They were not married. He was a man, known to be of some social standing. She was a woman of none. Four weeks he had waited before they had relented, but he had come every day to the monastery without fail.

She stood and bowed. He found that he responded in kind. Having left the estate, he had never dreamed that he could have left something behind there. It was as if, until now, their existence had been within an unbroken circle. Now he found himself on the outside, looking in. The bow, the hesitant step forward. He almost reached out for her as she sat down again to gaze at the still pool. And all the while he sensed that some part of him was hammering and hammering on a door that would now be closed to him forever.

"I was afraid you would not see me," he said, wincing inwardly that he had opened with this admission.

"Of course I would see you."

He settled on the bench beside her. She looked as if she probably belonged in a garden like this. By contrast, for all that he had a name and title, he was dressed like a soldier, a brute amongst the flowers.

"How are you?"

"A little better." She smiled. "I think I was lucky. I don't remember much about how we got back here."

"Takashi brought you."

"Takashi?"

"Is that bad?"

"I had thought he was dead."

"I had thought so too. I saw him fall, but there was an outcropping in the cliff. He said he thought he should have died. It took him forever to climb back up."

She stared at him surprised, the paint on her lips as bright as red berries. Then she pursed them and nodded:

"I should thank him then, that he came back for me."

"You may get a chance."

She looked at him, at his hand resting on his leg. Did she realise he was forcing himself not to touch her? Because to touch her would be to make her real. But that door was still closed. If she recoiled from him, he would be at a loss.

"Why are you here, Ryuu–*sama*?" she said after a time. A light breeze shimmered in the flowers. He gazed at her face in profile, at her determination not to look.

"Did you think that, because you lied, I would not come?" She pursed her lips again. "And anyway," he added, "I am inclined to believe in certain of your lies."

"You should not. There are towns and cities and people beyond Akayama. One day you will have to learn to live out there."

"Learn to live!" He shook his head, amused. "Already I think this town is becoming familiar to me." Mei glanced at him and he looked at her askance. "You think that I am such a child?"

"Not a child. Just, one who has much to relearn, and out here I can't..."

"Can't what?"

But she said nothing. It struck him then that other things had changed. She had once been full of tiny movements, from teasing at her sleeves to biting her lip, to looking about her as she spoke, or winding a finger absently in her hair. She was almost completely still now. Only the thumb and forefinger of her right hand moved, plucking at the frayed edge of the obi she wore. If she was aware of the change, she didn't show it.

Ryuu reached into his *kosode* and took out a small object wrapped in white cloth. He shook it into his hand and held it up for her to see: a small jade seal:

"Do you know what this is?"

"No," she said.

"Nor do I, but Arata wanted it and, for that alone, I think it has monetary worth. How much, I don't know, but we would need to start somewhere. If we could afford land, a small freehold...I don't yet know if I can make things well with the governorate, but I will have to try. People know my name in Edo. I would not be without allies."

"I see," she said gently.

"I think it is a possibility," he said, brandishing the seal as if she might recognise something of its potential, but she only stared blankly and all at once he felt like a fool. It was nothing: a piece of stone. He was talking about rebuilding his household. Where would he even begin? And if he could travel to Edo and clear his name, what of her? "I want you to come with me," he said, as he rewrapped the seal and returned it to his shirt without meeting her eye. "Would you do that?"

"I can't travel yet."

"Two weeks more they said." He stared at his hands in his lap.

"They are generous. I do not yet feel strong."

"We would go first to Edo. To the shogun. It must be done, but after that, we could start afresh."

"Build a house, on a mountain?" she said, so very very softly.

"You don't understand, Mei. We have our whole lives–"

He felt a wave of heat pass through his chest as she took his hand. Her smile sad as she pressed it to her cheek, eyes closed:

"There will be ladies at court who will fall in love with you, and they will love you with honest hearts, and you will be happy," she said.

"I..." He hesitated as her words sunk in, then took his hand back. Her own remained suspended where she had held it.

"Why–why would you say such things?"

"We had barely six weeks, Ryuu. Now you will have a lifetime, and there is so much that you will be."

The sunlight had gone from the garden, he thought; the gentle sounds of water and of birdsong too. He sat with both hands flat on the stone bench, watching the wind ruffle the suddenly colourless flowers. Four weeks he had waited to see her and still he had not come close.

"I'll tell Takashi you send your thanks."

"You should. I'm grateful."

"Maybe I'll visit again tomorrow."

With that, he rose and turned away. He thought he would probably never forgive himself, but he didn't look back. No force on earth could have made him look back.

赤山

"Did you send him away?" The girl asked.

She was a bright, smiling creature, a little younger than Mei, but plump from a life well–lived in the service of the surgeons. She wore her hair in tails on either side of her smile. Alive in a way that many people in this town were not. They called her Ito and she tended the women here, who were brought to live or die or give birth.

Ryuu had, it seemed, become a talking point. "Every day he came for you. You can't just turn him away!" The young girl watched their guest leave through gauzy drapes, the same drapes that surrounded the bed in this room, making it a box hung with gossamer. Mei steadied herself against the window frame. "They say he's the lord of an estate nearby. Is that true?"

"He isn't a lord."

Ito turned to look at her. Mei felt no physical pain for now, though movement was difficult. Still, as a matter of habit, when she stood she pressed one hand to her belly, to the invisible wound in her side. The scarring might fade a little in time, but she would not forget.

"Does it hurt?" Ito asked and Mei glanced up.

"No. Not anymore."

The girl smiled:

"Then, when you are better, will you go with him?" She turned away from the window and folded her hands behind her, swaying on the spot. "I would that a man like him fell in love with me."

"It is not that simple. We are not in love, you see."

"Then why does he come here?" Ito goaded her.

"Because he does not know it yet." Mei watched him cross the grounds and leave the monastery through the front gate. He joined the thin flow of traffic on the trade road and became just one more figure in the crowd. The air smelt of fresh rainfall. But it always rained in Okiri. "Sometimes when you wake, it takes time for a dream to fade. That's what he is."

"You were in love with him once then," the girl said.

"No, just with someone like him."

赤山

"I heard you were leaving," said Takashi. He was leaning in the doorway. Ryuu, it appeared, decided to ignore him a little longer.

The room in the inn felt small, but perhaps that was because there was something about Ryuu's nature that filled it. Six weeks had passed and he had recovered well. Takashi had started to see the similarities between him and his brother: both full of rapacious energy; both creatures of a compelling disposition. And while he had come to loathe Arata's ability to manipulate him, Ryuu on the other hand, seemed capable of genuine compassion. Takashi had been surprised too at how much the young man had come to depend on him. Surprised and touched.

Mei had recovered more slowly. She had fought an infection for nearly three weeks after a surgeon took the bullet from her body. Ryuu had gone to the monastery every day since and Takashi pitied him. When her life hung in the balance, Ryuu had not given up, but she had become a compulsion for him, so that he seemed at times to be little more than a moth buzzing at a flame. It was not want of character on his part; he was certainly not weak nor even, Takashi suspected, easily led. But he had nothing to fall back on. No experiences; no decisions. No regrets, even. Only her.

Then Takashi had watched as all that changed and his energy had become frustration, then anger.

He didn't visit the monastery again.

There was very little Ryuu needed to pack. He was taking some clothes Takashi had given him; he had a sword and a cloth bag to wrap it in for the journey. He was trying now to tie it neatly save that an excess of passions seemed to have interfered with the symmetry of the knots. That was another thing. He was not yet learned in hiding his thoughts. He was angry today and thus it imbued his every motion. "I think you're rash," Takashi said. "You still have a price on your head in Edo and, if I don't return at the end of summer with your head, they will send others like me."

"If they're anything like you, I doubt they'll cause me much trouble."

"Hah. I did say 'if.' I'm still considering it as an option." The fabric bag tore beneath Ryuu's fingers and he hissed something incomprehensible. "You really are charming," said Takashi: "I know what she sees in you."

"Did you have something important to say?"

"Hm." Takashi scratched his chin: "Are you still intending to go alone?"

"I told you, it's her choice."

"It's a fool's choice. Where are you going to go?"

"To the *bakufu*. I need to clear my name."

"You could travel under another. Does it really mean that much?"

Takashi knew, as he spoke, that it did. There was a reason that he himself went by his family name, despite a dead father and a broken lineage that few now would remember. It was a mark of Ryuu's respect for him that he did not turn that fact back on him, even in anger.

"While I travel I will have to use another, but forsake it forever, no," Ryuu said firmly. "That's why I will go to the shogun."

"Might I offer my own humble advice?" asked Takashi. Ryuu looked up. "Disappear. Just for a while. Most of the people in this town believe Akayama is dead; soon Matsuda will send soldiers to this estate and you will not be able to stand against him. If you go to the shogun in your current condition–"

"I don't need your advice!"

"–You cannot go there and show them fear and expect them to have mercy on you!"

"I will not show them fear then!"

Takashi rolled his eyes. Ryuu bore little resemblance to a nobleman, but he did succeed in retaining an ungodly sense of entitlement. It made offering him advice an exercise in supreme patience.

"With the greatest respect, you are afraid of everything, Ryuu – from leaving this place to going out alone. Before you show your face in court you need a better understanding of what you're facing. And for god's sake, take the girl."

Ryuu turned towards him with a strange expression in his eyes:

"She would have gone with you, you know. When she offered to do so, that wasn't just to save my life. She would have gone with you, Takashi."

"I know," he said. His own desire felt hollow and hard to understand. One day he might let himself consider the idea that, for a few short weeks, even he had discovered a need for someone. That she had never been his made it all the more bittersweet. "That's no foundation for the future though," he muttered.

"I don't think it was because you threatened me. I don't even think it was founded on coercion," Ryuu admitted.

"Who said anything about coercion? I was talking about pity. Pity is an ugly reason to love." He gave a sad smile.

"It is better than lies."

"Are you telling me you're not just the smallest bit curious about who she really is?"

Ryuu looked away.

Takashi wondered what was going through his head. Ryuu had talked about leaving often, but it was as if he had worked himself up to this, like a child in a tantrum. It was an act of defiance. Perhaps some of that was directed against Mei, but the greater part, Takashi suspected, was against the circumstances in which he found himself. Afraid or not, Ryuu was not the kind of man who would be content holed up in a small town or bound by a false identity. So it surprised Takashi that, when the young man turned back to him, he seemed calm.

"I meant to give you something before I go." He took a little cloth-wrapped bundle out of his pack. "You paid for my room here. You paid for the medicine. This is the least I can do." He handed it to Takashi who unwrapped a small jade seal. "Perhaps it would go some way if you ever did decide to, you know, stop...be someone else, I suppose."

Takashi smiled at the gift. Mei would likely approve. He didn't know if he was ready to step back from the game yet, of lords and clans, honour and name. But he knew one thing: since leaving the Red Mountain, he had no longer found himself racked by hesitation. Whatever he chose, he knew, he would not regret it.

"You still insist on going then?"

"Yes," said Ryuu.

"To Edo?"

Ryuu tugged the bag onto his back, but, when he looked up, the lines had gone from his face and his eyes seemed the colour of a clear sky:

"Thank you, Takashi," he said.

"To Edo? Hey, if not to Edo then where?"

"Wherever fate leads me, for now."

Ryuu smiled and, after a moment, Takashi smiled back ruefully:

"Give her my regards then."

赤山

Mei woke, certain that she was back on the mountain, until the smell of damp assailed her senses. Even the incense could not stay the rot in the walls of the hospital wing. It tasted of the worst of all her days, of fever and unimaginable pain. The mountain and the sky seemed never to have existed in this world of walls and pallets and blankets, bowls of clean salted water that stung like venom when they washed the wound in her stomach.

"Just tell her farewell. She might see me."

It was definitely his voice. She sat up and listened, holding her breath. Outside one of the monks told him no, he was not permitted to visit her.

He didn't argue.

She rubbed the sleep out of her eyes, feeling a mixture of disappointment and relief as she listened to Ryuu's footsteps receding. Then she rose to watch him through the gauze curtain. He had a bag slung over one shoulder and was dressed for the road, his hair in a loose topknot. He looked like a vagabond, she thought, and a little knot of muscle contracted at the base of her ribs as she realised he was leaving..

He reached the trade road.

And turned towards the mountain and the valley beyond.

She frowned.

This was wrong.

He was meant to go to Edo. He was meant to go to the court. He was meant to be someone, Akayama Ryuu, *daimyo* of the Mountain, someone who would have a chance to remake the world in a way that she had never had.

Then why was he so stubborn?

The monks didn't stop her, though several did follow her at a distance as she hastened across the garden to the gate and paused only briefly to gather her bearings. People flowed back and forth on the trade road, dressed in all manner of travelling costumes, from rags, to leather armour, to broad flat hats. They carried burdens or wheeled carts or stumbled under the weight of sedan chairs. The town was alive and humming its own song as the fresh rain dried in the roadside grasses.

She caught up with him on a small bridge on the edge of town; he was resting against it, as if he had been waiting for her all this time.

"Where are you going?" she demanded, aware that, by raising her voice, she attracted glances from the crowd. He said nothing, but unfolded gracefully from the spot where he had been leaning and began to walk away. "Where are you going?"

Glancing back, he said:

"There is a town in the valley, thirty miles to the west of here that I want to see.".

She followed along behind, slipping her hands into her sleeves:

"It's not a town; it's a village, and you don't know the way."

"Somehow," he said, "I think I'll find it."

Epilogue

A bright day greeted the two travellers.

Ryuu enjoyed sleeping in the open air. The sky was pale. A tiny beetle crawled up a grass stem just inches from his nose and everything smelt like the gardens in summertime, but when had there ever been another time? It had always been summer.

Yesterday they had passed the village where Mei was born.

They'd walked for another half a day, but he'd not wanted to go much further because Mei had been silent. He'd not known if she was still angry at his decision or whether her injury gave her pain, but he had called a halt to their journey.

They had camped in the shadow of some trees, beneath a sky full of stars.

Last night, she had sat watching the flames. He had gone to find something to eat and returned with a handful of mushrooms: a paupers' supper. Tomorrow he might try his hand at hunting. The world felt especially vast these days.

When he'd looked up, Mei had been crying. The tears had slipped down her cheeks in two bright lines, but her eyes had been unfocused, staring into the darkness, as if she were a statue with rain on its porcelain cheeks:

"I promised I would make a story for you, that you would be...a great hero. You were meant to be much more than this."

"Did I ask you that? To make a story for me?" He'd stood up then, and gone to crouch before her: "It was a most extraordinary story, Mei."

And it had been. Just a story. Just an extraordinary story.

So now he lay there in the morning dew, thinking about her; thinking about them and who they were. Travelling companions, yes, but, if he was honest with himself, they no longer felt like lovers. She was more a stranger to him than he had really let himself believe. And he too, as much as he had hoped it would not be so, was a stranger to himself. He was walking through a world as glistening and bright as it might have been on the first day of creation.

With a sigh he sat up, and found her next to him in the grass, already kneeling and watching the edge of the forest.

"What are you doing, Mei?"

"Keeping watch," she said turning towards him. Her arms were wrapped around her knees, her hair mussed by sleep. And he remembered a woman who had watched over him at night in the house, perched in the window frame. He remembered the night she had first lain beside him.

"Did anyone come by?"

She shook her head then wrinkled her nose and smiled:

"You have grass in your hair, Ryuu–*san*."

"Ah." He picked it out as he stood up and sprinkled it over her hunched figure, wiping his hands, walking carelessly past. "As have you."

She laughed, but when he crouched to prepare their travelling gear and glanced back over his shoulder, she was holding one of the blades of summer dry grass and was twisting it between her fingers, sometimes lifting it to her nose as if to catch the scent of trapped sunshine, and her face was sad again.

They spent most of that day trailing through the woodland and it wasn't until afternoon that the trees thinned and they found themselves on the edge of another valley. There was grass now as far as the eye could see, here and there broken into a patchwork by fields of crops and thatched fences, tumbledown houses and cattle grazing peaceably in the sunlight.

They walked through village after village, greeted sometimes with smiles and sometimes with curiosity.

Ryuu felt like a child. It would take time for him to grow accustomed to this aspect of the journey: new places, new people. When he turned his attention to Mei though he was pleased to see that she too was showing an interest in the world around her, her eyes visibly brighter than the day before.

The sun turned the grass gold and the sky white from horizon to horizon.

She removed her shoes to more easily balance on a low wall at the side of the road, all broken mud bricks and clay. And, as she picked her way along, she asked him where they were going.

"I don't really know. I suppose we'll know when we get there."

"What are we going to do then?"

"I don't know."

"Well, who are we going to be?" she asked and he turned to look at her, her silhouette afire with the sun behind.

She laughed as if the question had meant nothing and, after a moment, took his hand for balance. Though she had always been so very sure–footed.

Her fingers were warm and light against his palm, gripping tightly if he tried to move away.

They walked that way, through the brightest part of the afternoon, then on towards the fading light.

If it really were possible, he thought, to fall in love with the same person twice, then no doubt everyone would choose it. Over and over. And over again.

Printed in Great Britain
by Amazon.co.uk, Ltd.,
Marston Gate.